Privacy is a Foreign Word in Supino

Privacy is a Foreign Word in Supino

A NOVEL

Maria Coletta McLean

Toronto, Ontario, Canada
www.inanna.ca

Copyright © 2023 Maria Coletta McLean
Except for the use of short passages for review purposes, no part of this book may be reproduced, in part or in whole, or transmitted in any form or by any means, electronically or mechanically, including photocopying, recording, or any information or storage retrieval system, without prior permission in writing from the publisher or a licence from the Canadian Copyright Collective Agency (Access Copyright).

We gratefully acknowledge the support of the Canada Council for the Arts and the Ontario Arts Council for our publishing program. We also acknowledge the financial support of the Government of Canada.

Cover design: Courtney Hellam

Privacy is a Foreign Word in Supino is a work of fiction. All names, characters, businesses, places, events and incidents in this book are either the product of the author's imagination or used in a fictitious manner.

All trademarks and copyrights mentioned within the work are included for literary effect only and are the property of their respective owners.

Library and Archives Canada Cataloguing in Publication

Title: Privacy is a foreign word in Supino : a novel / Maria Coletta McLean.
Names: McLean, Maria Coletta, 1946- author.
Series: Inanna poetry & fiction series.
Description: Series statement: Inanna poetry & fiction
Identifiers: Canadiana (print) 20230530540 | Canadiana (ebook) 20230530559 | ISBN 9781771339629 (softcover) | ISBN 9781771339636 (EPUB) | ISBN 9781771339643 (PDF)
Subjects: LCGFT: Novels.
Classification: LCC PS8625.L42923 P75 2023 | DDC C813/.6—dc23

Printed and bound in Canada

Inanna Publications and Education Inc.
210 Founders College, York University
4700 Keele Street, Toronto, Ontario, Canada M3J 1P3
Telephone: (416) 736-5356 Fax: (416) 736-5765
Email: inanna.publications@inanna.ca Website: www.inanna.ca

This book is dedicated, with love, to my youngest daughter, Kathryn McLean, and her husband, Robert Rebeck and their lovely children: Julian, Audrey, Samuel, and to Miguel Gomez-McLean, as well as to the inimitable Paige.

Another Bride, Another Groom

AT LA CASA BELLA, BIANCA was buttoning her best lace dress. Earlier, her husband, Fortunato had offered a comment when he'd seen her ironing it. "White?" he'd asked. "For a wedding?"

"Someone should be wearing wedding white and the bride certainly isn't."

"But *bella*, do you think it's appropriate?"

Bianca arched an eyebrow in his direction.

"Okay, okay," said Fortunato. "I'll go and see how the girls are doing."

She returned to buttoning her dress but the fabric strained a little at her waist.

Bianca took a deep breath, and held it; yes, that was better, but then the lace resisted again when she tried to fasten it across her breasts. She exhaled sharply and popped a button. Now she had to undo all the pretty mother-of-pearl buttons in order to step out of the dress and rummage in her sewing kit for some unbreakable polyester thread. Two things were certain and she might as well face up to them: cotton thread wouldn't hold the button against the strain of her breasts, and her swollen breasts meant only one thing. Another pregnancy. Damn that Fortunato with his sweet talk and his persuasive gifts. Double damn him!

The last of the ten o'clock bells tolled from the church tower and inside the Kennedy Bar, Pietro the barman announced, "Closing time."

The few regulars drained their espressos, popped the last bites of croissant into their mouths. Just as Pietro was turning the sign from open to closed, the Lavazza deliveryman entered carrying a box of coffee beans.

"Closing?" asked the deliveryman, glancing at the bell tower and then at his watch. "It's ten o'clock in the morning."

"Special day," said Pietro. "Let me put this box inside so I can get on my way."

The deliveryman looked up and down the cobblestone street. A few cats stretched out on the stone wall beside the church, a soccer ball lay abandoned beside the fountain, a sheet of newspaper fluttered half-heartedly on the fence. The village of Supino looked as sleepy as the opening shot of an old black and white Fellini film.

"What's going on?" asked the deliveryman.

Pietro checked the deserted street, turned up the palms of his hands. "Nothing."

"So why are you closing?"

"Oh," said Pietro. "A wedding today."

"Not you, is it?" joked the Lavazza man.

Pietro didn't laugh at the joke, he didn't smile, he just said, "The farmer."

"The old one? With the donkey?"

"Ha," said one of the customers as he brought his cup to the counter, "Did you think the farmer was already married?"

"To his donkey, perhaps?" said another. "He did buy Zeus that new straw hat last fall."

"Our groom bought himself a new suit. Brand new," said the tailor. "And a vest. Latest style. New shirt. New tie."

"And he ordered prosciutto all the way from Parma," added the butcher. "Whole leg for the wedding feast."

"From Parma," said another as he kissed his fingertips, as if he could already taste its salty sweetness.

"My wife says the *bomboniere* are imported too. From Sulmona."

"Sulmona's not a foreign country, you know. It's *in* Italy," reminded the deliveryman. Sulmona was in fact only 140 kilometres from Supino. Half a tank of gas, there and back.

Several villagers shook their heads. Someone said, "Who drives that far for candied almonds that you could buy at the *pasticceria*? All candied almonds taste the same."

"My wife says these ones are *speciale*."

"*Speciale* waste of money. Have you seen the price of gas?"

The regulars shook their heads once again, placed some coins on the counter to pay for their coffee and were halfway out the door when they suddenly stopped. Had they heard correctly? Was someone making a joke? "What?" they said. "*Scusa*?" "What did you say...?" And they turned to look at the cobbler, opened their eyes wide, nodded toward him.

Those two words, *imported wine*, bounced around the bar like a rogue Ping-Pong ball before they crumpled to the marble floor. Lay still. Not deflated, just shocked. Every villager, made their own wine from local grapes.

"Not French wine?" asked one, with eyebrows lifted.

"Tell me it's not Greek," added another, with a hand to his forehead.

"From Abruzzo. Right next door. Montepulciano..."

"That's a good wine," said young Bruno, but he worked in Rome as a hotel doorman so of course his views had grown more global. "Always popular at weddings."

"Well, you only get married once," said Pietro, "or maybe twice."

"But seriously, are you really closing for a wedding?" The driver motioned to the regulars, who were halfway out the door. "What will your customers say when they see the closed sign?"

"Nothing. They'll be at the church."

"*All* your customers?"

"You're new here in Supino," said Pietro. "In this village when someone from our neighbourhood gets married, we all go to the church. Wish them good luck. And since the farmer's my friend, I will go back to his orchard afterwards for the wedding dinner. Others will come later for a drink, or a dance or two. Stop by if you wish."

"Stop by? I have deliveries to make," said the Lavazza man. "My job's to deliver coffee beans, not to dance in some farmer's field."

"I see," said Pietro. "That's your priority? Deliveries?"

"Of course. It's my job."

"You must be from Roma."

"I am. So what?"

"My condolences," said Pietro as he accompanied the customers and the deliveryman out the door.

At the farm, preparations for the wedding were underway. Zeus had been lathered and rinsed and brushed and now, Nino the farmer held some fancy ribbons in his hand and patted Zeus's mane as if ribbons and donkey hair had some connection. Zeus eyed the netting warily. He gave a disapproving shake of his head.

"I know, I know, brides and grooms don't usually arrive in donkey carts," Nino said to Zeus as he braided the netting into Zeus's coarse mane. "But these are modern times, my friend, and you are not just any old donkey, so we must make a new tradition."

Nino shook his head at all these modern ideas. Of course, he'd grown modern too: he'd planted three rows of miniature carnations in his vegetable garden. And he'd picked the flowers that morning: some to be delivered to the church; some for his bride to carry; a sprig for his own lapel, and three pink ones for Zeus's hat.

"Be still, my friend," said Nino as he checked his watch. "As soon as I finish with you, I'll put on my new suit and we'll be on our way. *Stare calmi*."

Assunta, wearing her Sunday dress, came out of the farmhouse and said, "Let me take the flowers to the church for you."

Her father said, "But I already have them in the cart."

"I know, but you aren't dressed yet and I have time. And I want to do something."

"You've done enough already. Organized the food with Pietro.

Arranged for the band. Those *bomboniere* that you ordered all the way from Sulmona."

"That's nothing. I'm good at organizing, you know that."

"You get it from your mother—God rest her soul—too bad she didn't live to see this day."

It was a moment when you must either laugh or cry, and Nino and Assunta chose laughter. Even Zeus added a snort of laughter, or perhaps it was impatience. Assunta wiped her eyes with a small lace handkerchief that had once belonged to her mother and Nino did the same with a cotton square that had his initials embroidered on the corner. Zeus stamped his foot once more and they got busy: Assunta loading the flowers into the Fiat Cinquecento and Nino going into the house to wash and dress in his brand-new suit.

Nino thought his Sunday suit still looked presentable but Assunta had said it was old-fashioned. Assunta said that double-breasted jackets with wide lapels were out-of-date. Assunta said the trouser legs were too wide. Nino liked the old style but to please his daughter, he made the trip to the tailor's. At first he thought he'd just get his suit tailored but while waiting for the tailor to mark and measure, he'd caught sight of a grey pinstripe fabric. A doctor or a businessman might choose that material but perhaps pinstripe was appropriate for a farmer too. After all, a wedding was a special occasion.

That morning, Nino had spent an hour in Fortunato's barber chair and now that he was washed and dressed and looking in the mirror, he was quite pleased with his reflection. "Not bad for an old man," he said to himself, and then, he pulled his handkerchief from his pocket once more to dry his tears.

"Zeus," he called as he opened the farmhouse door. "We must be on our way." Still he took a moment to admire the setting that Pietro the barman had created in his small orchard: the ten tables laid with white cotton, the dozens of wooden chairs tipped against the tables, waiting, the jars of wild flowers that Assunta had gathered, all under the apple trees. "See that, my friend," he said to Zeus. "Today I will be a married man and you, Zeus, will be a donkey for two. We're very lucky, my friend. *Avante.* Let's go."

At the bride's house, Elena sat before the mirror while her neighbour Rosa buttoned a row of pretty pearl buttons from neck to hip. She folded the soft lace collar that circled Elena's neck. Rosa clasped the string of pearls, grown more luminescent with age, and she reached for the wedding veil.

"This is such a lovely veil," she said. "These tiny pink carnations are perfect and when they open a little, as the day goes on, they'll look more and more beautiful. Just like you. *Che bella*, Elena. You are a beautiful bride."

The most Elena could offer was a tiny nod of her head. If she tilted her head too much, the tears would surely overflow. At sixty-five, she was a bride for the first time—about to marry Nino, a widower of many years. The decades could not quell her excitement. Today, she was dressed in a rose-coloured gown and about to be crowned with a circle of miniature carnations and baby's breath. Of course, there would be no babies in this marriage, but they had Assunta, the best daughter anyone could ever want and they had Rosa's seven-year old, Carlito, who they thought of as a grandson, so they were lucky, so very lucky.

Through the open window, they heard the tapping of Zeus's hooves approaching on the cobblestones. "He's here already," said Rosa, as she gathered up the hairpins. She gave Elena a quick kiss on the cheek, "See you at the church, *bella*," and boom! She was gone. Elena stared at the woman in the mirror. That morning, she'd spent an hour in the hairdresser's shop and now that she was washed and dressed, she stared at her reflection, admired her soft brown curls the hairdresser had gathered at the top of her head and said to herself, "Not bad for an old woman." Then, she heard the knock on her front door, a door that bore a large net bow and ribbons that danced and sparkled in the sunlight, and she opened it to greet her groom.

Meanwhile, across the street at Rosa's house, there was tension in the autumn air. Seven-year-old Carlito had endured the same indignations as Zeus. He too had been scrubbed and brushed

and now, Rosa brought his new clothes—all stiff and scratchy.
"This collar," said Carlito, "is choking me. I can't breathe."
"*Stare calmi*," said his mother. "I have to put the tie."
"You mean the noose? Help! Help! You're strangling me."
"What's all the fuss?" asked Claudio, adjusting his cufflinks as he came into the room.
"First of all," began Carlito, "Mamma is making me wear this stupid white suit. I told her white is a colour for babies and I'm already seven. And a half. Now, she's trying to strangle me with this tie that makes me look like a clown. I begged her to let me wear a grey suit, like Clark Kent but no, I have to wear baby white..."
"Listen, Carlito, you'll have a nice carnation for your lapel—Nino's bringing it and..."
"Flowers are for sissies, Claudio. You know that. Superman wouldn't wear a flower not even when he was Clark—"
"Carlito," warned Rosa, "That's enough." And she picked up the hairbrush and approached his mass of curls.
Carlito covered his head with his hands, "Oh no."
"Be thankful you're not Zeus," said Claudio. "He's having his hair braided with flowers and ribbons."
At the church of Santa Maria Maggiore, the wedding guests lingered on the *piazza*. Don Vincenzo joined the crowd and instructed the two altar boys to watch for the cart so he could cue the surprise—a trio of musicians, all sporting fedoras with white satin hatbands for the occasion and engaged to play Frank Sinatra's latest hit, "You Make Me Feel So Young." The Mayor wearing his striped sash of red, green, and white was there; Elena's neighbours and Nino's neighbours were there; the barber, Fortunato, and his daughters had just arrived. "Bianca will be here soon," he said to no one in particular. The girls in their matching flowered dresses ran to greet Carlito, who stood near the door yanking at his shirt collar.
Above the buzz of voices came Sinatra's lyrics. The villagers clapped loudly as Nino, agile and energetic as a young man, jumped from the cart. He grasped his bride's waist and swung

her down to stand beside him: arm in arm, they led their guests into the church.

Inside was the combined scent of carnations and incense, the soft sounds of wool trousers stretching as men genuflected before the altar and the gentle hush as women folded down the kneeling pads, the warmth of beeswax candles, and then a shuffle at the door as the band stopped playing and stepped aside. Now the bride would stand framed in the doorway for a moment before she began her walk to the altar. The ancient organ wheezed a few soft preliminary notes.

Instead of the bride, Bianca appeared in the doorway—she waved her fingers at the expectant crowd as if to say don't pay any attention to me—and she swished slowly down the aisle in her white lace dress, the click of her satin shoes as constant as heartbeats on the marble floor. She wore her blond hair in the usual Grace Kelly chignon but today she'd tucked in a few sprigs of baby's breath—not to celebrate the pregnancy, you understand—just to soften the severity of the hairstyle. Instead of slipping silently into the aisle seat, she motioned to Fortunato and her daughters to stand up so she could step in front of them, one, two, three, and sit in the centre of the row. But a woman with a floppy felt hat sitting in front of her blocked Bianca's view so she stood again, which meant that Fortunato and the daughters had to stand up once again, and one, two, three, Bianca returned to the aisle seat.

As the organ sighed again the first few notes of the processional hymn, Don Vincenzo nodded to Carlito who walked to the back of the church, where he lifted the cord attached to the white carpet and proceeded back up to the altar as the carpet unrolled behind him. At the altar he genuflected, as Don Vincenzo had instructed, turned to the wedding guests and bowed, as Don Vincenzo had *not* instructed, and fairly flew down the aisle to sit with his mother and Claudio once again.

When the last of the communion wafers had been distributed and Don Vincenzo had given the final blessing and Nino and Elena had walked down the aisle as a married couple, Nino had a sudden change of heart and stopped in the middle of the *piazza*. "Elena," he said. "I don't think we should ride in the cart back to the farm. Don't you think it would be better to walk with our guests?"

"Of course," she said. "But Zeus?"

"He'll follow along like always," assured Nino.

For his wedding gift, Pietro the barman had organized a picnic meal rather than the traditional multi-course wedding feast. Various villagers passed plates and platters in a steady stream from the farmhouse kitchen to the tables beneath the apple trees until the tables were completely covered with plates of cold cuts, cheese, pickled peppers and eggplant, anchovies wrapped around capers, prosciutto wrapped around breadsticks, fingers wrapped around wine tumblers, arms wrapped around shoulders, guests rapt in conversation.

There were many toasts before Nino rose to speak. "My friends," he began. "Today, I am the luckiest man in the world and the happiest man in the world. It's time to dance." He and Elena joined hands and stepped from table to table accumulating willing dancers along the way, winding through the apricot and pear trees, ducking beneath the low-hanging apple branches, their gnarled branches heavy with autumn fruit, and twirling among the early evening shadows. The guests lingered long after the September sunset; the heavy bells of Santa Maria were ringing midnight before the guests rose to return to their homes. A million stars lit the way.

Il Tempo:
The City Newspaper

BIANCA THOUGHT THE *IL TEMPO* newspaper from the city of Frosinone was a waste of money but Fortunato said, "If people have to pay, they take it more seriously."

"But you pay for the newspaper, and let your customers read it for free. What do you call that?"

"I think of it as a courtesy for my customers," said Fortunato as he placed the newspaper on the small wooden table. "Gives them something to read while they're waiting their turn. Keeps them in the shop."

"You'd be better to put the money toward a third barber chair. That way you'd be making money not spending it."

Fortunato looked around his small two-chair barbershop, "There's not enough room for a third chair, *bella*. You know that."

"So let them read the village newspaper. It's free."

"But there's nothing of value in it. The city newspaper has articles about what's happening in Roma and Naples. It has all the soccer news."

Bianca slipped her cardigan over her shoulders, checked out her reflection in the mirror, tucked a loose hair back into place, and said, "I can hear all that news at the hairdresser's."

"Can you?"

■■■

Down the road, at Simonetta's hairdresser's shop, Bianca flipped through the local news and tossed the paper onto the table a few minutes later.

"I see you don't subscribe to the new city newspaper from Frosinone," Bianca said to Simonetta but before the hairdresser could answer, the mayor's wife interrupted, "Why don't you, Simonetta? We're part of their new distribution area."

Bianca responded, "The only reason we're included in their new distribution area is for them to make money off of us."

"Oh, I'm sure there's more to it than that," said the mayor's wife, fluttering her newly trimmed bangs. "My husband put an ad from the City Hall to welcome the newspaper to our village."

"So that's how he spends our tax dollars," said the hairdresser.

"Rosa and Assunta put an ad for their water-bottling plant. So they think it's worthwhile," said the mayor's wife. "Pietro put an ad for his bar."

That night, Bianca slipped the new, city newspaper from Fortunato's barber's leather chair into her herb bag and carried it home. While Fortunato was at the bar playing Scopa with his friends, she read the soap-scented news.

"Politics, sports, traffic crash, who cares?" she muttered but she stopped at the City Hall ad. It was nice. A good-size rectangle bordered in red, white, and green. Not too showy but impressive enough. Then, she saw the ad that Rosa and Assunta had placed for the water-bottling plant. It was in the shape of a stubby water bottle. Very simple with a logo that asked, "Why not drink more?" and answered its own cheeky question: "It's good for you."

That line, "It's good for you," haunted Bianca's dreams that night so that she woke in the morning from a restless sleep. But she had an idea. Her herbs were good for people and her knowledge of herbs might be worth advertising if it could bring more people to her shop above Fortunato's barbershop. She decided to combine two errands into one afternoon trip to the nearby city of Frosinone: she'd go to the doctor who would tell her what she already knew and she'd go to the newspaper office and place an ad.

The doctor's office was muggy and even though the woman beside her was coughing her germs into a handkerchief, Bianca changed seats. When she was called into the examining room, she was glad to have the excuse to undress and step into the loose green cotton robe. She closed her eyes throughout the examination and then, sitting across from the doctor at his desk, she answered his routine questions until she heard him say, "You're pregnant, Bianca. Congratulations." Bianca did not say thank you; she did not say she was pleased; she simply sighed and said, "I know."

"But what you don't know," said the doctor, "is that I hear two heartbeats. You're having twins."

"Damn that Fortunato. Double damn him!"

"It takes two to dance *il tango*, Bianca."

Next Bianca headed to the newspaper office, which smelled strongly of fresh paper and stale ink. A man sat behind an oak desk cluttered with manila envelopes, inkbottles, a few stray paper clips, an over-stuffed Rolodex, and a battered sign that said, "*Editore*."

"*Buongiorno*," said Bianca. "I'm here about an ad."

He looked at the clock before he responded, "You're early."

"There's a time frame?"

"Not exactly. Just that you're early. That's all."

There was a chair for visitors but the man didn't offer it to Bianca or even glance at it. He was shuffling some papers, searching for something.

"Just give me a minute. It's here somewhere," he said.

When he finally looked up, Bianca nodded toward the chair and asked, "*Permesso?*" but instead of apologizing for not offering her a seat, the man just waved his hand at her as if she was a pesky fly who'd found her way into his office, uninvited and therefore, unwelcome.

"Here's some free advice," said Bianca. "My mother always taught me that you catch more flies with honey."

"What's that supposed to mean?"

"It means that's not the way to speak to a woman who comes into your office. Don't wave your hand at me. You can't treat women that way."

"Oh, really?" asked the man. He leaned forward, crossed his arms on his desk. "Any other advice?"

Bianca sat down in the chair. She might as well rest a few minutes before she went on her way. It was very apparent that she wouldn't be giving this rude man any of her money for an ad. In fact, she wouldn't even bother to answer his question.

"What would you do in this situation?" continued the *signor*. "My neighbour came to my house last week to bring a death notice for the newspaper. I offered her a cup of tea and she said, '*Si*.' Then, when I brought the cup, she took one look at it and handed it back. Said she had to get going. When I looked in the cup, I saw that it was tea-stained. Pretty badly stained. Not very appealing. But I'm not sure how to remove the stain. English bone china, you know. Kinda delicate."

Bianca leaned back in the chair, fanned her face with her spotless handkerchief. "I'm not here to give you household tips. Don't you have a mother?" asked Bianca. "Ask her, the poor woman."

"She's dead."

"*Mi dispiace*. I'm very sorry."

A sadness settled on the *editore's* face and Bianca felt a moment of pity for him.

She put her handkerchief back in her purse and closed the clasp.

"How long ago did she die?" she asked. "If you don't mind my asking."

"Almost ten years now but the feeling's still the same, you know. Even though I'm a grown man, I think I would give anything just to have one more hour with her, drinking a cup of tea in the garden and talking."

"Your mother would tell you to put a little bleach and water in the teacups. Let them sit for 30 minutes and then wash them. Or you could use lemon slices if you have extra. Some people use baking soda but you have to scrub and you don't look like the kind who has patience."

"You're very honest. I like that." He flipped through the papers on his desk. "What did you say your name was?"

"Bianca." She stood up to leave.

"Of course, we'll change it for the column," he said, waving her to sit down again, pushing the papers aside. "Here's the set up. I'll mail you the letters every week in a brown manila envelope that says *Il Tempo* on the return address. It's important to keep your identity a secret. Your postmaster will think it's just a regular newspaper subscription. Inside will be the letters from readers asking for advice and a stamped envelope for you to send me your replies. Keep your advice honest and straightforward just like you did with me today and—"

"Just a minute. I think there's some—"

"If you're worried about the household tips, don't be. We don't get many of them. Mostly it's questions about how to deal with an interfering mother-in-law or worries because the husband is staying out late, and various aches and pains."

Bianca paused for a moment, on the edge of her seat. The man was offering her a job. Of course, Fortunato wouldn't want her to accept a job. What would people say? That he couldn't provide for his own family? That she wore the pants in the family? That it was scandalous for a woman to work outside the home to make money? Unless it was charitable work for the church or to help out in the husband's business. Well, she had no problem taking the money—but that wasn't the appeal. She considered it an act of true compassion—to share her wisdom with others. Anonymously, and with kindness: Bianca was trying to be kinder toward others, but people could be such fools.

"I know how to use herbs to cure aches and pains," assured Bianca. "Or how to cause them."

"Well...okay. But before we go any further, I have to tell you the pay's not great. It's ten *lire* a column for three columns a week. We're thinking of an extended column on Saturday but we'll have to see how it goes. And everything is confidential. No one should know you're the advice columnist for *Il Tempo*. Not even your husband." He looked directly at Bianca. "Is that a problem?"

"Problem?" echoed Bianca. "There are lots of things I don't tell my husband. Believe me, it's better that way."

"That's a good line, believe me. We can use that as the heading." He scrawled a few words on a paper. "'Believe me, advice from... now the name. How do you feel about '*Cara* Juliet'?"

Bianca brushed her fingers beneath her chin in that universal dismissive Italian gesture that meant there was nothing more to say. Then she said, "People from our province won't listen to advice from Juliet. She was a Northern Italian."

He tapped his pencil a few times. "What about 'Dear Anna'? There's an advice columnist in America called 'Dear Ann' and everyone loves her."

"What do I care about a woman in America? Italians might have similar problems but our solutions are always better." Bianca sat forward in her chair and lowered her voice. "Do the *Americani* even know how to remove a curse or ward off the evil eye?"

There was a quiet moment while the man considered the question. Above them a fan swirled the warm air half-heartedly. "What about Minerva, Goddess of wisdom?"

Bianca smiled. "Also Goddess of War," she said. "Not 'Dear Minerva,' though. Just Minerva. That's enough."

"So, it's a deal?" said the *signor*, holding out his hand.

"One more thing," advised Bianca before she offered her hand. "Next time a woman comes in, offer her a chair."

"Sorry, you just caught me off guard. I wasn't expecting you to be early," said the *editore*. "Would you like a cup of tea before you go?"

"Maybe next time," said Bianca with a smile. "After you've bleached the teacups."

■ ■ ■

On her way back to the village, Bianca stopped in to see her mother. The *signora* Lucrezia lived in a large home surrounded by apple trees. Even though her mother didn't drive, she'd had a circular driveway that she'd seen in the movie, *Gone with the Wind*, made for her own house. But there was no house servant to open the front door for Bianca, no cook to offer her a cool glass of *limonata*; there was however a grand staircase that led to the second floor. Bianca found her mother on the balcony that overlooked the south orchard where the apple trees were heavy with autumn fruit and Erminio, the gardener, was up on a wooden tripod ladder with a canvas sack strapped across his chest.

Bianca had agreed to keep her advice column secret so she couldn't explain to her mother why she wanted to borrow her mother's maid. Bianca needed one day a week to concentrate on the letters, and she'd have to ask her mother for a favour without telling her the reason. So she was forming the question in her mind but before she could speak, her mother did.

"You look paler than usual, *bella*," said her mother as she kissed Bianca's cheeks.

"I've been to the city. I'm a little tired, that's all."

Her mother held her at arm's length and looked her over.

"Are you putting on weight? Your ankles look swollen. I've warned you *bella*, once you gain one kilo, it's easy to gain two and then it's bigger dresses and a thick waist and no husband wants a wife with a…"

"Mamma, okay, I know all this. I came to talk to you. I need a favour."

"Anything, my dear, you know that." *Signora* Lucrezia motioned to the bench. "Remember, I don't babysit."

"It's nothing like that, Mamma," began Bianca with a sigh as she sat on the bench, crossed her arms to hide her widening waist. "Could you loan me your maid one day a week? What's her name again?"

"Why do you need a maid? Antonietta's old enough to help with the housework. Why, when I was twelve years old—"

"You were taking piano lessons and dancing lessons, and flirting with the boys."

"Yes, those girls of yours should be doing that too. Antonietta always has her nose in a book and Giuseppina—must she always play with Rosa's boy? Do you want her to grow up to be a *maschiaccio*?"

"Mamma, she's only eight years old. All little girls are tomboys at that age."

"I wasn't."

"What's the maid's name again?" asked Bianca.

"Teresa. But you'd be better off with her sister. The sister's good with babies."

Bianca ducked her head; questioned her mother through lowered eyes, "Who said anything about babies?"

"Bianca, please, your breasts are fighting to pop the buttons off your blouse."

"It's worse than you think, Mamma. Twins."

"You'll never get your figure back." Lucrezia waved her hand, beyond the orchard to the blue horizon, to show that Bianca's slim figure was gone forever. Then she added, "What's the matter with you? Don't you have any self-control? After the birth, get your tubes tied."

"Mamma, it's a sin."

"Sin. I'll tell you what's a sin. Having babies year after year. Two is enough. You'll lose your figure, then you'll lose your husband and then you'll become... You worry too much about sin. Easy for the priest to make the rules. He—"

"God makes the rules, Mamma. The priest is just following them."

"It's the same difference. He doesn't have to take care of all these babies. Let the doctor tie your tubes. Do the penance. Then you're done with it."

A Change of Routine

AFTER ROSA HAD WALKED CARLITO to the schoolyard, where the nuns fluttered and cooed like grey mourning doves among the children, she stopped at the Kennedy Bar for her morning cappuccino. Pietro lifted a croissant from the tray and placed it on a plate, then he foamed the milk. Pietro was an expert at gauging his customers' moods so he nodded at Rosa, and then even though he could clearly see that everything was not okay with her, he asked. "*Tutto a posto?*" and Rosa lied and said, "*Sì*."

Even after nothing more than croissant crumbs covered the plate and streaks of espresso foam marked the bottom of her cup, Rosa lingered. The church bells rang nine-thirty before she lifted her bag and walked down the road to the Acqua di Santa Serena water-bottling plant.

The parking lot was almost deserted; the drivers had already loaded up their trucks and left to make their deliveries. Inside, Claudio was on the phone. Rosa went to the small counter in the corner and began to sort the morning's mail. In a minute, with the mail in her hand, she went down the hall to their office, Assunta's and hers.

"Some invoices for you," said Rosa as she handed over the envelopes. "That was a lovely wedding, Assunta. One of the nicest I've ever attended."

"Yours will be just as nice, Rosa."

"Mine?" asked Rosa as she pulled out her chair and turned it toward her friend. "*Certo*. It's almost seven years since Elgidio's disappearance. So Rome will issue an official death certificate. Surely, you and Claudio plan to marry." And when Rosa didn't answer. "Don't you?" asked Assunta.

"I'm not sure." Rosa shuffled the last few envelopes, changed their order according to size, changed it back again. "Marriage changes people. Something shifts. Maybe it's the balance of power or the constant compromise or something. I don't know." But of course, Rosa did know about marriage, and compromise, and heartbreak. She'd married Elgidio on an impulse on the night of a full moon and during her three-year marriage, she'd learned about compromise and power. "It seems to me that compromise is always the woman's job. She also gets the heartache. And the power? It's on the man's side, not the woman's."

"But it wouldn't be that way with you and Claudio," assured Assunta as she straightened the envelopes into a neat pile. "You've worked out a good system over the last few years, haven't you?"

Rosa rolled a blank sheet of paper into the typewriter. "Yes," she said. "So maybe it's best to leave things the way they are."

"But Rosa, Claudio living here at the plant? You and Carlito living at the house? You can't go on like that forever."

"Can't I?" she asked, her fingers poised above the typewriter keys.

"Of course not—it wouldn't look right. Once Elgidio's declared officially dead, you and Claudio are free to marry. Do the honourable thing. That's expected."

Assunta waited for the clickety-clack of Rosa's typing to pause, waited for the sound of the typewriter carriage as it swung back to the left, waited for Rosa's response. The tiny typewriter bell rang and Rosa said, "Who cares about traditions and expectations?"

Assunta reached over and placed her hand on Rosa's arm. "You must care," said Assunta. "Otherwise why aren't you and Claudio living together right now? Why is he returning here every night like he's a bachelor? Why are you living alone with Carlito at your husband's house like you're a widow or...?"

Rosa lowered her hands from the keys and tried to explain something that wasn't really clear to Rosa herself.

"I'm tired of this village and their old-fashioned traditions," began Rosa. "Must I marry as soon as some official says Elgidio is dead in order to appease all the women watching out their windows each night to make sure Claudio has left my house, my bed?"

"What's the matter with you this morning?" asked Assunta.

"I don't know," replied Rosa. "Nothing. Let's forget about marriage and get some work done."

Assunta slit open a few envelopes but Rosa lingered, tapping her fingernails on the desk instead of on the typewriter keys. She lifted the Frosinone newspaper; put it back down.

"Our ad in the newspaper," began Rosa. "It's kind of cheeky —drink more—but I was thinking, 'Will people drink more?' I think we need some sort of incentive. A chance to win a prize, for example. Maybe they could mail in the label with their name and address to be part of a lucky draw."

"People would object to paying for a stamp," said Assunta.

"Of course," said Rosa. "What if the back of the label told if they were a winner?"

"Maybe. We'd have to be careful that the person couldn't see through the bottle and see if they're a winner. Otherwise they wouldn't buy."

"Of course," said Rosa.

"And there'd have to be lots of chances to win. Like one in ten. The villagers like good odds."

"Of course," said Rosa. She didn't want to give up on the penny-pinching villagers. "There could be lots of small prizes, like win a free bottle of water, and then, a few bigger ones like win a free case of water, and then the grand prize."

"The grand prize would have to be money," said Assunta.

"Of course."

"Or a trip."

"A trip would make a person buy ten bottles of water instead of one," said Rosa. "The chance to get away from here."

Assunta raised the idea at the weekly meeting. Rosa suggested that the grand prize should be a trip to Napoli.

"Why is it always Napoli with you?" asked Claudio. "There are other cities, you know."

It was just the four of them at the table: Rosa, Claudio, Assunta and Gino. Gino was the son of the village banker; his father had invested heavily in the water bottling plant and Gino was heavily invested in wooing the only daughter of the family who owned the village hardware store. With Claudio, he'd been an enthusiastic business partner in their Roma bar and pizzeria, and now he was just as eagerly involved with the water-bottling plant, not just for his own future but to prove himself to the girl's father. Gino had already picked out the ring at the village jewellery shop: Claudio had come with him and inspected the rings as well; they'd sworn the owner to secrecy. Threatened that they'd take their business elsewhere if word got out that they'd been looking at engagement rings. "Of course," said the owner. "*Certamente.*" He solemnly shook hands with both the bachelors even though they all knew it was an empty threat—there was no other jewellery store in the village and the shops in nearby Frosinone were too expensive. Nevertheless, if you couldn't trust the village jeweller to keep quiet, whom could you trust?

When Rosa had suggested Napoli and Claudio had responded with annoyance, Gino had raised his eyebrows at Assunta, but she'd just shrugged. A little lover's quarrel perhaps. Or just some stress about—what? Neither knew nor did they want to ask.

"Win a trip to Roma?" asked Gino, but he answered his own question. "Roma's too close. And not really romantic enough. Except, of course, after midnight, in Trastevere. How about Florence? Or Venezia?"

"Venezia," said Assunta. "A city that's associated with water, and *amore*. A perfect match."

She looked at Rosa and Claudio but Rosa didn't turn her usual bright smile in Claudio's direction, and Claudio only reached out to rub the back of his neck.

"So, it's decided," declared Gino. "The grand prize is a trip for two to romantic Venezia. Meeting adjourned."

Rosa and Assunta left the office at four. Their routine was to pick up Carlito from the schoolyard and walk up the hill together. Then, Assunta walked past Rosa's house and carried on home to her father Nino's farm. But this afternoon, Assunta suggested a coffee and an ice cream, so Rosa knew something was up. As always, Carlito had to check if they had any new flavours and now, he was debating between watermelon and cantaloupe to accompany his beloved chocolate. When they were finally settled at a table, Assunta gave her news. "I'm moving."

"What?" said Rosa.

"Where?" said Carlito.

"Why?" said Rosa.

"I want to give my father and Elena some space," said Assunta. "Newlyweds don't need a spinster daughter hanging around like the proverbial fifth wheel."

"You can have my room at my house," said Carlito. "I'd love to live on the farm. Nino's giving me three rows to plant next year, and I'm going to plant—"

"Shush, Carlito," said Rosa. She handed him a napkin to wipe his face. "Let Assunta finish her news."

"There's more?" asked Carlito. "Are you getting married too?"

Assunta laughed. But then her face grew serious, and a little pensive. Who would she marry?

"Even better," she declared. "I'm moving into Elena's house. I'll be living right across the street from you."

"It's too small," said Rosa. "And it needs a lot of work—It's too small," she repeated.

"No, it's not," said Carlito. "Elena lived there and she's a lot fatter than Assunta."

"Isn't anyone happy to have me as their new neighbour?"

"Of course. Of course. Just tell me you'll have some work done on the place. Put in some modern touches. A new bathroom, for sure."

"All of those things," said Assunta. "Bathroom. New paint. Polished floors and..."

Carlito lost interest in the conversation. He ran to the corner to join in the impromptu soccer game. Rosa and Assunta talked on about renovations. Assunta showed Rosa some kitchen designs she'd sketched in her notebook and soon the church bells were ringing for the six o'clock mass and Claudio was headed up the street, briefcase in hand.

"Just like the old days," he said. "My two favourite women talking plans to improve the village. What activities are you plotting? High-wire acts over the *piazza*?"

Over the past three years, since Claudio had returned from Roma, to live in the village, he and Rosa had set up a routine. Claudio came to Rosa's house for dinner, spent some time playing soccer with Carlito before dinner and some time playing cards with Carlito before bed, and then he spent some time with Rosa after Carlito was asleep. By midnight on any given night you could hear him whistling softly as he walked back down the road to his grandparent's farmhouse.

When he and Gino had agreed to be managers of the new water bottling plant, they'd arranged to renovate the farmhouse. Now there were offices on one side and his living quarters on the other. Out the back, the barn also had an addition to accommodate the delivery trucks. Finally, they'd added a brand new building to house the bottling plant itself. So, Claudio divided his life between his office and his home at his grandparent's farm and his time with Rosa and Carlito at her house. Usually he tried not to mix business with pleasure but tonight, there was a lot of silence at the dinner table, so he broke his rule.

"Gino's going to run some numbers tonight to see how many bottles of water will have winning tickets for the smaller prizes," he said to Rosa, and when she didn't respond, he added, "That will tell us when we should attach the ticket for the grand prize."

"What's the grand prize?" asked Carlito.

"A trip to Venezia."

"I've heard about Venezia," said Carlito. "Giuseppina told me they have water there instead of streets and I told her she's crazy."

"Carlito, you should be nicer to Giuseppina. She's a good friend to you, and she's right. Instead of streets they have water canals. Everyone travels by boat." Rosa gathered the plates and stood to take them to the sink but Carlito's questions kept her standing at the table.

"How do they get to school?"

"Boat. Or they cross a little bridge built over the *canale*."

"Is there a *piazza*?"

"A grand *piazza* with a very tall clock tower where two black statues stand like guards. And every hour they hit the bell to make it ring. One ring for every hour. And the sound echoes through all the little streets and canals to tell the time." Rosa took the plates to the sink and returned with a small plate of *biscotti* and the fruit bowl but before she could go back for the fruit plates and the knives, Carlito asked another question.

"Does everyone have their own boat or is there an *autobus* boat?"

"Most people have their own little boat. There's a big boat called a *vaporetto*. People buy a ticket just like riding the *autobus* and the *vaporetto* takes them back and forth, along the *Canal Grande*, to the mainland. There's a garbage boat and a fire engine boat and a boat that comes every day with fresh fruits and vegetables—like a floating store."

"Why didn't we ever go there, Mamma?"

"I don't know. I guess I never thought of it. Would you like to go, *bello*?"

"Of course. When?"

Later that evening, after Carlito was asleep, instead of Claudio and Rosa spending time in her bedroom, they sat on the hard kitchen chairs facing each other across the bare table and had a little talk.

"I can rearrange things at the plant," suggested Claudio "and come to Venezia with you and Carlito," but Rosa was shaking her head before he'd even finished his proposal.

"The three of us spend so much time together—it would be nice for me to have him to myself for a little while."

"You had him to yourself for four years." Claudio's voice was a little harsh. To be fair, all the years he'd been living and working in Rome, Rosa hadn't told him he had a son. To be fair, Rosa had never received Claudio's letter and the enclosed *lire* for the train ticket asking her to join him in Rome. So, of course, she hadn't come, hadn't even answered. To be fair, Rosa thought Claudio had deserted her. So they'd been separated for four years.

"And whose fault was that?" Rosa asked, pushing back her chair.

Claudio reached his hand across the table. "I'm not saying it's anyone's fault. I'm just saying that I'd like to come."

"And I'm saying I'd like it to be just the two of us—Carlito and me—like it used to be." Now Rosa's voice was a little harsh; perhaps harsher than Claudio's had been. As if she wanted to instigate a fight.

Claudio checked his watch but it wasn't the late hour that deterred him from responding. He knew something was bothering Rosa just as surely as he knew that asking her would result in only silence. When she was ready, she'd tell him. So she'd take Carlito to Venezia for a week and he'd stay in the village and even though they'd be miles apart, her words, "like it used to be," would linger in the air between them. Linger as surely as the silence between thunder and lightning.

■■■

Two young men in their painter's whites came into the bar. After Pietro took their order—double espresso, cornetto stuffed with chocolate— he asked about their painting job.

"Almost finished," said one. "And believe me," here he stopped to tap his heart with the palm of his hand, "I'm sick of the colour brown."

"Which room are you painting brown?" asked one of the high school girls sitting in the corner table where their textbooks sat unopened.

"*Tutto.*"

The word *tutto* passed among the customers. "Every room?"

asked one. "Whole house?" asked another.

"*Tutto*," repeated the painter. "Every room, every wall."

"Why would anyone paint their whole house brown?" asked the electrician. "Wait, what shade of brown? What's the official name? Something kind of golden, like autumn leaves?"

"Dark like beech tree bark?" asked the coffin maker. "Or light like pine?"

"Birch?"

Pietro guessed, "Espresso? Cappuccino? Latte? Please don't tell me it's this dull new colour from America—*caffè Americano*."

The grocer tossed in a few words too: colour of bread crust? Whole wheat flour? Chick peas?

The painters laughed. "The colour of dirt. Not rich earth like the vineyard, not mulched earth. Earth like a desert. Like sand. As boring as a *biscotti* without even a sliver of an almond or a dried cherry. That's her choice."

"Maybe," said the coffin maker. "That explains why she's a spinster. She likes drab and boring."

When the laughter died down, the teenager from the corner table said, "Like there are no drab and boring men in this village for her to marry?"

The men regarded one another but they kept their suggestions to themselves because the electrician was adding even more news. News as shocking as a loose plug producing sparks.

"She's asked me to put three new electrical outlets in the house."

"Three outlets! The house only has three rooms. Why does she need three more outlets?"

"Does she also want a higher electricity bill?" asked the postman. "Because that's what I'll be delivering. Where does she want these extra outlets?"

"One in the kitchen," began the electrician.

"*Va bene*," said Pietro. "An extra outlet in the kitchen is a good idea. Handy for a toaster, or a little radio or..."

"You can toast bread in the fireplace," said the grocer. "Free."

"Another in the bedroom," continued the electrician, and he

paused for a moment before adding the next bit of information, "To plug in the special lamp ordered from Roma. To sit on her night table. A lamp with a neck as long as a goose, so she can read in bed at night."

"That explains why she's a spinster," repeated the coffin maker. "That's what she wants to do in bed at night? Read?"

Once more the teenager gave her opinion. "What's wrong with reading? Maybe she likes to read books *romanzo*."

The coffin maker didn't answer. The teenager was too young, too innocent to understand how different reading about romance was from actually having a romance. Any spinster would do well to have a man in her bed rather than a book.

The room grew quiet save for the rattle of spoons against cups, the bite into the crunchy cornetto, the splash of crumbs on the metal tabletops. Pietro broke the silence by asking about the third electrical outlet. One for the kitchen, one for the bedroom—what room was left?

"One in the bathroom," said the electrician. Heads turned his way. Eyebrows lifted. Eyes widened—surely he was joking?

"There's a light in the bathroom, no? You flick the switch and it comes on *automatico*, no? Why would anyone need an electrical outlet in the bathroom?"

"Maybe she's thinking of an electric fan," suggested Pietro. "To blow the steam out of the room."

"That's what a window's for," said the grocer. "You open the window, the wind comes in, the steam goes out. Completely free."

None of the men could think of either a reason for an electrical outlet in the bathroom or a joke about how you might use it. The teenager in the corner knew the answer. "Hairdryer," she said.

"Hairdryer?" repeated the coffin maker. "Hot air to dry your hair when the sun shines free every day?"

"What do you know?" asked the electrician. "You're as bald as a bocce ball."

The talk moved on to other things. Soccer, politics, elections—none of the news that interested the teenage girls. They'd finished their drinks and were gathering their books when Claudio came into the bar. Claudio always added a layer of excitement to the otherwise boring village chatter. Sometimes he talked about Rome. He'd lived there for a few years and he still returned to buy his suits, his leather shoes, records for his stereo. Sometimes if you walked towards Rosa's house in the evening, you could hear the music from Claudio's records flowing out of the open window, and if you walked slowly enough from the old fountain up *via condotto vecchio*, the music would follow you up to the new water fountain. Often they heard, "On An Evening in Roma," and they'd chat about all the things they might do on an evening in Rome.

So although Claudio was old, by their standards, he wasn't ancient like the coffin maker or the grocer. Right now, he was talking to Pietro about Venice—what Italian city was more romantic than Venice? None. As they listened in to the conversation they came to understand that Claudio wasn't going to Venice but only his *amore*, Rosa, and her son Carlito were going. That was odd. Claudio and Rosa were like the Romeo and Juliet of Supino—star-crossed lovers—but with a happy ending pending. Rosa's husband, Elgidio, who everyone said was a crude and boastful postman had disappeared seven years ago. And now that seven years had passed, his widow, Rosa could remarry. That's where Claudio came in because who wouldn't want to marry him? He was handsome and smart and sexy like Gregory Peck in *Roman Holiday*. So why would Rosa go on holiday without him?

Venezia: La Serenissima

CARLITO HAD GROWN TIRED OF asking how much longer and now he sprawled across the seat, half-asleep with his head against Rosa's arm, but as soon as the train slowed, he sat upright and asked once more. "Look," said Rosa, pointing out the window, "We're here." Carlito kept his face pressed against the glass as the train travelled over a peninsula with the waters of Venezia sparkling on both sides but then, when the land reappeared and the train slowed again amongst a tangle of railroad tracks and low stone buildings, darkened with soot, he said, "That's it?"

"No, no, *amore*," she assured him. "There's more."

They grabbed his knapsack and her travel bag and joined the crush of passengers leaving the train, walking in a quick line to the station. Rosa stopped Carlito just before the exit doors. "Now, we must go slowly so we don't miss anything."

"*Si*," he replied, but he was tugging at her arm nonetheless. As soon as they stepped through the doors, the pulling stopped instantly. "Oh!" he said. "Oh." His eyes were wide.

Travellers milled around them but Carlito stayed rooted to the cement step of the train station, taking it all in. "Listen," Rosa said. "Can you hear the water?"

Carlito heard footsteps; he heard newspaper boys calling the headlines; he heard the impatient *caw, caw, caw* of seagulls and then, he heard it: the sound of the waves licking the sides of the canal as greedily as a cat lapping milk in a ceramic bowl. "Let's go," he said as he tugged Rosa to the water's edge.

Carlito stopped at the tollbooth and studied the prices posted there. "Listen to this," he called to Rosa. "There's a price for adults, for children, and for luggage. Did you hear me, Mamma? Even the luggage has to pay!" Then he stared down the length of the Grand Canal: he took in the array of boats; the crowded cafés that lined the waterway; the shiny red geraniums dangling from window boxes. Notes from an accordion reached them and a flotilla of gondolas appeared around the bend. At the front of the first gondola, a man stood with his legs spread wide, playing his accordion and singing "O Sole Mio." Within the gondola, a group of Japanese tourists snapped the singer's photo while all along the walkway, others snapped photos of the gondola stuffed with tourists. Carlito laughed. "It's like a show," he said.

Looking around he asked, "Why aren't there any children here?"

"They're still in school," reminded his mother. "We'll see some later. Let's find our hotel now." She reached into her pocket, produced a small business card and studied the address. "Do you want to walk, *amore*, or take the *vaporetto*?"

Carlito watched the *vaporetto* pull up to the floating station, unload a group of tourists and suitcases and load up with others. He reached in his pocket to finger his folded *lire*. Claudio had given him five *lire* and Carlito wanted to spend it wisely. "Let's walk," he said, hiking his knapsack up on his shoulders. He stopped a few metres away at a gelato stand but the place was crowded and the prices posted were high. They turned into a side canal where the streets were narrower and the shops fewer. A few more twists and turns and they were lost.

Following a narrow pathway between ancient buildings, they came to a dark canal and a small bridge. "One, two, three..." Carlito counted the thirty-one steps to the other side where there was another narrow pathway between more ancient buildings. At the end, some sunlight and another canal. Carlito ran ahead to watch a low boat sidle up to the side of the canal and bump gently against the moss. As effortlessly as a bird leaves a branch waving in the breeze, one man jumped from the boat to throw a thick rope around an equally thick pole cemented into the cobblestones. The second man started to unload long, narrow boxes, which the first man lined up on the walkway. Then he too jumped from the boat and the movement caused the water to slap the sides of the canal like a reluctant reprimand.

Once the men had removed the lids and propped them under the boxes, Carlito and Rosa admired their display: red roses, yellow calla lilies, orange tiger lilies, carnations, Gerbera daisies, and forest green ferns. In the quiet, the rattle of a metal door unfolding as it opened echoed across the water and returned. A man pushing a small wheelbarrow inspected the flowers. In quick succession, he pointed to a flower or a fern, gave a number, "*dodici...diciotto...*" and pointed to the next. *Lire* changed hands; flowers filled the florist's wheelbarrow and the florist leaned against the building and lit a cigarette. As quickly as they'd created the display, the men dismantled it but before they could step back into their boat, Rosa said, "*Scusa, signor*, do you know this address?" She held out the card with the name of the hotel but the man just shrugged, "Ask the florist," he advised. "He knows every address in Venezia." And with a push from his oar, they slipped away.

"Another one," announced Carlito, pointing to a second boat filled with a man, a woman, and a strong scent of peaches. The woman stepped to the sidewalk and accepted crates of fruit from the man. Another riotous display of colours. From across the canal, women emerged from houses with ancient walls covered in wisteria. The opening of their front doors—swish—caused the flowers, pale as sun-bleached lavender, to sway wistfully in the warm Venetian air before their reflections returned to the dark waters of the canal.

While the women chose their fruit; while the man weighed their purchases on a dented, handheld scale; while the woman collected their *lire* and offered change; while Rosa consulted with the florist for directions to the hotel, Carlito watched the water lapping the metal sides of the vendor's boat, and waited for another to arrive. By the time, Rosa had her directions, Carlito had seen two more: a small motorboat piled high with luggage and a long narrow boat steered by a gondolier who held his cigarette in one hand and his oar in the other while bottles of wine clinked happily in wooden cases crowded in the hold.

"We have to walk over the bridge and cross two more canals before..." began Rosa, explaining the route to the hotel.

"Let's buy some peaches," suggested Carlito. "In case we get hungry along the way."

In the first *piazza*, which was very small with neither a statue nor a fountain nor a cluster of tourists, they sat on the bench and ate their peaches. The scent of baking bread wafted into the *piazza*; a pushcart vendor set up a display of postcards; a flock of pigeons settled on the cobblestones and somewhere in the distance, church bells announced three o'clock.

"Shall we go, *amore*?" asked Rosa and they were off again walking through the shade of the narrow streets, the sunshine of two more *piazzas*, and over numerous bridges spanning numerous canals like rows of basket-handle arches.

The hotel was small. A reception desk, a rubber plant, and a spiral staircase occupied the first floor. With a skylight illuminating their way, they climbed to the fourth floor and opened the door to room 4B. It was dark inside and before Rosa could locate the light switch, Carlito had already found the handle that rolled up the shutters. The afternoon sunlight streamed through the French doors and flooded their room. The balcony was *minuscolo* but the view was *enorme*. Carlito pointed it all out: the train station, the Grand Canal, the grand *piazza* with the bell tower, the churches everywhere. "Let's go," he said. The room was too small for him with all of Venezia to explore, so down the spiral stairs they swirled and out again into the warm afternoon air.

They arrived at the *piazza* just as the school bells announced dismissal time. Carlito claimed a table at the outdoor café while Rosa went to the counter to order. By the time she'd returned with drinks and snacks in hand, the *piazza* was crowded with children and parents. "You see those boys?" asked Carlito, and Rosa knew without even looking that it would be a group of boys passing a battered soccer ball from one to another, and that as soon as Carlito had downed his snack, he'd be joining them.

Rosa signalled the waiter, ordered *acqua frizzante* but it was a stranger who sat the bottle of water, with a glass teetering on the top, on her table. "They're busy," he said, "so I brought it along with my drink."

"*Grazie*," she said, but no more; she needed a few minutes to gauge his intention. The stranger pulled up a chair at the next table and shook out his newspaper. He sat sideways so he could watch the activities on the *piazza* but he didn't say anything else. Rosa studied him as she lifted the glass and allowed the bubbles to caress her lips. He was wearing a suit, but not an Italian one, his hair was sprinkled with grey and he needed a trim. Beneath the table was a shopping bag with a shoebox. He wasn't Italian yet he didn't seem like a tourist. A businessman perhaps, although he wasn't hurried at all.

Carlito, red-faced and sweating, returned to the table. "Good game?" asked the businessman.

"Break," explained Carlito, motioning to the other boys lined up for drinks. He eyed the man's shopping bag.

"Are you on vacation?" he asked.

"I'm travelling."

"Travelling where?"

"Carlito," warned Rosa. "Let the man read his paper."

"I don't mind. Let me introduce myself. I'm Anthony—or I guess you'd call me Antonio." He offered his hand to Carlito.

"I'm Carlito. You can call me Carlito."

They both looked at Rosa. "Rosa," she said, extending her hand. "Don't let us disturb your reading."

But Antonio folded his paper and placed it on the table. "Have you been in Venezia long?"

"We just arrived," replied Carlito. "We've only seen three boats, some gondolas, and a *vaporetto*."

"I see. I guess you're going to go to Saint Mark's square and feed the pigeons."

"I guess not," said Carlito. "We didn't come to Venezia to feed pigeons. We can do that at home. We're going to watch the statues ring the bell every hour. Mamma's going to buy some glass and I have five...some *lire* to buy something too. Maybe a mask. Like Zorro. And we're going to ride in a gondola but not until late when all the tourists have gone back to the mainland. Mamma wants to listen to the quiet."

"There's a gondola repair shop near here. I think you might like to see that. Actually, I'm not quite sure where it is. I found it by accident when I was just walking."

"How long have you been here?" asked Carlito.

"Five days. In a few more days, I'm going to catch the train and go south for a while."

"We live south," said Carlito. "In a village. But there's nothing to see there. Are you going to Roma?"

"I've been to Roma but I wanted some quiet, so I came here."

"Why are you travelling by yourself?" asked Carlito. "Don't you have a family?"

"*Scusa*," Rosa said to the businessman before she turned her attention to Carlito. "Sometimes, little boys ask too many questions."

"It's okay," said Antonio. "My boys were the same."

Two boys ran past the table and in a flash, the soccer game was back on and Carlito was in goal and Rosa and Antonio were alone, at separate tables. "May I?" he asked, gesturing to her table. He had boys; he wore a wedding band; Rosa decided he was just being friendly.

They met the businessman again that evening as they walked to a restaurant that the hotel manager had recommended. "*Locale*," he'd promised them. "*Autentico*." But the manager hadn't mentioned that the restaurant would be almost impossible to find.

"Well, hello again," said the businessman.

"We're lost," announced Carlito. "And I'm pretty sure we passed this way already. Do you know this restaurant?"

Rosa held out the card; Antonio shook his head.

"I went to a good place last night," he said, "But now I can't seem to find it."

They stood together on a small bridge and leaned against the railing. The evening air was still warm but a small breeze came from the canal. In the silence, they could hear the chimes of churches announcing eight o'clock. The scent of barbecued fish wafted toward them. "I'm hungry," said Carlito. Without discussion, the three of them left the bridge and turned down the first walkway. Shopkeepers were closing their stores, sliding metal shutters down to the cobblestones, attaching formidable locks with equally formidable keys. "*Buonanotte*," floated in the air.

"I'm hungry," repeated Carlito, and as if by magic, a small lantern blinked on, throwing a pale beam of yellow light across a small sign.

"*La Lanterna*," read Antonio. "It *could* be a restaurant." He pushed open the scrolled wrought iron gate. "Or someone's home," he added with a laugh.

At first, they heard only their soft footsteps on the pathway, then they heard the clink of silverware and the tinkle of laughter and finally, they heard a voice, "Table for three?"

They ordered the fish. Despite her warning not to fill up before his dinner arrived, Carlito ate most of the bread sticks from the breadbasket.

"It's the soccer," said Antonio. "It makes a boy—I mean a player—hungry."

"What did you do today?" asked Carlito.

"I wandered around an art gallery and admired the paintings. I bought some postcards."

"Will you send them to your boys?"

"No, no. I bought them for souvenirs—instead of taking my own photos. What did you do?"

"We tried to find the gondola repair shop you told us about but we couldn't. Were you making a joke with us?"

"Of course not. I'll get the directions from my hotel man and take you there myself, if you want."

"Tomorrow?"

"If it's okay with your mother."

But instead of turning to Rosa to get her permission, Carlito asked another question. "Where do you live when you're not travelling?"

"I'm from the U.S. But I sold my house in New York and I'm travelling. So right now, I don't really live anywhere. I'm a citizen of the world."

There was something wrong with Antonio's voice. His words were meant to be funny but his eyes were sad. What exactly was a citizen of the world? And where were his boys while he was travelling? And his wife? Carlito wanted the answers to all these questions but before he could ask, the waiter came with the fish and by the time he'd eaten his, he'd also grown so tired that he lay his head on his mother's lap and fell asleep.

"*Scusa*," said Rosa. "He's too inquisitive and perhaps I've indulged him too much."

"Are you raising him on your own? Don't answer if you find me too inquisitive," laughed Antonio.

Rosa took a moment. The sky was black but expectant, waiting for the stars to step out. She could change the subject but Antonio seemed like a stranger who knew how to listen without judgement. He seemed like a man who was carrying his own heavy secrets.

"My husband disappeared a few years ago," began Rosa, twisting the gold band on her finger. "I don't mean he ran off, I mean he disappeared. He was a bit of a drinker—actually he was a big drinker—and he got lost on the way home from the bar and I don't know. The police think he fell in the river and drowned but they never found his body. But no, I'm not raising Carlito alone. His father...well, it's a long story."

"He's a bright boy. Obviously full of curiosity," Antonio said, and then he attempted to change the subject. "And he loves soccer but I think all Italian boys love soccer, right?"

"Perhaps. Do all American boys love baseball?"

"Or football, yes. Mine weren't any different. The oldest was a quarterback. Actually he was just heading to college when..."

The waiter arrived to clear plates and offer coffee. Antonio ordered brandy. Rosa waited. Every time he'd mentioned his boys, he'd used the past tense. He hadn't mentioned his wife yet he wore a wedding band.

"There's something about the Venetian night," he began. "And Carlito reminds me a lot of my youngest. Charles, his name was Charles." Antonio's voice choked up a little. He swirled his brandy, took a small sip, swirled some more. "The oldest was named Samuel. They were just regular American boys, you know? We had this life—friends, barbecues, church on Sunday. And then, one day, everything changed. In an instant, my whole world turned upside down. A policeman came to my office. I knew him—Johnny, Johnny O'Malley. I thought he was coming to sell me tickets to some fundraiser, although he'd never come to the office before. 'I'm sorry, Anthony,' he said. I remember he took off his hat. 'There's been an accident. Your wife and the boys were taken to...hospital.' I remember I stood up, grabbed my keys. 'Let's go,' I said as if we had no time to waste and Johnny put his hand on my arm, 'Take it easy. I'm sorry, Anthony, they didn't make it.' I yelled his words back at him, 'Didn't make it? Who didn't make it? Not Jane. Not Samuel. Not Charles. Who didn't make it?' His hand on my arm was like a vice turning tighter and tighter with every word. He told me the boys were dead on the scene. Jane had died en route to the hospital."

Rosa put her hand over her mouth; her eyes were wide with shock and sympathy. She couldn't imagine it. What could she say? She put her hand on his arm and then just as quickly removed it.

"That was last year. I quit my job. I sold the house. But I couldn't seem to make a plan. The doctor said it was shock and I said, 'No kidding?'" Antonio's laugh was bitter. "He prescribed a long vacation. He said, 'Travel for a while. A change of scenery.' So here I am. Wandering around Europe, like a lost soul. Looking for something I lost but knowing I won't ever find them."

"Oh dear," said Rosa. "Oh dear." Her hand was back on his arm, patting.

"When I saw your boy today, I swear it was the first time I smiled in weeks. I hope I haven't upset you with my story. I don't usually burden strangers with my sorrow but you told me about your husband's death and so—"

"It's different for me," said Rosa. She straightened her shoulders and continued, "I never loved my husband. I married in haste and I had lots of time to regret it. And the more I regretted it, the worse things got with the marriage. My husband was a jealous man and eventually I gave him reason to be jealous. I had an affair. Another mistake. I should have just left and gone back to Napoli. I have an uncle there who would have said, 'I told you so,' at least once a day, but he might have taken me in."

"So you stayed? Because of Carlito?"

"No, my lover—Claudio left the village before I had a chance to tell him that I was pregnant with Carlito. So I pretended Carlito was my husband's son. It's a small village. No room for *madre single*, a woman raising a child on her own. And then, when Carlito was still a baby, my husband disappeared or drowned or both— it doesn't matter and I was left alone with a boy to raise."

"And the other man? Did you ever hear from him again?"

"He came back three years ago. Said he'd just found out that my husband was dead and that I had a son. Well, we have a son. Carlito was almost four when Claudio came back and Carlito looked so much like Claudio that anyone would know he's Claudio's son. Still the villagers pretend he's my husband's son and I pretend that they don't know and Claudio lives in the village and comes to my house every night and everyone pretends that nothing's going on. It's a small village. They stick to tradition even when truth is staring them in the face."

"Does your boy know?" asked Antonio, looking into his brandy snifter as if the answer might be there in the amber liquid.

"No."

"Will you tell him?"

"I don't know. I want to do what's best for Carlito but it's really not my decision to tell him or not tell him. He'll hear. As long as we live in the village, someone will say something and he'll hear."

"Perhaps, best if you tell him, then? What's your—Carlito's father—say?"

"We've been fighting about it lately. He wants Carlito to know. He wants us to tell him together. Tell him that Claudio is his real father. Tell him his mother was unfaithful."

"That's a heck of a situation," said Antonio; he tipped the last of the brandy into his mouth. "What will you do?"

"I think I'll have that brandy now."

Almost seven years had passed since Elgidio the postmaster had disappeared in the night. At first, no one was particularly concerned because Elgidio had taken to drinking too much and getting lost on his way home. Sometimes he woke up in Nino the farmer's field, other times in his own backyard or behind the post office. It didn't matter where he found himself; the facts remained the same. He'd been unable to get his wife Rosa pregnant even though they'd been married for over two years. There'd been rumours that he was impotent and his wife was unhappy and then, rumours that Rosa was having an affair with Claudio. The same night that Rosa told Elgidio she was pregnant, Claudio left the village. What did that mean? Since the baby was born, Elgidio had drank even more because every time he looked at their son Carlito, he saw Claudio's face looking back at him. Looking like that Cheshire cat in the story book that Carlito liked. That smile that no one could describe or understand or interpret. Elgidio drank to forget all those things, drank until he too smiled like the Cheshire cat. That's what he was doing on the last night anyone saw him; he was inspecting his reflection in the river that ran deep behind Nino's farm. He was so tired; his throat was so dry. The river was a pillow where he could lay his head and drink, feel the icy cool water soothe his parched throat. The river was black as tar; he closed his eyes, opened his mouth. He remembered the relief of the cold water numbing his thoughts, erasing his worries. He sank lower into the river, his head heavy on the water, and he felt nothing as he floated downhill.

When Elgidio failed to turn up at his home or at the post office the next morning, and Nino found Elgidio's hat hanging on his grapevines, the village police searched the riverbanks from Nino's farm down to the pastures outside the village where the river forked. They found nothing. The police chief phoned to the nearest villages and asked them to keep an eye out for a body. And then they waited.

At the bar most of the men were in agreement. "The police chief couldn't find a body without a map."

"The river was moving very fast last week. All that spring rain. Elgidio's body would have reached the *Mediterraneo* by now,"

"Hard for the widow without a body," said the coffin maker. He didn't add that without a body, he couldn't build a coffin. Building coffins was how he made his living. Then he added, "How's she going to live?"

"Maybe they'll give her Elgidio's job at the post office," suggested the young man who was now a hotel doorman in Rome. Apparently he'd forgotten how village life worked.

"Sure, right after they offer her the mayor's job. What's the matter with you? This is Supino, not Roma. A woman can't run the post office."

"There's no death certificate unless they find the body," said Pietro. "That means no coffin, no funeral, and no pension for the widow." Someone suggested Rosa could sell the house but Pietro reminded them that the house was in Elgidio's name so she couldn't sell it for seven years. The men shook their heads at the idea that you couldn't sell your own house.

"Seven years?" someone repeated.

"Until he's declared officially dead," explained Pietro as he gathered glasses, emptied ashtrays, ran his bar cloth over the tabletops. "No pension, no sale. Nothing to do but wait."

"Elgidio made a mess of his life when he was alive," said the coffin maker, "and he's created a worse mess now that he's dead."

"What was he doing by the river in the first place? His route is his house, the post office, and the bar."

"Maybe he got lost on his way home," said Pietro. "It wouldn't be the first time."

"I'll tell you one thing for sure," said the coffin maker. "Once he fell in that river, he moved faster than he ever had in his life."

There's No Place Like Home

BIANCA HEARD FORTUNATO CHATTING WITH the postman; she heard the thud of the mail on the counter; she heard the whoosh of the beads, which hung on the doorway, as they separated. And swung back together again: click...click...click. And then, Fortunato called up to her, "Some mail for you, *bella*." She fairly flew down the stairs. Her heart was pounding—it must be the first of her Ask Minerva letters from the newspaper office—but when she saw the envelope in Fortunato's hand and the questioning look on her husband's face, the pounding stopped.

"From the newspaper office in Frosinone," said Fortunato as he read aloud the return address. His tone was questioning.

"For me?" asked Bianca, breathless, with a little tilt of her head, a lift of her eyelashes.

"It says, '*signora* Bianca Corsi.' There's no doubt about it—that's you."

Bianca turned up her palm and her smile. "*Grazie*," she said but Fortunato didn't put the envelope in her outstretched hand. Instead he said, "It feels heavy."

"Of course, it's heavy," said Bianca. "It's a newspaper."

"Why is the office sending you a newspaper? I'm the one who subscribes." Sometimes Fortunato could be curious, stubbornly curious, in thinking up questions. Fortunately, Bianca could think up lies just as quickly. But she was trying to be more patient, kinder, so she tried to pacify Fortunato. Her words would still be lies, but they'd be pretty lies, reassuring ones.

"It's a gift. I went to the office in Frosinone to enquire about an ad for my herb store. They said they'd send me a newspaper so I could inspect the other ads and decide if I want to place one of my own."

"But we already get the newspaper. They didn't need to send you one." Fortunato lifted the envelope in his hand, as if he was weighing it, once, twice. "Why is your newspaper in an envelope? Mine doesn't come in a—"

"Because it's a gift. Because they want me to spend my money on an ad. Because they think my husband is *signor curioso*. What's the matter with you, Fortunato? Do I pick up every piece of mail with your name and ask you why this and why that? No. Because I have other things to do. Better things to do. Give me my mail and get on with your own business. Shave someone. Cut their hair."

With a shrug of his shoulders, he motioned to his empty barber chair.

"So, trim your own moustache. Or stand outside so people can see you're available. Or put your own ad in the newspaper. But leave me alone."

Fortunato handed over the envelope. Then he stepped outside and leaned against his barber pole, his mind spiralling just like the red and white stripes of his pole.

A few minutes later, Bianca brushed past him. "Wait," he called out. "Where are you going?"

"See you later," she replied and she waved her envelope at him.

By the time, Bianca had walked up the circular driveway that led to her mother's house, she had decided to tell her mother everything about her secret job as an advice columnist for the Frosinone newspaper. Sometimes, honesty was warranted.

"Ask Minerva?" said her mother. "I don't understand. Ask her what?"

"Anything they want to ask, Mamma. My job is to give them an answer."

"But what if they want to know about personal things? Problems in the bedroom or how to get money out of a husband with a tight fist or what to say to a nosy mother-in-law."

"I'll tell them."

"Bianca, think for a moment. Men read the newspaper too, you know. If you tell a wife to slip a few *lire* out of her husband's pants when he's asleep, men might start counting their money..."

"—Mamma, I'll deal with all of that when the letters come in. Here," said Bianca, in an attempt to reassure her mother, and herself, "let's look at some right now. But first, I need to ask a favour."

"What is it this time? Remember, I don't babysit."

"It's nothing like that, Mamma. I just want to ask if I can have the letters sent to your house instead of mine."

"I'm disappointed you didn't think of that already, Bianca. What were you thinking, having them sent to the barbershop? Your husband doesn't need to know all of your business. Haven't you learned that yet? And don't stick your finger under the flap—you're likely to break a nail that way—let me call Teresa to bring the letter opener."

Within a few minutes, the mahogany table in the dining room was covered with letters of various shapes and sizes and Bianca's mother had sorted them according to the quality of the envelopes. Then she picked one up. "This one has perfect penmanship," she said. "Open it first."

"'Dear Minerva,'" read Bianca. "'My life is almost perfect. I have a wealthy husband who gives me everything I want. I have a big house filled with the finest furniture and closets full of the finest clothes. I even have a fur coat...'"

"—A fur coat?!" said Bianca's mother. "Obviously the husband is having an affair."

"Mamma, please, we don't know that. Let me finish."

"Fine. Find out for yourself. You'll still learn the truth before this stupid woman," and she flicked her lacquered nail at the notepaper.

"'But something doesn't seem quite right,'" Bianca continued reading. "'My husband now has business meetings two nights a week and he comes home rather late. Even though he complains about these meetings before he leaves, he seems happy enough when he returns—I hear him singing in the shower. Then he comes to bed and falls asleep almost instantly. Last week, he went to his meeting without his briefcase—he left it in the front hall—and when I asked him about it, he got very angry with me and demanded to know if I had opened it. Of course, I had not.'"

"Don't read anymore, please!" Bianca's mother leaned back in her chair, the back of her hand draped across her forehead. "This woman is giving me a headache. Does she not wonder what her husband didn't want her to see in that briefcase? Anyone would tell her there was either a jewellery box or an invoice for some jewellery that the wife never received but this woman is so stupid she'll think that her husband is going to surprise her with a gift and the real surprise will be—"

"Mamma, please. I can't get any work done if you keep interrupting me. Let me finish."

"Tell her the only business men have in the evening is with other women. Ask her if her husband is that Don Giovanni—Lorenzo... I forget his last name but I hear he's romancing the new hairdresser who is jingling more jewellery than a—"

"First, I have to read what kind of advice she wants."

"Of course, maybe she wants to be blind as well as stupid."

"Okay, Mamma, why don't I put this letter aside for now and we'll open another one. You pick. Thank you. Yes, it is a nice envelope. Yes, I noticed the black edging. Okay, okay, pass me the letter opener. All right, here's what the letter writer says, 'My uncle Tony is so angry at my uncle Domenic that he says he will strangle him with his bare hands the next time he sees him. Some problem about property and money owed and...well, that doesn't matter. Now, another uncle—Luigi has pneumonia and the doctor says he won't live long and my aunt is worried about the funeral. Because both Uncle Tony and Uncle Domenic will come to Uncle Luigi's funeral to pay their respects but if they are there at the same time, Uncle Tony may try to strangle Uncle Domenic.'"

"*May try?*" repeated Mamma. "What is the matter with these people? Didn't she write that the uncle said he *would* strangle the other uncle? Why is she writing 'may try'? Of course, he will try—does she expect him to lose face within the family? You can't go around saying you're going to strangle someone and then when the opportunity arises, do nothing."

"But Mamma, at a funeral?"

"What better place?"

"You don't think it's disrespectful to take everyone's attention away from the dead uncle?"

"It depends. If he's any kind of responsible man, he'll have to keep his word. I don't understand her problem. What does she want you to do?"

"Give advice. That's my job. To give advice."

"Wait," said Bianca's mother. She leaned forward in her chair, whispered to her daughter even though they were alone in the silent dining room, "Do you think the letter writer is that gossip who lives next door to the pig farm? She's a jealous woman, that one. I'll bet she's more interested in what's going to happen to the property when the man dies. I remember she wanted to buy part of the land and the pig farmer wouldn't sell. I wouldn't be surprised if she didn't cause his illness in some way. The berries of the *bella donna* are in bloom now and they can injure the lungs. Well, you know that. What illness did you say he had?"

"Pneumonia, but that's not the point, Mamma. The woman is looking for advice about..."

"Tell her to mind her own business. Stop planning a funeral for someone who's still alive. Have the decency to wait until the man's dead before she starts coveting his property."

"I don't think you understand, Mamma. She's worried about one uncle killing another at a funeral."

It was at that moment that Teresa arrived with the tea tray and Bianca quickly pushed the letters into the brown envelope and tucked it under her chair.

"I'll finish these later," she said. "Do you think I might keep them upstairs? You're not using that room at the back of the house, are you, Mamma? The one with the desk?"

"Use it if you want. I never go in that room. Maybe Teresa mops it once in a while. I'll remind her to clean it properly."

It took Bianca several days to settle on her first three responses for the newspaper. She thought they should be different topics, not all romance or family problems but a nice mix of questions and wise answers. She typed out her responses on her father's old Olivetti and kept a carbon paper copy in the top right hand drawer of the desk. After she sent the first responses back in the stamped envelope that the newspaperman had included, she began to wonder how people would react to the column. Of course, she'd hear their opinions at her weekly hairdresser's appointment.

In the Mood for Love

WALKING HOME FROM WORK, ASSUNTA met up with the florist and his wife as they were closing the metal grate of their flower shop, barring the window display that featured fluffy white ostrich feathers in bronze pots and silk poppies drooping out of silver vases.

"A good day?" asked Assunta.

"Giuseppe Tomei died this morning so funeral flowers for tomorrow," said the wife.

"Nothing but red roses," added the husband. "A basket of roses from each of the children and a rosebud rosary from the grandchildren. A giant cross of roses from the wife. So a good day for us but not so good for Giuseppe."

"Ey!" called Fortunato from across the street. "Funeral for Giuseppe?"

"Tomorrow at eleven," said the wife. "Church of San Nicola."

Fortunato locked his barbershop door, patted his striped barber pole for good luck, and joined the others.

"A good man," said Fortunato.

"Four children—all married," added the florist. "Seven grandchildren—all boys."

"I hear Bianca is expecting," said the florist's wife. "Maybe a boy for you this time."

"I'm not sure we'd know what to do with a boy," laughed Fortunato. "But we'll see what the springtime brings."

The florist and his wife left Fortunato and Assunta at the corner, wishing them *buona sera*.

"Going to check on your new house?" Fortunato asked Assunta. "I'll walk along with you, if you don't mind."

"Of course. How's Bianca, the girls?"

"Antonietta is at the *liceo* this year. Did you know that? She takes the bus into Frosinone every morning with the other teenagers. I can hardly believe it, you know? It doesn't seem that long ago that we were that age."

"Almost twenty years, Fortunato."

"Impossible! How can we be that old? Of course, you still look like a teenager, Assunta." Fortunato ran his fingers through his thick hair. "My hair is turning grey."

"That's a distinguished look on a man," said Assunta. She didn't say that hers would have strands of grey as well if not for the hairdresser's skill.

Fortunato and Assunta walked past the green grocer, already closed; they said, *"buonanotte"* to the shoe-store owners, started up the slope to the T in the road where the telephone booth stood like a Swiss guard.

Fortunato said, "It seemed that it was a happy time when you and I were at the *liceo*, don't you think?"

"How do you mean?" asked Assunta. Her heart beat faster.

"I don't know. Before all the responsibilities of marriage and children, I guess."

"I don't have those responsibilities, Fortunato, you always forget."

"*Scusa*, Assunta, I'm a fool. You must be feeling a little lonely tonight with your father and Elena away. And Rosa and Carlito away too."

"Maybe." Just for a few moments, she let her mind linger in those long-ago days when she and Fortunato, along with the other teenagers, boarded the blue bus for Frosinone and travelled the half hour to the *liceo*. How Assunta had loved him; how Fortunato had never noticed. Except for the strands of grey in his coarse hair, Fortunato looked much the same—a sturdy boy with a friendly smile. So long ago—all ancient history. They turned up *via condotto vecchio*. Five more houses and Assunta would be at her new home.

"Remember that time that Cosmo Boni kicked his soccer ball to someone on the school bus and they missed the pass?" asked Assunta. "And it hit the front windshield and landed in the bus driver's lap."

"Of course. The driver stopped and yelled at all of us. When we got to the school, the bus driver went into the office with Cosmo—the ball too—and Father Augusto called his house and Cosmo's father came to the school."

"Remember how we actually heard his father's footsteps thundering down the hall and *il professore* tapped his ruler for attention but we all ran to the door and looked out anyway?"

Fortunato laughed. "We would not have heard it all if we'd stayed in our seats—Cosmo's father yelling at him and at the bus driver too. Dragging Cosmo down the hall by the back of his jacket."

"And you and your friends, Fortunato, laughing in your sleeves. Poor Cosmo."

"What—poor Cosmo? He had three days off school. I think he spent the time practicing for the school team; we won that year so it all turned out for the best."

They were both laughing when they arrived at the door of Assunta's new house. "No lights," said Fortunato. "Do you want me to come in with you?"

Across the street, beside Rosa's house, someone scraped the balcony door open a little. Someone else turned down the radio.

"I can do it," said Assunta. "I'm just going to check on the paint job. See if the workers are finished."

"Close up the windows when you're done," advised Fortunato. "It's a little damp tonight and you want the paint to dry. When's your father coming home from his honeymoon? It's almost chestnut harvest time and I know he won't miss that."

"He and Elena will be back at the end of the month. Rosa and Carlito will be back next week." Assunta's voice was as flat as a glass of ginger ale left sitting too long on the counter.

"Oh yes, Giuseppina has the map of Venezia open at the house, trying to guess where they might be each day," said Fortunato. "Of course she imagines every trip is by gondola. What about you, Assunta? No desire for a trip to some faraway city?"

"I was in Genoa in the springtime, remember?"

Fortunato shook his head, "But that was for work, wasn't it? I meant for pleasure."

Assunta imagined herself in Venezia, travelling by gondola on a night like this with the sun just setting and the stars waiting to make their entrance. She'd be alone in the boat, of course, except for the gondolier singing, "O Sole Mio."

Assunta shook her head, hoped the teardrop would be too proud to fall. Fortunato pulled her sweater tighter across her shoulders, "Don't want you to catch cold," he said. "I best be getting home."

"Say hello to the girls," called Assunta. "And Bianca," and her voice was loud so the neighbours wouldn't feel the need to report to Bianca that Fortunato was lingering at Assunta's new house as if it meant something, their being together, when Assunta knew it meant nothing. Just like when they were young.

She looked across the street at Rosa's house: it too was dark and lonely.

As Assunta climbed the steps to her new house, she could hear Fortunato's whistle grow *piano, piano* as he headed home. Down the street someone closed their shutters and latched them tight. The roar of a motorcycle headed up the hill: the girl sitting on the back turned to stare at Assunta just as Assunta wiped aside her tear. She turned the key in her front door; heard the click as it unlocked; heard the echo as it bounced off the neighbour's wall. Across the street a shadow in a window stopped to look. Assunta turned on the light; went inside; closed the door quickly and that bang echoed in the street just like the sound of unlocking her front door had done. She told herself that these were the sounds of life in the village and she would have to get used to them.

All her life, she'd lived on the farm and every day she left the prying eyes and ears of the village behind her when she walked to the tranquility of her home. Only buttercups and poppies bowed their heads to her when she passed; no one noticed her arrival except for her father Nino and Zeus the donkey and they were mostly interested in what she might make for their supper. But once she started living in the village, her neighbours, whether they were visible or not, would be her constant companions. The sounds of her every activity would be available to all who cared to watch or listen. Her neighbours meant this as a kind of caring for her well-being, for her safety, for her spinster status, she knew this...and yet, on this night, it chafed.

Inside the house smelled of paint. Assunta kept her distance from the freshly painted walls as she climbed the stairs to her bedroom. Maybe she'd been wrong about the colour. The paint chip said "cappuccino foam," but it was beige. Everything was beige. The workers had installed the full-length mirror on the back of the bedroom door but they hadn't installed the light fixture yet. Even in the half-light from the open bathroom door, when she looked in the mirror, Assunta saw that she looked tired. She closed the windows to keep out the night air but she couldn't keep out the thoughts that her life was as beige as the walls and her reflection confirmed that. Even after she locked the door and headed to the farm, melancholy accompanied her.

Zeus the donkey was happy to see her, happier still when she forked the hay into his trough. The chickens were glad she was home, clucking loudly as she sprinkled their feed. The dog rubbed his head against her leg as she unlocked the farmhouse door. But it wasn't enough.

She took some leftovers from the fridge but didn't bother to turn on the stove to heat them. Instead, she decided it was cool enough to light a fire. Assunta sat with her cold dinner on her lap and watched the flames and thought about Fortunato heading home to wife and family; thought about her own father, remarried at sixty-five and honeymooning with Elena. At the bottling plant, Gino was set to propose to his girl; Claudio wanted to marry Rosa. Everyone was coupled up except her.

She returned her plate to the kitchen; she wasn't even sure what she had eaten—cold sausages, cold potatoes and cold peas?—and opened the top cupboard where her father kept the brandy. Maybe the brandy would warm her since the fire hadn't. That's what she told herself but really she wanted the brandy to silence her chattering mind and knock her off to sleep, which she hoped would be dreamless.

When Fortunato unlocked the door at his house, Giuseppina was already on the other side, pulling it wide open. "I've been waiting for you. Dinner's ready."

Fortunato glanced at the table: there was a copper-coloured oak leaf at every setting so he knew that his oldest daughter Antonietta had set the table. Lately, she'd taken to adding these little touches of the season. "*Bella, bella mia,*" he said to her. As Fortunato reached the kitchen sink to wash his hands, Bianca finally spoke. "Hurry up. The pasta's getting cold." Her face was fuller now that she was expecting but he didn't dare mention it because although he thought it made her look more feminine, Bianca thought she looked bloated. Her waist was gone. "You look tired, *bella*. A long day?" asked Fortunato and since Bianca didn't respond, he made a suggestion, "I was thinking you might like to change your hours at the herb store. Maybe open only two days a week instead of three. What do you think?"

"Maybe," said Bianca.

"Also, I was thinking," continued Fortunato, "that we could clear out the things from that extra bedroom upstairs and I could paint it for the babies."

"Paint it pink," said Antonietta.

"Paint it blue," said Giuseppina.

"And if it's one of each?" asked Bianca. "One of you will have to share your room."

The girls pointed at each other but they laughed.

Bianca dished out the pasta. The sweet scent of simmered tomatoes combined with the strong scent of Romano cheese filled the room.

"Yellow," said Fortunato. "Canary yellow. A nice, bright colour. A happy colour for boys or girls. What do you think of that, *bella*?"

"*Si*, if yellow guarantees two happy babies, that's the colour we want."

"Yellow, it is," said Fortunato and turning to Bianca, he said, "I walked Assunta to her new house this evening and she seemed a little sad."

"I would think she'd be happy—to have a house to herself and time to herself."

"I think she's missing her father. And Rosa and—"

"Do you want to look at the map?" asked Giuseppina. "I was thinking they might have gone to the Lido beach one day where all the big fancy hotels are."

"Maybe they'll see a movie star," sighed Antonietta. She was thirteen and Hollywood-obsessed. "That's where they all stay."

"And how do you know where the movie stars stay when they are in Venezia?" asked Bianca.

"Oh, someone at school said—"

"What someone? Do they have a name?"

"Of course."

"And what is it?"

"Okay, okay, it was Gianni—"

"Gianni Capobianco! I knew it. How many times have I told you to stay away from that boy? We're not sending you to the *liceo* to talk to boys. We're sending you to learn things. Important things—not where movie stars stay. As if that Capobianco boy knows anything about movie stars or Venezia."

Bianca twirled her spaghettini and lifted a forkful to her mouth. The conversation was over, or it would have been, if Antonietta hadn't said, "I can't just ignore the boys at the *liceo*. That would be rude."

"No, that would be smart," replied Bianca. She pointed her fork at Antonietta. "They'd learn soon enough that you're there for education not romance."

"You're so mean..." began Antonietta.

"Antonietta," warned Fortunato, motioning with his fork to her plate.

"Why don't you just send me to a convent and get it over with?"

"Don't think I won't young lady and—hey, Antonietta, you get back to the table."

"Let her go," said Fortunato. "She's just upset. It's hard to be a teenager. Don't you remember when we were at the *liceo*, Bianca?"

"I remember that Carmela always talking to the boys and the next thing you know she's a married woman at sixteen. Then seven months later, a baby arrives. I remember Carmela's mother saying, 'Premature,' and my mother saying, 'A nine-pound premature baby! A miracle.' As if anyone was fooled."

"Assunta and I were speaking of the *liceo* tonight too. It bothered me a little to see her looking sad. I wonder why she never married and had a family of her own."

"Maybe no one asked her. Or maybe it wasn't the right person who asked her," said Bianca. "Maybe she has a secret lover living in the next village. What do we know?"

"If she had a lover, in the next village or the next country, we'd know all about it. There are no secrets in this village. You should know that by now, Bianca."

"Maybe she's married to her work like these American women in all the magazines."

"Work can't keep you warm at night," said Fortunato, reaching for her hand, raising it to his lips to kiss.

"It also won't give you babies," said Bianca but she was smiling. "Are you going to buy the paint tomorrow?"

"Funeral for Giuseppe Tomei tomorrow."

"What?"

"He died today. Didn't you hear, *bella*?"

She'd been at her mother's and missed the news. In that moment, Bianca decided two things: she would keep her herb store open the usual three days a week so she could keep up on what was happening in the village, and she would mix up a potion for Assunta. Some kind of love potion. Nothing too strong. Assunta couldn't deal with that but something that would make her more interesting to men. The problem was how would she administer it? It was not as if she and Assunta had tea together or...well, she'd think of something. She always did.

The following morning when Fortunato went to the Kennedy

Bar for his ten o'clock espresso, Pietro was just getting ready to read a letter to Minerva from the newspaper.

"This Minerva," said Pietro, "it's like she's here having coffee with us every morning. An invisible customer."

"What do you care?" asked the grocer. "Maybe she doesn't pay for an invisible coffee but she brings lots of us here, just to hear her advice."

"Pretty bad advice, I'd say," said the coffin maker.

"Let's hear what she has to say first," said Pietro with a shake of the newspaper to announce the first letter and Minerva's response: "'Dear Minerva: I met a man who wants me to go away with him for the weekend. To the beach in Positano. It's in another province and no one would know us or know we weren't married. Is it okay? Signed, In Love.'"

"'Dear fool, You might be in love but I guarantee your Romeo is in lust. Men are only interested in one thing and it's not three little words, it's three little letters. Tell him that if he wants to take you away to another city, he'll have to stop at the church first and put a wedding band on your finger. If he says yes, then you can say yes. If he says no, you say goodbye. Didn't your mother teach you anything? Minerva.'"

The regulars all voiced their opinions.

"So suspicious."

"I can't believe they pay her to write such answers." The butcher banged his hand on the table; the street sweeper added his judgment.

"Obviously, no one ever asked her to go to the beach."

"Spiteful, if you ask me. Bitter—like last year's wine," said the postman. He leaned back in his chair and made a suggestion, "Wants to get back at all men just because no one invited her to the seaside, or anywhere."

Several of the men laughed and began telling their own stories of women who'd accepted invitations and those who did not. When Fortunato left the bar to return to his barbershop, the air was still thick with tales of romantic conquests and secret liaisons. *Le relazioni* both real and imagined.

The Bottle-Cap Salesman

IT WAS ONLY THE SECOND day of Rosa and Carlito's trip to Venezia and Assunta was missing her friend. Half a dozen times during the day, she'd started to leave her desk to walk to Rosa's and then, she'd remembered and sat back down again. In fact, she had just sat down once more when Enzo the bottle-cap salesman came out of Claudio's office. He stopped at her desk.

"Do you have a few minutes?" Enzo asked as he straightened his tie. Assunta put down her pen and looked directly into his eyes before she spoke.

"Yes, but Enzo, you know I don't make the decisions about new suppliers. That's Claudio's job."

"I know. It's something else," he said, and he stuck two fingers under his collar and pulled a little as if he needed some extra room to allow for his next words. "I just thought it's getting close to lunch hour. I can't do any more calls until after four. I'm hungry and if you're hungry, I thought we might have lunch together." When Assunta didn't answer right away, Enzo made another suggestion, "Just name the restaurant and I'm happy to take you there."

Assunta laughed. There were no restaurants in the village and she was pretty sure that Enzo knew that. Plus, she usually brought her lunch to work. Enzo was now nonchalantly tossing his car keys in the air and catching them while he waited for her response. Her usual bagged lunch was waiting for her in the fridge. Before she could say no thank you, she surprised herself and said, "Sure. Why not?" and he dropped the keys and scrambled to pick them up and when he rose, his face was flushed and his smile was wide. Assunta smoothed her hair and her grey wool skirt and reached for her matching sweater, which was hanging on the back of her chair.

He drove a forest-green Alfa Romeo, which was highly polished and smelled like something vaguely familiar. Before Assunta had identified the scent, Enzo rolled down his window and the autumn breeze arrived and ruffled his hair at the back of his neck.

"Where would you like to go?" he asked as if he was a genie from an Arabian tale rather than a bottle-cap salesman from Italy. "Your wish is my command."

They were headed out of town, approaching a café attached to the gas station. Assunta said, "We could get a *panini* and a coffee there."

"Why don't we drive into the next town," Enzo suggested. "I have a customer in Ferentino and there's a new restaurant close to his business. Why don't we try that?"

Assunta fidgeted. After all, what did she know about this man other than the fact that he was a salesman who came monthly to try to convince Claudio to buy his bottle caps and Claudio always told him that he was happy with the company they used and they shook hands and then, the next month, Enzo appeared again. She didn't want him to think that she had any influence over Claudio's decisions; maybe agreeing to lunch had given him the wrong idea. But Enzo wasn't talking about bottle caps; he was talking about the opera. He was planning to get tickets for an opera in Verona next month and planning to spend a weekend there.

"My friend Rosa is near Verona right now," said Assunta. "She and her son Carlito have gone to Venezia for ten days."

"Ahh, Venezia," said Enzo. "She's so beautiful, so mysterious and now her fame has spread so far and she attracts so many tourists. I think she casts a spell on the visitors and they go back home and tell all their friends and the friends come and they too fall under her spell. The serenading gondoliers seduce them.

She's playing a dangerous game, attracting all these tourists; soon there will be no room for Venetians. They'll be overrun by the *Americani*."

Assunta smoothed her tweed skirt and looked at her palms for a moment as if they might contain the answer. She said, "I take it you don't like the *Americani*."

"I love Americans. I just love our way of life more than theirs and they threaten that."

"Venezia attracts tourists, that's all. Isn't that good for our economy?"

"Spoken like a true American—for them, it's always about money. Some things are more important than dollars."

"Not when you don't have a job. Not when you're hungry."

"Venetians have managed for thousands of years. They're experts at importing goods and—wait a minute, I almost missed my turn. There's the restaurant on the right. We can finish our talk inside."

But they didn't. They got settled into a corner table right next to a long, narrow window with a restricted view: a tangled quince tree and a wooden bench. Assunta said something about the bench looking like one that her father had made years ago just after her mother had died and then she got talking about her father's recent marriage to Elena and she told Enzo about her plans to move out of her father's farmhouse and into Elena's small house in the village. She spoke about it as if the move was an adventure and she said she was excited to be living alone for the first time in her life but somehow her voice cracked a little and she had to take a sip of her wine. And then another.

Enzo reached across the table and patted her hand. "How is it that a lovely girl like you never married?" he asked. "Wait," he said, answering his own question. "You were too busy taking care of your father after your mother died, right?" and Assunta nodded because it was easier to agree with that noble suggestion rather than admit that no one had ever asked her. "And all the men who were in love with you got tired of waiting and married someone else, right? I'll bet they look at you now and wish they'd waited just a little longer."

Assunta wasn't sure that Enzo was aware that he'd left his hand on hers but she was very aware of it. He kept it there until the waiter came with the pasta. Even then, he withdrew slowly and she was a little disappointed when he did.

"What about you?" she asked. "Why aren't you married?"

"I travel too much with my job. I never met the exactly right girl. My brother married and had children so my mother is happy. I met a girl in Sicily once and I thought about marrying her but my mother almost had a heart attack when I mentioned Sicily—as if it was a completely different country, like Africa, and I got tired of the tension. I'm a man who likes peace. So, I'm a happy bachelor eating lunch with a beautiful woman—not a bad life at all."

They talked all through lunch and even after the waiter put the bill on the table and hovered nearby, Assunta didn't realize they were the only customers left in the restaurant. She had a vague recollection of hearing the church bells ringing and a clearer memory of the waiter coughing several times and a very clear vision of glancing at her watch and seeing that it was a quarter past four. "*Madonna*," she said. "Claudio will think I have deserted him. And the deliverymen... I have to get back to work. Right now."

Enzo put some bills on the table and lifted her sweater from her chair but when she put her arm into the sleeve, she realized that he had squeezed the cuff and her hand was trapped inside. "I won't let go until you promise to have lunch with me again," he said with a smile and a light tone but also with a look in his eye that she couldn't quite decipher. Was he actually interested in her? He'd been coming into the bottling plant for four or five months now and never offered more than a *buongiorno*. Why now? "Please say yes," he said, and Assunta interpreted his look as loneliness. And she knew loneliness.

They arranged to meet the next day at the same restaurant. Enzo said he had business in the area and would she mind driving there herself to meet him? Of course, he would be happy to come to the bottling plant and pick her up, if she preferred; it was just that he would already be in the town, near the restaurant and if she didn't mind ...

She didn't mind. In fact, she preferred to meet him outside of the village. That way she could keep the lunch dates to herself. Rosa was in Venezia and who else would she tell? She thought about that question the next morning when she stopped at the dry goods store and bought a new sweater, which she immediately draped over her shoulders to ward off the morning chill, and when she decided on the spur of the moment to stop in at the hairdresser's, that's where she met Bianca.

"New sweater?" asked Bianca. "That's a good colour for you, Assunta. What is that? Eggplant? Merino wool?" Bianca reached out to touch the fabric but Assunta ducked under her arm and into the hairdresser's.

"It was on sale," said Assunta.

"Really?" asked Bianca in a voice that suggested that she knew Assunta was lying even if she didn't know why. "What are you doing here anyway?" asked Bianca. "It's not your day for a wash and set." Before Assunta could think of another lie to explain her presence in the hairdresser's shop on a Wednesday instead of her usual Thursday, the new hairdresser approached in a puff of lavender perfume.

"Did you read this?" asked the new hairdresser, waving her bangles and the newspaper in her hand. "Listen. 'Dear Minerva: My son is running around with a girl from the city. Now the woman of the *tabacchi* store tells me he bought a bottle of perfume, and had it gift-wrapped, but it hasn't shown up at our house so obviously it's a gift for this girl. Also the roses from my garden keep disappearing. I asked my husband a dozen times to speak to my son but my husband says, "And say what?" What do you advise, dear Minerva?'

"'First of all, don't worry. Second, say nothing. Every mother knows that a boy will run around with any female that allows him to kiss and fondle and do whatever he wants—all for the price of a bottle of cheap perfume. This girl is as common as parsley. When it's time to marry, he'll choose someone whose mother is watching her every move. So let the boy have his fun. Let the girl have her perfume. And let your husband have some peace. Minerva.'"

The Wednesday morning regulars offered their opinions.

"What kind of woman needs to write to the newspaper to get advice she could get anywhere? I think they made up that letter."

"Really? I thought it might be the butcher's son. He's always polishing up the Fiat."

"We could ask the pharmacist's wife. See who's buying condoms all of a sudden."

"The boy's not stupid. He buys them in the city."

"Maybe he gives the girl money and she buys them."

"He better be careful. You can't trust a girl from the city. Those city girls will prick a condom as surely as a thorn will jab your finger. He won't think the rose is so sweet when she tells him there's a *bambino* on the way."

"Are you ready to wash my hair now?" said Assunta turning to the new hairdresser.

But it was Bianca who responded, "What else does this Minerva say?"

"'Dear Minerva,'" read the hairdresser. "'There's a new barber in town and suddenly my husband is going for a trim every two weeks instead of once a month. And he puts on a clean shirt when he goes there. And he tips the barber as much as the cost of the trim. When I ask him about it, he says the new barber is supporting a widowed mother who needs the money and I need to be more generous. What do you think?'"

"It's not Fortunato's barbershop," said Bianca. "The letters aren't necessarily from *our* village, you know."

"Hey!" said Assunta. "New hairdresser, are you going to trim my hair or am I just sitting in this chair to listen to you gossip? I have things to do if you don't."

"*Scusa, signora.* I'm getting the scissors right now. Oh, look at the lovely thick hair you have. Let me just trim the bottoms nice and even. Such strong, healthy hair. You're so fortunate, *signora.*"

"*Si*," said Bianca. "I'm *signora* Fortunato!"

"Come," said the owner, Simonetta and she led Assunta to the back of the shop where the sinks were located. "Let me wash your hair. I have this new shampoo that smells delicious and makes your hair shimmer."

■ ■ ■

When Assunta pulled into the parking lot at the restaurant where she was to meet Enzo for their second lunch date, she saw that his car was already there. And when she opened the restaurant door, he was standing inside near the entrance chatting to the owner. The owner lifted his eyebrow and lowered his voice. Enzo turned. "Assunta," he said. "Here you are! Let me tell you my plan." But Enzo was interrupted by the waiter who came swinging out from the kitchen with a bottle of wine. The cork had been removed but tapped back in again. In the other hand, he carried two stubby wine glasses, one stacked inside the other. He handed the bottle and the glasses to Enzo with a wink. "*Grazie, grazie*," said Enzo, as he reached for the wine and turned back to Assunta. "Come," he said and he headed for the door. Assunta took a quick look at the owner but his face revealed nothing. Behind him the waiter swung through the kitchen doors again with a tray held high and the owner hustled into the main room to unfold a serving table. The restaurant was already half full of guests but there were several empty tables. Wait. Was that Pietro, from the Kennedy Bar, eating a plate of pasta? She turned back to Enzo, put up her hand to say *momento*, but Enzo was already gone so Assunta too went out to the parking lot.

Enzo was leaning against his car, leaning very casually as if he didn't have a care in the world, yet there was a tension in the air. "A little change of plans, if you don't mind," he said. "Come, let me explain on the way." He held open the passenger door and was behind the steering wheel before she'd smoothed her skirt and set down her purse. "It's such a nice day," he began. "I thought why not take Assunta on a picnic? Would you like that, my dear? There's a pretty little spot down near the river with a willow tree. Lots of shade. What do you think?" Assunta didn't know what to think. Was that Pietro she'd seen at the restaurant? And had he seen her? She'd thought she and Enzo would be eating in the restaurant and this sudden change of plans made her a little uneasy. Or maybe it wasn't the change of plans but Enzo's uneasiness that she'd picked up on. "Is everything all right?" she asked.

He said, "It is if you are willing to picnic with me."

He was right. The weeping willow tree growing close to the river's edge provided lots of shade and the trunk stretched so wide that you could have privacy if you wished.

That's where Enzo set up his picnic. There was veal cutlet on a bun that had been wrapped in double layers of aluminum foil and rolled inside a gingham napkin. There was a wedge of olive oil cake spiked with candied orange peels, also wrapped in aluminum foil. There was a bosc pear and a small bottle of water. Finally there was a white box from the bakery in Ferentino with *amaretti* cookies inside. "Is it to your liking?" he asked as he used his penknife to slice the veal sandwich in two.

"It's very nice," said Assunta. "Did you prepare it all?"

Enzo paused for a thoughtful moment before he lifted the bakery box and laughed, "Not the cookies. But let's talk of other things. Let me pour you some wine first."

They must have spoken of other things but Assunta only remembered that his fingers touched hers when he handed her the glass of wine; again when he passed her half of his sandwich. She remembered that he laughed and said, "You have some sauce on your lip. Allow me," and he touched the corner of her mouth with the gingham napkin and his fingers lingered there.

Enzo leaned toward her; she leaned too; the movement ended in a sweet tomato-scented kiss, and then a longer kiss, that promised to be the beginning of many things.

■ ■ ■

Like many things in Venice, they came across the pasta-making storefront by accident. In fact they were lost. Rosa had been looking for the sweater shop they'd seen earlier in the day and Carlito had been watching for the glass store that sold small glass creatures that he could afford with his money from Claudio, and Tony, the American, was just walking with them, stopping now and then to take a photo of yet another canal, another gondola, another wavy reflection of the three of them staring at the water.

"I wish my camera had a recording device," said Tony. "I'd love to tape the sound of the water slapping against the moss every time a boat goes by."

"This morning we saw the garbage boat right outside our hotel window. It made a lot of noise," said Carlito. "You could tape that—it was all clunking and banging."

"*You* make a lot of noise," said Rosa and she reached out to tousle his hair and he escaped to the other side of the canal and stood waiting on the *piazza*. Tony pointed his camera in Carlito's direction and Carlito immediately made his Superman stance with hands on hips, chest pushed out.

"I better catch up to him before he starts looking for a phone booth where he can change into Superman," said Rosa.

"He's a boy with a lot of imagination."

"Yes, he's like his father in that way," said Rosa, and then she stopped because she meant Claudio, her *amore*, who was a natural storyteller and not Elgidio, her husband, who was completely without imagination. She didn't want to clarify; in fact, she didn't want to think about when and how she might tell Carlito that Claudio was his real father. What was real anyway? Nothing in Venice was real, that's for sure. Even standing on the stone bridge hearing the soft sounds of water lapping the moss-covered canals, the echoes of church bells and the calls of pigeons, Venice retained its secrets, the impossibility of its existence. A city built on water? Hundreds of bridges straddling hundreds of canals. Impossible. Yet here they were.

As if Tony could read her mind, he said, "It's unreal, isn't it? So hard to explain. The silence—that's my favourite—the midnight silence of this place. I wish my sons..." He didn't finish his sentence and he didn't need to because Rosa understood his sorrow; his dead sons, his dead wife accompanied him like daytime ghosts.

"Your boy's getting restless," said Tony as he pointed to Carlito who was now jumping from one foot to the other, trying not to fall over as he edged closer to the water's edge.

"*Attenzione*," called Rosa and they joined Carlito and turned down a side street and stopped before a wide window with a crew of Venetians in white caps and aprons making pasta. There was a giant machine with an equally giant dough hook kneading the pasta dough. There were pasta machines like old-fashioned washing machines with rollers that flattened the dough into long narrow sheets. There were cutting machines that turned the sheets into various pasta strips.

"Those are Claudio's favourite," said Carlito pointing to a flat strip.

Pappardelle? "They're *your* favourite," said Rosa.

"We're the same," said Carlito and he looked down the narrow street. Where was that glass store? "I'm going to buy Claudio a surprise gift." Tony opened his mouth to say something, and then he closed it again. He didn't know Rosa that well but he knew her well enough to know she wouldn't welcome his opinion on telling Carlito that Claudio was his father. Rosa was a jumbled mix of sensibility and superstition. Sometimes she was very practical, like when she talked about the water bottling plant or the plans for the village flower show, but other times she was ruled by the phases of the moon. Usually when they related to romance. She actually believed that the full moon had blinded her on the night in Naples when she'd agreed to marry Elgidio. She barely knew him; knew only that he had a secure job and a home and was offering to share them with her. That's what she had said but at the same time, she was obviously very in love with Claudio, had loved him for a long time and yet still was hesitant to marry him. Partly because she'd had a bad marriage with Elgidio; partly because she knew she had to tell Carlito the truth before they married. That made sense to Tony but Rosa had also talked about getting some advice from a fortune teller she had consulted once in Naples. And she wasn't joking. She'd be a lot to handle, unless you were in love with her, and Tony was not ready to be in love with anyone.

After Carlito had found the right glass shop and spent a lot of time making his decisions and counting his money and swearing Tony to secrecy about one of the gifts Carlito had bought, they sat in another *piazza* and ate gelato.

Carlito ordered his typical chocolate and for the second flavour, he'd added pistachio. Rosa had ordered *melone* with chocolate shavings and Tony had maintained his usual order of basic lemon, this one with grated lemon rind in it. "You'd think they'd all taste the same," he said. "After all, lemon is lemon." And both Rosa and Carlito had answered simultaneously, "No it's not."

"They don't have this flavour in Supino," said Carlito, pointing to the pistachio.

"Your village likes the traditional flavours?" asked Tony, and Rosa and Carlito both shook their heads. "Sometimes Claudio grates orange rind on our chocolate gelato at home. You can't find that at the gelato store."

"I'd like to see your village," said Tony.

"You can take the train there," said Carlito. "That's how we got to Venice."

"Get off at Supino station?" asked Tony.

"There's no Supino station," said Rosa, with a shake of her head. "Ferentino is close."

"And then? From Ferentino station?" Both Rosa and Carlito made a circular motion with their hand, and Rosa said, "You know. Ask around."

■■■

Assunta was having a whirlwind romance: she and Enzo had had lunch together, a picnic together, watched a film together in the darkness of the Frosinone cinema followed by coffee and conversation, under the stars, at a tiny café. This was their fifth date and Assunta was looking forward to it. Today's sweater was indigo blue. At the restaurant, the waiter led Assunta immediately to the same table. He brought the same brand of mineral water and the same Castelli Romani wine that they'd drunk the first time. Enzo was on his feet as soon as he saw her; he lifted her sweater from her shoulders but before he folded it over the back of her chair, he held it to his face for a moment.

"It smells like you," he said. "What is that lovely scent?"

"A blend of cedar and rose petals," said Assunta. She blushed a little. "I bought it at the herb store in the village."

"Ahh, so you know Bianca," said Enzo.

"Everyone knows Bianca. In fact, I just saw her this morning at the...in the village."

"I bought some lavender from her herb store—for my mother—last Christmas. The daughter wrapped it for me in a little bag. A sweet little girl. I get my hair cut at Fortunato's barbershop there sometimes. When I'm in the area."

"Yes, Fortunato and I went to school together," said Assunta. She admired the round bowl of her wineglass, and inhaled the heady scent of wild mushrooms and oak before she drank. "We've known each other all our lives."

"Really?" asked Enzo leaning forward to hear her response. "I thought he was older than you. How'd he end up with Bianca?"

"He fell in love with her. That's all. And love is—"

"Blind?"

"Bianca's very beautiful."

"Yes, she's a cool beauty all right. Very detached. A good business woman but not very warm."

"They seem happy enough. Maybe Fortunato's warm enough for both of them."

"Maybe, but let's not talk about them."

Like all their dates, the time flew by. They ate veal stew; they had salad. Assunta listened to Enzo's stories about his different customers and his various travels. He asked her about her favourite opera; he asked if she'd been to the outdoor opera in Roma or in Verona. She told him she'd been to Roma to see *Pagliacci* with her father, but it was a long time ago. And the story and the songs were so sad; she hadn't gone again.

"Maybe it was just that opera," said Assunta. "And Roma is always so jammed with people and cars and...well, you know."

"In Verona, they're performing *La Bohème*, which is perfect of course. The story's just another version of Shakespeare's *Romeo and Juliet* and Verona is the birthplace of that play. We can go and see Juliet's balcony—it's quite ordinary really but when you imagine her standing there with Romeo on the cobblestones beneath it, well, you can't help feeling the romance of it all. *Scusa*, Assunta, I get all sentimental about the opera. Shall we order some dessert?"

"Perhaps," said Assunta. Did he say, "*We* can go..."? Would she? Would she go to Verona with Enzo for the weekend if he asked her? "Perhaps"—that's what she had answered, "Perhaps." But they'd been talking about dessert, hadn't they? Not a weekend in Verona.

A weekend in Verona meant more than a train ride. It meant a hotel room and an understanding that they'd be spending the night together and he hadn't mentioned anything about his intentions or if he had any and what did it matter anyway? She was a grown woman. She could do what she wanted. She could go away for a weekend with a man even if they weren't married. Whose business was it anyway?

"Pardon?" she said.

"I asked if you wanted the *torta*, or would you rather the tiramisu?"

"I can't decide. What are you having?"

"You choose," he said. "Whatever you want is fine with me."

Later that afternoon, while she was tallying the drivers' invoices, she thought about how solicitous he was with her. He always asked her to choose; he'd say, "Whatever you want." She liked that about him. Actually there were many things she liked about him: he was prompt and attentive; he asked about her life, like, "When is your friend returning from Venezia?"

"Two more days."

"When is your father coming back from his honeymoon?"

"Next week."

"When will your new house be ready?"

"Soon."

The last question bothered her a little because she could not have him come to her new house—all the neighbours would see and talk. But he hadn't asked to come to her house. Did it matter? Were their dates outside of the village convenience or secrecy? His invitation to go to Verona—suddenly she felt a chill. He was a handsome man. Was he embarrassed to be seen with someone so ordinary?

"Enzo," she asked the next time she sat down at "their" table. "Why don't we meet in the village?"

"What village?" asked Enzo, filling her wine glass.

"Supino."

He put down his wine glass; looked at her intently. "What's this?" he asked. "Are you tired of eating here?"

"No, no. It's nothing to do with the restaurant. This place is fine; in fact, I like to think of it as 'our place.' But I was also thinking about how we only meet outside of the village. Like a secret rendezvous. And I wondered why. That's all."

"I have appointments in this area. There are no restaurants in the village. I don't want to take you for a quick *panini*. I want to see you surrounded by linen tablecloths and flowers. You belong here"—he gave an expansive sweep of his manicured hand—"among businesspeople, not construction workers and truck drivers grabbing a quick bite. What's this all about, Assunta?" Then, like an insignificant afterthought, he added an extra question, "Did someone say something?"

She laughed. "Who would say something? No one knows I'm seeing you." For the moment she had forgotten that she lived in a village where privacy was a foreign word. She remembered the day they'd had the impromptu picnic; the day she thought she'd seen Pietro in the restaurant. Was it Pietro? Had he seen her? And so what if he had?

"So what's the problem?" Enzo sat back in his chair as if he had all the time in the world to listen to her concerns. And exactly what was her concern?

"I thought, perhaps, you didn't want to be seen with me, for some reason."

"Are you joking?" he asked and he shot forward and grabbed both her hands. "Let everyone see me with you. People will look at you and then at me and say, 'The lucky guy—what does she see in such a man?' Name the place you'd like to go—anywhere in your village or mine or a hundred villages throughout Italy and I'll take you there. Let the whole world see us. You choose. Anything you want. Tell me. Where would you like to go, Assunta?"

He waited for her to answer but she remained silent. Enzo looked at her; he repeated his question, "Where would you like to go, Assunta?"

"Verona," she said. "I'd like to go to Verona with you."

And so it was decided. Enzo said he'd take care of everything: the train tickets, the opera tickets; the hotel reservation.

■■■

At the Kennedy Bar, the talk was mostly about Giuseppe Tomei's funeral the week before

"Too many flowers, such a waste of money," said the coffin maker. "You could hardly see the box—and it was mahogany." The coffin maker couldn't understand why people would pay for an excellent hardwood like mahogany, with its wonderful dark grain, and then cover the wood with roses and common inexpensive ferns. "Everyone knows Giuseppe had four children," said the coffin maker. "Why spend all that money for four giant baskets of roses?"

"And don't forget the long rosary made of rosebuds from the seven grandsons," added the grocer. "Another expense. And for what? To show the love of his grandsons? Better to give the money to the grandsons than to the florist."

But then the florist came in and the conversation stopped. But only momentarily because the grocer asked the painters about Assunta's house. "Painting all done?" he said. "Every wall the colour of the desert?"

"Actually," said Pietro, "the colour's cappuccino. A nice neutral shade. Once she hangs some photos and..."

"Photos of who?" asked the grocer. "Zeus, the donkey?"

"Actually," repeated Pietro but he stopped. He was going to say that he'd seen Assunta, wearing a pretty sweater the colour of sunflowers, in a restaurant in Ferentino just a few days ago. At least he thought it was Assunta but before he could continue, Fortunato took up the rest of Pietro's sentence.

"I think Assunta's feeling a little lonely with her father on his honeymoon and Rosa off to Venezia. I walked her home last week and..."

"—what did Bianca say about that?" asked the grocer, rubbing one finger across the other.

"We're not teenagers anymore," said Fortunato. "A married man can have a friend, an old friend."

"An *old* friend? That's what you call her? No wonder she's depressed, painting her house brown, always dressing like a sparrow."

"I saw her today," claimed the grocer, even though it was not quite true. His wife had seen Assunta and told him, "She was wearing a new skirt the colour of pomegranates."

The men looked at each other, looked for agreement or suggestions to the meaning of plain Assunta wearing a red skirt. Was she seeing someone? Inspired by her father's late marriage? Decided it was time to catch an *amore* of her own? Was there anyone new in the village? Or newly single?

"Davide's cousin is visiting from up north. He's single."

"He'd want a housewife not a working woman."

"The new bank teller? From Tivoli?"

"Not interested in women."

"What about the shepherd? Is he married?"

"No, and he doesn't want to be. All he cares about is his sheep."

"I think he's interested in the woman who makes cheese and owns that little house on the mountain."

"What's the matter with you? He's interested in selling her milk. That's all. To make cheese."

"She can balance trays on her head—that's an advantage."

"What advantage? Assunta can balance numbers. No man is interested in balancing acts—unless it's a circus act."

Pietro was only half-listening to the jokes and philosophies twirling around the bar. Had that been Assunta at the restaurant? Had she seen him and then left? That was definitely not like Assunta. Unless she didn't want him to know she was there. But why would she want that to be a secret? They could have eaten together. Unless she was meeting someone else? But if she was, why leave? Unless she was meeting a man and *he* was a secret. Pietro felt uneasy about the whole thing. He was rather protective of Assunta; she was a bit vulnerable and a little innocent in some ways. Smart in business and household tasks but inexperienced in the ways of romance and love. At least that's how Pietro saw it. Like a big brother. Looking out for a younger sibling. Pietro wished Rosa was here; he could count on Rosa to advise Assunta. Or warn her.

The Engagement

WHILE ROSA AND CARLITO WERE in Venezia, Claudio and Gino returned to the village jewellery shop. Gino had already been to talk to Carla's father, to ask for her hand. "You're lucky that Rosa's father is dead," he told Claudio. "It's nerve-wracking to go and talk to the future father-in-law. My hands got all sweaty and I heard myself talking nonsense about the weather, the soccer score—anything but what I was doing there. Then, after too many coffees, I noticed my hands were shaking and I felt like I was going to throw up so I finally got down to the business of explaining why this man should allow me to marry his daughter. Halfway through the conversation, I started thinking that if I were the father, I'd kick this *cretino* out of the house. He was worried that I'd spent time in Roma running the bar with you and now I was back in the village running a completely different company and why wasn't I a banker like my father? What did I study in school? And when I said I hadn't finished the university course, he looked at me like I was some sort of undependable *vagabondo* who never finished anything he started. He even asked my views on divorce."

"And what did you say?" asked Claudio.

"I lied, of course. I said that even though the government intended to make divorce legal in Italy next year, I was against divorce. Said it was bad for the family. Said it was anti-Catholic. Then, he asked if I went to church and I didn't think I could lie about that so I just said, 'Easter and Christmas. Weddings and funerals. My mother attends every Sunday.'" Strangely enough, that seemed to satisfy him. He asked about my plans for the wedding. This is how he said it: 'What are your plans for the wedding of *my only daughter*?' Of course, I said I planned to leave every detail entirely to Carla and her mother. So he shook my hand and said, 'You can pick up the ring now.'"

"So he knew about the ring?" said Claudio. "I thought the jeweller was keeping that information private. He said..."

"Private? In Supino?"

Claudio nodded. "When are you going to give it to her?"

"Tonight. Why wait? I'm taking her to Frosinone to the new rooftop restaurant. She'll like that. And after dinner, we'll take our coffee on the rooftop garden and I'll give her the ring. Then we'll go to her parents' house and have champagne. I already arranged it with her mother. I've got to remember to go to the florist. A bouquet of red roses for each of them. And hide them in the trunk so Carla doesn't see. It'll be a springtime wedding. I don't want to wait until the fall. And neither does she. What about you? Are you picking up the ring today?"

"Not yet."

"Why not? There's no father to ask. You've already chosen the ring—and it's a beauty. What's the problem?"

"Something's not right. Rosa's first marriage was—let's say, difficult, so she's worried about a second marriage."

"But, you're not Elgidio. He was one of a kind—and I don't mean that in a good way. She should be glad to be rid of him and happy to have you."

"That's what I think. But you know what, Gino? She's not happy to have me. That's the truth of the matter and now, I'm rethinking it. I don't want to marry someone who's not anxious to marry me. I don't want to have to talk her into it and then spend my whole life making sure she doesn't regret it. That's too much pressure."

Gino glanced toward the back of the shop before he asked his next question but the jeweller was still back there polishing the ring.

"And the boy?" asked Gino.

"Yes, Carlito's a great boy. We make a good family, and we could have one or two more. I wouldn't mind that at all but Rosa ... well, she doesn't seem to know what she wants and I'm just getting tired of waiting."

"Is there more to this story, Claudio? Have you met someone else? Have you seen that new hairdresser? *Bellissima!*"

"No, she's a party girl. I want a woman. I want a family. I want the life my grandparents had. It's an old-fashioned idea and I'm as surprised as anyone to hear myself say that it's what I want, especially after saying, for so long, I didn't want that predictable life but...I don't know...maybe, you grow up a little and see things differently. I want Rosa but is it too much to ask for her to want me too?"

"You wouldn't think so but my situation is simple. Yours seems complicated."

"Only because she's making it complicated." The jeweller reappeared with the ring box balanced on his palm like a waiter balancing his tray. When he opened the box to show Gino, the diamond shimmered on its sea of inky-blue velvet.

"Wow," said Gino. "*Spettacolare.*"

Gino had his ring in his jacket pocket when he opened the door and Claudio and he stepped out into the autumn sunlight.

"So, what are you going to do?" asked Gino.

"I don't know," replied Claudio with a resigned shrug. "Wait, I guess."

Afterwards they went to the bar for a coffee. Pietro flipped over the espresso cups quickly; pushed the button on the *Gaggia* machine and slid the cups out before the last drops fell. He pointed to the sugar bowl with one hand and unfolded the newspaper with the other. Gino and Claudio joined Fortunato at the corner table but they couldn't really talk because all around them, everyone was waiting to hear the latest Ask Minerva column in the Frosinone newspaper.

Pietro wiped the counter with a damp bar towel and then he knocked his knuckles on the marble. "*Attenzione,*" he called. "A letter from Minerva." Then Pietro began to read, "'Dear Minerva:

PRIVACY IS A FOREIGN WORD IN SUPINO

I've been married for almost fifteen years. We have children, a house, the usual things but my wife doesn't pay much attention to me anymore. It's always what the children need or the house needs or she needs and never about what I need. Maybe this is the way marriages go after so many years together.'" Pietro stopped for a moment; his eyes scanned the customers. All men. Most married. Many for a decade or so. Everyone was listening intently, so he continued, "'Meanwhile, there's this other woman who is always kind and attentive with me. She asks about my work and my interests and she really listens when I respond. I don't want to cheat on my wife but I'm tired of feeling like I'm invisible unless she needs something. Are you married? Do you have any experience with this sort of thing? Lonely in the Village.'"

The men looked at each other.

"'Dear Lonely in the Village: Yes, I have experience with bored husbands trying to make a little time on the side with unsuspecting single women and my marriage is none of your business. You ask the question, I give the answer: that's the way this column works. Marriage works this way: you promised to love and honour and cherish. When is the last time you made her feel cherished? Once you give your wife the things that you crave, she will return them to you. And a nice piece of jewellery doesn't hurt either.'"

"That's last week's column," said the postman, reaching for his bag of letters.

"*Si*," agreed Pietro. "But here's the reply from the poor husband, who took her advice."

The postman put his bag back down. The other customers leaned forward as Pietro spoke, "Listen to what the husband says this time: 'Minerva: My wife didn't like the jewellery. She demanded to know why I was giving her a gift when it wasn't her birthday or our anniversary. She asked if I was having an affair and who was the other woman? Things got so bad that the neighbours were banging on the door telling us to shut up. Needless to say, I slept on the couch. Thanks for nothing. Lonely in the Village.'"

Several customers started banging on the tables as if to drown out Minerva's advice but Pietro raised his hand again. "There's more. Here's a reply from someone who calls himself a faithful reader: 'Re: your advice to Lonely in the Village. My wife cut it out of the paper and put it on my dinner plate. I asked, "What kind of new food is this?" and she slammed the pan on the stove and slammed the door on her way out. She took the kids to her mother's house and said she's not coming home. I asked my secretary for advice and she recommended, like you, a trip to the jewellery store and so we went there on our lunch hour and she helped me to pick out some coral earrings. I sent them to my mother-in-law's house with a delivery boy but he returned the box with a note. It said, "So, you take your secretary *signorina* Stupida to the store to pick out jewellery for your wife? I knew you were having an affair, you #$#!!!" Minerva, your advice stinks!'"

"She may have lost a faithful reader with her useless advice," continued Pietro, "but she gained one too. Here's the last response: 'Minerva: Thank you for your column giving advice to Lonely in the Village. My business has improved tremendously. The jeweller.'"

"Surely it's not as bad as all that?" Gino asked Fortunato. "You've been married for a long time. Have you had to buy her jewellery just to get some attention?"

Fortunato thought about the pearl necklace he'd given Bianca nine months before their younger daughter, Giuseppina, was born. He thought about the cameo pin he'd given her, as a surprise, three months ago. It had come with matching earrings and some interesting gossip he'd heard about the new hairdresser, and now Bianca was expecting again. He looked around the bar. Were all these men who had children remembering the same gifts and the same births and the connection between the two? Or was it just him? Just Bianca? He thought about Assunta. She always asked about his barbering business; she was interested in his opinions about politics and current affairs. She never gave him unsolicited advice. Of course, she was a friend. Perhaps if he'd married her, she'd have become like Bianca. But maybe not. How was one to know until it was too late?

"Women like attention," began Fortunato, "and they like jewellery and they like to flaunt their gifts to other women. It's complicated. They criticize other women who are always showing off the gifts their husbands have given them but at the same time, they want the same things, and more. If the mayor's wife has a fur stole, they want a fur coat. I don't know what to tell you, Gino. Times are changing—new ideas coming from America about equality and working women. All sorts of nonsense and new notions, if you ask me," said Fortunato. "Take a woman like Assunta down at the water-bottling plant. She buys jewellery for herself. Do you think it's sad that she has no one to buy nice things for her? Or do you think it shows a modern, independent woman?"

"What do *you* think, Fortunato?"

"I've been married long enough to know that it's dangerous to say what you think in some situations. So I don't have any opinion on anything."

"*Mamma mia!*" said Gino, turning to Claudio. "Is that our future, my friend?"

"I don't know. I think I'll be like Fortunato here and have no opinion on anything. Except maybe if I'd like another coffee."

When Fortunato went to the cash to pay, Pietro hesitated for a moment, kept the change in his hand until Fortunato looked up. "I thought," began Pietro. The cappuccino machine exhaled a hiss of steam. The cups resting on the top jostled for space. "I thought I saw Assunta at the restaurant last week."

"Restaurant?" said Fortunato. "What restaurant? Did you say Assunta?"

"In Ferentino. She came in. Then she left."

"What are you talking about? Assunta doesn't go to the restaurant in Ferentino. She doesn't go in and then go out. Are you sure it was Assunta?"

"I thought so. I thought she saw me, then she left."

"Then it wasn't her. If she saw you, she'd come and say hello, no?"
"Yes."
"So it wasn't her," said Fortunato.
"I think I'll ask her," said Pietro. "Just to be sure."
"Sure of what? Wait. Maybe you need to write to this Minerva woman."
"Maybe that's it," said Pietro. "Maybe Assunta is this Minerva woman."
And they laughed. Fortunato pocketed his change. Pietro washed his hands, and wondered.

■ ■ ■

Claudio met Rosa and Carlito at the train station at seven. Rosa was distracted; she was concerned about the luggage, the carefully packaged bag of Venetian glass, the careless crowds pushing. Carlito talked nonstop.
"...*vaporetto*...gondola repair shop...*traghetto*...met a man..."
"You met a man?" repeated Claudio.
"We can tell you all about it when we get home," said Rosa in a voice that seemed like a warning to Carlito and a promise of half-truths to Claudio.
"It's funny how a train ride can tire you out," said Rosa. "You're only sitting but somehow, you're exhausted."
"Yes," said Claudio. "Funny."
"I'm not tired," Carlito assured them. "I'm hungry."
Claudio suggested that they stop at the *trattoria* to eat. It seemed a safe place for conversation and he knew there was no food at Rosa's. He should have asked Assunta to shop but he hadn't and so, they'd stop.
"Did you know?" began Carlito. "They don't make spaghetti the same in Venezia? The sauce tastes different and they stick a meatball on the top. Mamma said they do it for the tourists. Spaghetti and meatballs. Together. And listen to this, Claudio, they have a menu just for tourists posted on the window and all

it has is pizza, spaghetti, lasagne, and breaded veal cutlet. None of the good stuff. Mamma had to talk to the waiter and get him to bring real food like *vongole* and—did I tell you about the soccer in the *piazza*? Every evening we would go there and I played with the same boys. We saw the gondola repair shop. Did I tell you about that yet? And the big clock in the grand *piazza*—there were so many tourists there, Claudio, it was like you weren't even in Italy at all but in some—"

"Eat your dinner," said Rosa but Claudio noticed she wasn't eating hers. She turned down the waiter's offer of coffee; she said she'd make coffee at the house. She said she was just tired. She said of course she was glad to be back. Of course.

"And I brought you a present," Carlito said to Claudio. "Wait till you see it."

"You and your Mamma are my presents," said Claudio. He smiled at Rosa but she was still rearranging the *risotto* that remained uneaten on her plate.

Assunta was locking her front door when they arrived at Rosa's house. Rosa hurried to open the car door; Assunta hurried down her front steps; they ran to hug each other.

"How are you?"

"I've missed you so much."

"Let me look at you."

"A good vacation?"

Carlito tapped Claudio's arm and winked. "Women," he said as he rolled his eyes.

"Yes," said Claudio. "And we men will unload the luggage and carry it into the house." Rosa and Assunta went straight to the kitchen to start the coffee, assemble the cups, loosen the sugar, which had hardened a little in the humidity. Carlito rummaged through his luggage. "I brought you something," he said to Claudio.

"Let me guess," said Claudio. "A soccer ball? A gondola? A shirt with stripes?" but Carlito was wise beyond his years, at least in some ways.

"It's a real souvenir—hand-blown glass. I watched the

glassmaker myself. The fire was so hot that his face was red all the time. Like a monster. A monster who makes beautiful things. Here it is!" and he held up a ball of bubble wrap.

"You didn't have to buy me anything, Carlito. The money was for you to spend on yourself." Still he was touched by the boy's generosity and his anticipation as he watched Claudio unroll the wrapping to reveal a goldfish with an impossibly long tail that rose and curled as thin as spun sugar.

"Mine's in a fish bowl," said Carlito, unwrapping the second package to expose a gold fish caught in a solid bowl of clear glass.

"How did he make that?" asked Claudio.

"Magic," said Carlito.

"*Caffè*," called Rosa and they walked into the kitchen with their fish balanced on the palms of their hands, and stood with one hand behind their backs and the other outstretched, and in unison bowed to the ladies, unrehearsed. Like father, like son.

After the coffee, the women remained in the kitchen while Carlito and Claudio returned to the living room to play checkers. Claudio unfolded the board and waited; usually Carlito lined up the checkers

"Why do you keep staring at me? Do I have coffee on my chin or something?" asked Claudio, with a wipe of his chin and a wink at Carlito.

"I'm looking at your hair. It's exactly the same colour as mine," said Carlito. "And it's curly like mine."

"So, are you setting up the checkers or not?"

"Did you know my father? Did you live here when he was alive? Why did you leave the village anyway? Why didn't you live at the bottling plant like you do now? And..."

"Whoa, whoa! That's a lot of questions all at once."

"You can answer one at a time."

"Okay, let's see."

Claudio dropped the black checkers, one by one, on the back row. "Of course, I knew Elgidio because in this village everyone knows everyone else." More checkers for the middle row.

"That's the way it was then and that's the way it is now." Now the front row of checkers. "It's like you know Bianca's daughters, Antonietta and Giuseppina, and you know kids from school and neighbours and the families of the butcher and the barber."

"Antonietta and Giuseppina *are* the barber's family."

Claudio turned the board slowly and began to line up the white checkers in the back row, the middle row, the front row. He wanted to be careful with both his actions and his words.

"Yes, of course. So, the point is that everyone knows everyone in the village so of course I knew Elgidio... He was the postman so he knew everyone too..."

"Mamma said he was the post*master*. That's different than just an ordinary postman."

"Your mother is right. Elgidio was the postmaster and I was a postman—did you know that?"

Claudio moved a checker from the front row to the edge; Carlito mirrored Claudio's move before he answered.

"I thought you and Gino owned a bar and a pizzeria with a pizza oven from Naples. That's what Mamma said."

"Yes, but that was later in Roma. You know there's no pizzeria in Supino. The water-bottling plant wasn't here either when Elgidio was alive. We started that after Elgidio died. Well, not right after. Let's see, it was four years later. Yes, you were four when I came back to the village."

Claudio sat with his elbows on his knees, fingers tapping while he considered his next move. He moved his checker forward and to the left: Carlito moved his forward and to the left. They zigzagged across the board while the conversation continued.

"Why'd you come back?"

"I heard that Elgidio had died and I wanted to pay my condolences to your mother and I ended up staying."

"Mamma said that my father died when I was a baby."

"Yes, that's right. I came back one time when you were a baby but I didn't know you then." Claudio put his finger on his checker, moved it forward, and then changed his mind and slid it back. "In fact, I didn't know your mother had a baby. I came back because my grandparents died."

"Which grandparent died?"

"Both of them. *Nonna* one day and *nonno* the next."

"I didn't know they could do that. I hope Nino and Elena don't die like that. Then I wouldn't have any grandparents."

"You know they're not really your grandparents, don't you?"

"Mamma said they can be my grandparents if I want them to be. And I do. So they are."

"I see."

Claudio moved his checker; Carlito followed like a shadow. When Claudio saw an opening where he could jump Carlito's man, he didn't.

"Did you know Mamma before you went to Roma?"

Claudio squirmed, put his hands on the chesterfield as if to stand but then sank back in his seat.

"Carlito, I already told you and you know anyway. Everyone in Supino knows everyone else. That's like me asking you if you know the grocer—of course you do. Everyone does. That's where they buy their groceries. I was the postman so I delivered mail to your mother's house."

"Why did you stop being the postman? Giuseppina says that's a good job because you have a uniform and when you get old and don't work anymore, they still pay you."

"Giuseppina knows a lot for a seven-year-old."

"She's eight."

"Well, that explains it."

Carlito jumped Claudio's man and then jumped a second one, landing in the safe corner, ready to slide in whenever Claudio moved his man out in the centre of the board. "Can I ask you something else?" asked Carlito and Claudio waited because it didn't matter what he answered, Carlito would ask anyway. "Do you know anything about falling in love?"

"A little."

"Can you decide who to love or do you just get struck by Cupid's arrow and there's nothing you can do about it?"

"How do you know about Cupid's...?"

"Giuseppina."

"Of course. You have to be careful, you know, because Giuseppina is Bianca's daughter..." Claudio moved his checker from the last row. "So maybe she slipped you a love potion."

"That's not funny." Now Carlito slid his checker, waiting in the corner, into Claudio's newly emptied spot and added, "King me!"

"Bravo," said Claudio. "Now, about love—it's a strange thing, Carlito. Love's a mystery. We are attracted to someone for all sorts of reasons and it doesn't matter if they're older or younger..."

"I'm not talking about Giuseppina. And she's only one year older than me. That's nothing. If I wanted to love her, I would."

"Well, that's the thing. We don't necessarily fall in love with the 'right' person. That's what I'm trying to tell you. There's some kind of chemistry involved and we're attracted to someone and boom! That's it. We're in love and we want to be with that person and that person only."

Claudio slid his checker forward cautiously and as soon as he lifted his finger, Carlito jumped Claudio's man, landing in the vacant spot and repeated, "King me!" He looked up from the board and straight into Claudio's eyes.

"Giuseppina didn't say that Cupid's arrow had chemistry in it—is it like some kind of magic spell?"

"Cupid's not real. He's imaginary like Superman or angels or..."

"What are you talking about? Superman's real. He's just Clark Kent sometimes and Superman other times. Father Albanese said that just because you can't see angels doesn't mean they're not real. So it's the same for angels and Superman."

■■■

"They're so alike," said Assunta.

"I don't want to talk about it," said Rosa.

"Claudio was very lonely without you. I half-expected him to meet you with an engagement ring."

"I don't want to talk about that either."

"I see."

A few autumn leaves rustled on the windowsill as if they might like to come inside. On the shelf, the clock ticked steadfastly. Somewhere, beyond Rosa's yard, a nightingale whistled loudly, his song swelling among the night clouds. The clock continued to tick.

"I met a man in Venezia," began Rosa as she leaned forward and lowered her voice. "He's widowed and trying to create a life for himself. It made me think I should try to do the same. Maybe move back to Naples where no one knows us."

"What do you know about this man?"

"Not much. We had dinner together and got talking." Rosa folded the edge of the linen place mat over a few times and then unfolded it. "He told me his story and I told him mine."

"With Carlito there?"

"He was asleep."

Assunta hesitated for a second before she asked her next question, "Are you thinking of running off with this man?"

"Of course not. Just me and Carlito."

"To Naples?"

"Why not?" Rosa smoothed the place mat with her palm, put her hands in her lap, squeezed them tight.

"You don't have any family there."

"I have an uncle. A cousin."

"Do you mean the uncle that you always said, if you returned to Naples after your spur of the moment wedding to Elgidio, would only say four words to you—'I told you so!'"

"Yes."

"And the cousin?" Assunta had been twisting the sugar spoon in the bowl and now she sank it into the centre. A few crystals escaped and Assunta swept them into the palm of her hand.

"Probably the same," said Rosa. "After she showed me her perfect house and her perfect family and her perfect life."

Assunta walked to the sink, brushed the sugar grains from her palm and turned to face Rosa.

"So, what's the point? You told me you want to be less impulsive. I don't understand you. You've loved Claudio for years—even before Elgidio died— and even when Claudio was living and working in Roma and you were here raising your boy on your own." Assunta paused for a moment, swallowed an unexpected lump in her throat. "Sometimes I don't think you appreciate how much Claudio loves you, Rosa. You're lucky to have someone to love you so faithfully. I..."

Rosa interrupted. "You'll find someone to love, Assunta, it's just a matter—"

"Of time? Of good fortune?" asked Assunta, returning to her chair and crossing her arms on the tabletop. "Actually I met someone while you were away."

"In the village?" asked Rosa, leaning forward. "Who?"

"Do you know the bottle cap salesman? Enzo?" asked Assunta in a cautious voice despite an undertone of excitement bubbling beneath the surface.

"I know he's a...he lives with his mother, right? What do you mean you met someone? You already know Enzo."

"I know him differently now," said Assunta, the excitement breaking through. "We've been going out."

"Together?"

"Well, of course, together. Mostly lunch in Ferentino but now we've made plans to go away for the weekend together. Next weekend, actually." Assunta said, casually, as if she did this kind of thing all the time. "So I'm thinking of going to the *intima* shop in Ferentino to buy some new lingerie tomorrow morning."

"That was fast," said Rosa in a voice that she kept neither excited nor disapproving but purposely neutral.

"That's all you have to say?"

Rosa inspected her fingernails for a moment as if the answer might be hidden beneath the polish. Then she explained, "It's just that sometimes when the flame burns very fast and very bright, it goes out just as quickly."

"Just because that happened with you and Elgidio, doesn't mean it will happen with Enzo and me. You're not very supportive, you know."

"I'm sorry. Really, I'm sorry. I'm glad you have a romance. Don't pay any attention to me. It's just that love complicates things and I don't want you to get hurt." Rosa took another look at her nails. "Although there's no harm in going slowly."

"I've gone slowly my whole life. Thought carefully about everything. Always tried to do the right thing. Where'd that get me? Alone and about to move into a house for one. No husband. No children."

"But you have your job, your friends. That counts for something."

"That counts for a lot but it doesn't make you want to buy new lingerie."

So, it was decided that Assunta would go to the *intima* shop in Ferentino the next morning and Rosa would cover for her at work until Assunta returned.

"I'll be back before lunch," said Assunta.

"No lunch date?" asked Rosa.

"He's in Roma on business until Friday."

Rosa ran her fingers through her hair. "All gritty from the train ride," she said.

"Try the new hairdresser," suggested Assunta. "She's young and chatty but she gives a good shampoo."

The World According to Carlito

THE NEXT MORNING, CARLITO HEADED off to school but detoured to the barbershop where he lingered by the barber pole, pretending to tie his shoe. When Giuseppina came out, calling goodbye to her mother, Carlito called, "Hey, Joe,"

"Don't call me Joe," replied Giuseppina. "You know my name is Giuseppina."

"But it's Josephine in America. I'm giving you a nickname."

"What's Carlito in American? Maybe I can give you a nickname that you don't like."

"Okay, Giuseppina, *scusa*." They walked along together, past the butcher, the dry goods store. Carlito asked, "Do you think I look a lot like Claudio or do you think I look more like my father?"

Giuseppina stopped and studied his face for a moment until Carlito began to blush. "Well, you look a little like your mother but your hair is all wild and curly like Claudio's. Did your father have a lot of hair too?"

"In the photo he's almost bald."

"Maybe he had a lot when he was young. Maybe you'll be bald when you're old too."

"That's no help. And you didn't answer my question. Do you think I look like Claudio?"

"I don't know. Maybe a little." The continued their walk, up the small incline toward the jewellery shop. "Why don't you ask him?"

"I did but he didn't answer either. And I noticed something interesting—whenever Claudio talks about my father, he never calls him my father. He always calls him Elgidio."

"Of course, because that's his name," said Giuseppina. As always, she stopped to admire all the glitter and sparkle displayed in the jeweller's window.

"Do you know anything about getting married?" asked Carlito.

"I don't want to get married," declared Giuseppina. "I don't think it's worth the trouble. I'm thinking of becoming a detective lady or maybe..."

"I'm not asking about you," said Carlito, and then he blurted it out, "I want to know if a man marries a woman and they have a child—is the husband the child's father?"

"Of course. Who else?"

"Well...could it be someone else?"

"Do you mean can a woman be married to two husbands? I think that's a sin." They moved on but the next stop was the store that sold yarn and embroidery thread and they'd both agreed their window was boring.

Carlito clarified his question, "No, not two husbands. But could she have a baby with another man even if she was married to someone else?"

"No," said Giuseppina. They were walking now across the piazzetta of Santa Maria Maggiore and Giuseppina lowered her voice, "When you get married you have to make all these promises—that's another reason I'm not doing it—about being rich or poor and sick or healthy and something else about until death parts you. Then all the promises are off and you can do what you want." Beyond the church, the sidewalk narrowed but Carlito could still hear Giuseppina's words floating back to him as he followed her to the *tabacchi* store window. They always stopped here. Giuseppina was still talking, "But you couldn't have a baby with another man unless you married him because if you did, the baby would be a *bastardo* and no one would want to play with him."

"Wrong. A *bastardo* has no father."

"That's crazy. You have to have a father and a mother to make a baby. That's the whole wedding part."

"But is it only the husband who can be the father?" asked Carlito.

"I think it's only the husband who's *supposed* to be the father."

"And if it isn't?"

"Then they've broken the promises," said Giuseppina. "And they'll go to Hell unless they go to confession first and say a very big penance."

In the store window, the usual comics were displayed—no new editions yet. "In one of my comic books," said Carlito. "The archenemy always says promises are meant to be broken."

"If I make a promise, I keep it," said Giuseppina. "That's what promises are meant to be."

"Okay then, promise you won't tell anyone what I'm about to tell you?" asked Carlito.

"I promise," said Giuseppina, and she crossed her heart for good luck and stepped closer.

Carlito spoke softly, "I think Claudio is my father," and he felt his heart break a little because if that was true, he was now a *bastardo*.

Fortunato's New Customer

AFTER THE POSTMAN LEFT THE barbershop that morning, a steady rhythm throbbed and pounded its way up the spiral staircase to Bianca's herb store where the sound landed in Bianca's stomach, slap, slap, slap, and vibrated in her ears. Fortunato was tapping an envelope in the palm of his hand. Bianca waited. Finally he called up to her, "Some mail for you, *bella*." Bianca took the stairs slowly, hoping the newspaper office hadn't sent her something here instead of at her mother's address.

"From the newspaper office in Frosinone," said Fortunato as he read aloud the return address. "Why are they sending you mail a second time?"

"Why are we having this conversation again? It's my mail not yours."

"*Si*, it says *signora* Bianca Corsi—*signora* means you're married. Married to me. So it's my mail too."

"What? Are you crazy? Have the fumes from the shaving cream finally driven you insane? What is the matter with you?"

"I don't like my wife keeping secrets from me," said Fortunato. The slaps of the envelope against his palm grew louder. "I want to know what's going on with you and this constant newspaper mail."

"*Constante*? What do you mean by *constante*?"

Fortunato pointed the envelope at her and sliced the air between them. "Don't try to change the subject. And don't lie to me, Bianca. What are you doing behind my back?"

There was no point in holding out her hand for her mail; no

point in attacking him with questions; no point in refusing to answer or returning to her shop upstairs without the envelope in her hand. She'd have to be nice.

"Why don't you give me the envelope, Fortunato?" asked Bianca, holding out her hand. "I'll open it right in front of you. Before I read it to myself, I'll read it right out loud to you." Bianca patted her palm on Fortunato's heart. "No secrets," she said.

Bianca could easily invent and read out a fake letter thanking her for her newspaper subscription right on the spot if Fortunato handed her the letter without looking at it first but if he demanded to see the letter...*Mamma mia!* "Come sit here with me," she offered, motioning to the bench where the customers sometimes waited if Fortunato was busy. "Leave me a little more room, *per favore*, I am getting fat with these babies of yours." She sighed as she sat; she rested her hands on her swollen belly.

Fortunato opened the envelope only to find another envelope inside. The second envelope was addressed to *signora* Bianca Corsi care of the newspaper office. Somehow in the surprise of the moment, in the finding of one envelope inside another, in sitting beside his wife's warm body, in enjoying her soft tone, the second envelope ended up in Bianca's hands. She had tucked her head on his chest and he rested his chin on her blonde hair and inhaled the scent of lemons. He couldn't see the letter so he merely listened.

"'Dear *signora* Corsi, I am writing to you about your newspaper ad for your herb store in the village of Supino. I am not familiar with your village but I understand it's near the city of Frosinone where I lecture on occasion at the Frosinone *liceo*. My name is *signor* Franco Portobello and I am a Professor of Classic Literature at the University of Roma.'"

Bianca's voice, which had begun with hesitation, now hastened through the lines so that Fortunato had trouble keeping up with her but it didn't matter; he wasn't very interested in herbs; he was engrossed in the pleasure of sitting peacefully with his arm around his pregnant wife. He heard the rest of the letter in small phrases, "conference in Genoa...need to purchase various herb samples...advance order...availability of lovage, calendula... juniper... payment... appointment... at your convenience."

Three things happened in quick succession: Bianca's hands on his chest pushed Fortunato away from her, Bianca's dress swirled as she quickly climbed up the spiral staircase to her herb store, and her voice descended, "This is a very big order. I have to get started right away. Fortunato, I'll need about a dozen small sturdy boxes and some brown wrapping paper and more twine and..."

∎∎∎

Two weeks later a stranger entered the barbershop. He was a well-dressed man in his late sixties. He slipped his hand inside his tweed jacket and withdrew a small notebook from his inner pocket: then he pulled out a leather case and removed his eyeglasses. "*Scusa*," he said to Fortunato after consulting the paper. "I am looking for an herb shop located at *via...*" he rechecked the paper, "*numero...*"

"That's my wife's shop," said Fortunato. Something in the man's manner made Fortunato switch into a more formal style of Italian. "The shop is located upstairs."

"*Grazie*," said the man.

"My pleasure," said Fortunato. The man climbed the spiral staircase and Fortunato was left behind with nothing but the lingering scent of the man's pipe tobacco. Some traditional tobacco with a hint of vanilla.

The doorway beads clanked and Fortunato reached for his white barber's cloth and shook it expectantly but it was only Bruno the butcher from next door.

"*Mamma mia*," said Bruno with a quick look around the shop. "Did you see that car? It drove up the street purring like a giant cat and when the man turned off the engine, it sighed. Fortunato, did you see it? A Lancia Flaminia. Shiny as the day it came out of the factory! Where's the man?"

Fortunato pointed upstairs.

"Do you want to take a look at the car?"

Fortunato looked around his empty shop. "Why not?" he said.

By the time the man descended the stairs, Fortunato had admired the car, read the sports section, argued with Bruno about the chances of his team making the soccer finals, sent Bruno back to his own shop, and was now cleaning his combs.

"Can I help you with those boxes?" he asked the man. "That's quite a pile you have there."

"*Si, si,*" replied the man but Fortunato wasn't sure if he was agreeing with the number of boxes or Fortunato's offer of help. The man set the boxes on the counter.

"Do you have time for a trim?" the man asked.

Fortunato swept the seat of the leather chair with a soft brush before he gestured to it. "At your convenience, *signor,*" he said.

"My name is Portobello, Franco Portobello."

Fortunato shook the hand he was offered and gave his own name.

"You're married to the herb store lady?"

"*Si, si.* Married for almost fifteen years." Fortunato tied the barbering cloth around the man's neck. "Two beautiful daughters and two more babies on the way but I expect my wife told you all this." Fortunato ran his comb through the man's hair and reached for his scissors.

"Your wife looked very familiar to me. Did she study in Roma when she was young?"

"No."

"Lived in Roma for a while, perhaps?"

"No."

"Vacationed at Capri in August?"

"No."

Fortunato tilted the man's head forward so he could trim the hair at the back of his neck, hair that didn't really need a trim.

"What about you, *signor?*" Fortunato asked. "Do you live in Roma?"

"*Si.*"

"You studied there?"

"Studied there; live there; work there. I'm a professor at the university."

"Vacation in Capri in August, *professore*?"

"*Si*."

There was silence between them until Fortunato put down his scissors and brushed aside a few stray hairs, held the small oval mirror behind the man's head. The man nodded: Fortunato removed the cloth; the man reached for his wallet. After the bill was settled, Fortunato repeated his offer, "Now, *professore*, let me help you carry these boxes."

After they'd divided the boxes between them, the professor asked another question, "Tell me, Fortunato, do you know the village well? Can you recommend a good restaurant?"

"I was born here," began Fortunato as he stepped through the beaded curtain and onto the sidewalk.

"Really? And your wife too?"

"No. She was a teenager when she arrived with her mother. That was unusual to have strangers move to our village unless of course they marry one of the villagers. But Bianca's situation was different."

"How did she—they—happen to come to your village? If you don't mind my asking," said the professor. The professor seemed interested, Fortunato loved to tell a story, so he propped one foot on the base of his barber pole and began.

"More than twenty years ago, Bianca's mother bought a piece of land with some ancient apple trees on it near the edge of the village. She arranged to have a house built for her daughter and her. I remember my parents talking about it a lot that summer. It was unusual to have a stranger come to our village and build their own house and it was even more unusual that it should be a woman. A widow. I remember my mother telling us two things about that house. One was that it had a circular drive even though the *signora* didn't drive a car. And two, that it had a balcony that went all the way around the second floor. My mother was so impressed with that. You could go in or out of any room and have a different view every way."

"Shall we?" asked Fortunato, pointing down the street where

the *professore* had parked his Lancia. As they walked, Fortunato finished his story. "I remember my father was a little worried when he heard that an unknown widow had hired workers to build the house. He thought that the workmen might take advantage of her. You know, charge her too much, work too slowly, that sort of thing but believe me they soon found out like everyone in the village did that no one takes advantage of *signora* Lucrezia. Here we are. This is your beautiful car, right?"

The professor stopped. He swayed for a moment in the sunshine. Then he leaned his body against the side of the car. The boxes tumbled slowly to the cobblestones.

"*Professore*, are you all right? What is it? Too much sun? Do you feel faint?" Fortunato lifted his arms to rest the boxes on the roof of the car and then, just as quickly changed his mind, and sat them on the sidewalk.

"I'm fine. Just a moment of dizziness. Nothing to worry about," said the *professore* but he made no move to pick up the boxes or to open the car door. Instead, he said, "I'm not sure I heard the end of your story correctly. What did you say the *signora's* name was?"

"Lucrezia. Lucrezia Cavallo."

"An unusual name," said the professor.

"An unusual woman," said Fortunato.

They picked up the fallen parcels; Fortunato packed them into the back seat; the *professore* started the engine; it purred; he rolled down his window.

"Where did you say she built this house with a circular driveway and a wraparound balcony?"

"*Via case nuove*—the street of new houses— you pass it on your way out of town."

"*Grazie*," said *il professore*. "*Grazie mille*." And he was gone before either of them remembered about his request for a restaurant. Fortunato shrugged: there was no restaurant in the village anyway.

On the street of new houses, Lucrezia sat on the west balcony, reading, and even though she could feel the sun growing stronger, she wanted to finish the chapter before she put down the book and went into the house to see what her housekeeper, Teresa, had prepared for lunch. So she did. But when she rose to go inside where she would close the shutters of the balcony door to keep the house cool, she felt a little dizzy. Or did she get the order of events wrong? Did she first see the man's silhouette wavering near the gate? And then she got dizzy? The man was definitely not Erminio, her gardener. He was not the postman; he'd been by the gate earlier. He was not a peddler or a *vagabondo*. This man was well dressed; he was tall. And familiar.

The man put his hand up to shade his eyes or perhaps to get a better look at her at the same moment that Lucrezia did. She dropped her hand instantly. She stepped inside; she locked the door, closed the shutters; latched them carefully. Lucrezia knew she had not viewed a stranger; she had viewed the impossible— the return of Franco.

The Intima Shop

It was cool in the change room of the intima shop in Ferentino but Assunta felt flushed as she waited for the salesgirl to bring her a new bra to try. She glanced at her old bra, dangling on the hook; it was clean, of course, and still functional but a little worn out.

"Here we are," said the young salesgirl as she held up a bra that was the twin of Assunta's old one. Just a stronger shade of beige. The girl hooked and cupped and tucked.

"A perfect fit, *signora*," she said, pointing to the mirror.

Assunta shook her head. "It's too—" what was the word she wanted? "—uninspiring."

"Uninspiring?" repeated the girl as if she'd misunderstood. But Assunta nodded so the girl adjusted the straps a little, which raised the breasts; increased the cleavage. "Better?" she asked hopefully.

Assunta shook her head.

"I don't understand, *signora*. Is it the colour? It also comes in pure white, if you prefer."

"It's not the colour," said Assunta. "It's...it's just—would *you* wear it?" The salesgirl glanced from Assunta's full breasts to her own modest ones, "It's not my size, *signora*?"

"But the style. Would you wear this style?"

"Certainly not," replied the salesgirl and she took a step back as if she'd spoken too forcefully and there might be repercussions.

"Exactly. It's a bra for old ladies. Bring me something you'd wear."

"Are you sure, *signora*?"

Assunta swallowed hard. "Very sure," she said and as soon as the salesgirl had gone, she lifted her hand and fanned the blush from her face. The girl brought three bras: one black, one pink, and one red. Lots of see-through lace and shiny picot-edged satin. The black one looked like it was made of very fine fishnet.

"Oh my," said Assunta.

"We'll start with the pink one, *signora*," said the salesgirl as she cupped Assunta's breasts and hooked the back clasp. "It's called blooming spring rose. Everyone looks good in this colour." The salesgirl adjusted the straps: Assunta's breasts perked up; the salesgirl said, "It's very flattering for the skin tone."

Thirty minutes passed. Her old bra sat among the French lace and satin ribbons looking practical and dull. The change room chair was draped with bras and still, Assunta couldn't decide. She looked, once more, at the price tickets: they were all either expensive or very expensive. Assunta was a woman who'd been frugal her whole life.

Then the salesgirl came back into the change room with a handful of matching panties. They weren't much more than scraps of lace. Even though they were more expensive than the bras, they left less to the imagination. "I'm not sure," said Assunta, turning to the side. Scallops of lace bordered the tops of her legs. She looked very sexy.

"They're so expensive," said Assunta.

"It's not the cost, *signora*, that you need to think about," the salesgirl assured. "You only need to think about how they make you feel."

Assunta nodded; she was about to spend more than her weekly salary on underwear and she didn't care.

■■■

At the village hairdresser's shop, the air was heavy with the scent of shampoo and the chatter of waiting customers. Rosa looked around but didn't see the new hairdresser, Gabriella, who

Assunta had recommended.

Someone said, "Not in today."

Someone else said, "Better offer?"

A third said, "That romance can't end well."

A fourth predicted, "We'll hear all about it in Minerva's column soon enough."

They all laughed but Rosa had no idea what they were talking about. Rosa didn't know anything about the new hairdresser or her latest boyfriend but, obviously, Rosa hadn't been in the shop for a few weeks. Of course, Rosa knew that Minerva was the columnist in the Frosinone paper and she knew that everyone suspected that Minerva actually lived in Supino and the people who wrote to her lived here too and the villagers were forever trying to figure out the who's who of it all. The Supinese liked to know everything.

They all suspected that Rosa's husband, Elgidio, was not Carlito's father but Rosa wasn't sure that their interest was sympathetic. It was more about the *scandalo* of a married woman having an affair and then a baby, and *gratitudine* that they didn't have that problem in their family. Maybe it was smugness too. They'd never have their lover's baby and pass it off as their husband's. *Mamma mia*, when you put it that way, it sounded practically immoral rather than just bad timing, misfortune, and those dreamy purple clouds that streaked the sky on that afternoon eight years ago when she and Claudio...

The customers asked about her trip to Venezia and Rosa assured them that the prices in Venezia were outrageous and that the food was poor quality; it could never compare to the dishes that the villagers prepared. She said the wine was moderately good, particularly the white, but she quickly added the price so no one would feel upstaged by a Venetian white when they had husbands who grew and pressed their own grapes, grown in village soil, on the hillsides that led to Santa Serena mountain. She promised to bring photos once she'd taken the film to the photography shop in Frosinone to be processed into black and whites. And she didn't say one word about meeting Tony, the

Americano, because even though he was just a friend, he was still a man.

The owner gave her a lovely little massage along with the conditioner. "You know the travelling pushcart man who comes every month with linens and toys made in Taiwan?" asked the hairdresser but before Rosa could respond, Simonetta continued with her story. "This time he brought a Chinese wife—she taught me how to do this scalp massage in return for a trim—she has hair as straight and sharp as an arrow—and the massage feels very nice, doesn't it? No extra charge. A gift." Rosa knew that a "gift" from the hairdresser was a code for a "tip"—another idea *Americani*. Were they taking over the world with all these changes? She gave Simonetta an extra *lire*. She said, "Certainly, I'll say hello to Assunta for you as soon as I get to work." She didn't say, "She's not in this morning." She didn't say, "lingerie shop" nor "Ferentino" nor "weekend in Verona," yet she knew that soon enough, they'd know; they'd all know.

She bumped into Bianca on the way out, physically bumped into her but Simonetta had sprayed Rosa's flip hairstyle so thoroughly and Bianca's French twist was rolled so tightly that not a hair was displaced on either woman. Bianca asked about her trip and Rosa said, "You can hear all about it inside." And Bianca smiled, actually smiled, which bothered Rosa a little. It wasn't Bianca's usual mean, know-it-all smile but an almost friendly one. "I was at the bottling plant this morning," said Bianca but before Rosa could ask why on earth she'd been there, Bianca added, "but Assunta wasn't in."

"Just not yet," said Rosa. "It's still early."

"Is it?" asked Bianca, glancing at her wristwatch. "I'd say, '*Il tempo è l'essenziale*'—that's an American phrase, it means, 'Time is of the essence.'" And before Rosa could ask what the hell she was talking about, Bianca was on the inside and Rosa was still out.

When Rosa arrived at work, there was a note on her desk. No envelope; no signature; just a folded piece of plain paper. Pure white paper with clear black lettering: "*He's seeing someone else*" was all it said. Rosa stared at the words. She stared at the blank spaces between each word. She stared at the white paper, at the black letters. There it was in black and white. The words didn't leave any room for questions or doubt. Her heart began to knock on her eardrums in a steady warning: someone else, someone else. Had Claudio started seeing someone else while she'd been away?

"What's this?" asked Claudio as he came into her office, holding a note in his hand as well. Rosa dropped her note on her desk; she casually moved a manila envelope on top, swallowed her suspicions, squared her shoulders. "How would I know?" asked Rosa. Then she added another question, but her voice cracked a little near the end. "Is it like those notes you used to leave for me that said nothing—just blank pieces of paper?"

"We were going to write our own story, Rosa, remember?" Claudio's words carried more than memory; they carried loss. Sorrow. The hint of an ending.

Rosa paused before she answered, paused long enough to hide her worry, which was swiftly escalating. Her voice was soft and sad. "Yes, I remember."

Claudio lifted a business card with one hand, held the note open with the other, and read, "'I'm called away on business for a few days longer. Plans must be rearranged. Upon my return, I shall explain.'"

"No signature?"

Claudio flipped the business card over and held it between his thumb and index finger so Rosa could read it. *Prodotti di Metallo*: tins, lids, bottle caps. Lorenzo Caprara, *direttore vendite*."

"*Direttore vendite*? Since when is Enzo a sales *manager*?" she laughed, but then her voice grew cautious. "Why's he sending you a note?"

"I don't know," said Claudio. "It was on my desk when I arrived."

Suddenly, Rosa remembered that Bianca had been at the plant this morning. That's what Bianca had said outside the hairdresser's.

"Was Enzo here earlier?"

"Someone was," said Claudio. He held the note out to her. "Smell the paper." It smelled of lavender. Bianca never smelled of lavender but of intricate blends of bergamot and rose and—

Claudio tucked the business card back into the envelope, handed it to Rosa, and turned toward his office. Rosa hurried to her desk and pulled an invoice from the pile and pretended to read. Nothing made sense. Not the words on the page or the notes on the desk. Who were they for? *Mamma mia!* Rosa folded her arms on her desk; put her head down and waited. And waited. Waited until she heard the rustle of Assunta's bags filled with lingerie and tissue paper, and hope.

"*He's seeing someone else*," read Assunta, after Rosa had handed her the note, and Assunta's response was very clear, "No, he's not, Rosa. Claudio was miserable when you were in Venezia. The only people he saw outside of the plant were Gino and Pietro, down at the bar."

"Then, why is this note on my desk?" asked Rosa, but neither had an answer.

"The handwriting is a little familiar," said Assunta. "It looks like someone tried to disguise it."

"Who would try to hide their identity? Why not sign it?" asked Rosa. The note was not necessarily mean-spirited. In fact, it might be a kind-hearted warning so the person wouldn't be hurt. Therefore, it couldn't be from Bianca.

"Bianca said she was at the plant this morning and you weren't in yet," said Rosa. But the note that was left on Claudio's desk included Enzo's business card so that note had to be from him. Rosa passed Enzo's note to Assunta. Assunta was her friend, her best friend, and she didn't want to hurt her but if she didn't give her the note, Assunta might be hurt even more.

Assunta put her shopping bag beside her desk and then she moved it a little so the chair hid it. She leaned against the desk and shook her head.

"He's not married," said Assunta. "He told me that."

"I didn't say…" began Rosa. "He lives with his mother, doesn't he?" Rosa already knew the answer; she was trying to encourage

Assunta to keep talking. If Rosa gave her some support, perhaps Assunta would share, so Rosa said, "I'm sure he told you that too."

"Yes. He's been honest with me," said Assunta. She twirled her mother's gold ring that she always wore on the ring finger of her right hand. "He even asked me if I was seeing anyone." Rosa bit the inside of her lip to keep from saying one single discouraging word. Assunta continued, "I said no. Of course, I said no but perhaps I should have said more. Perhaps I should have said I would never accept a lunch date with one man if I were seeing another."

"Of course," said Rosa. She was dying to ask: "Did you ask Enzo if he was seeing anyone?" but Assunta was already a little annoyed with Rosa for not being supportive and Rosa didn't want to make matters worse. On the other hand, matters would be a lot worse if Rosa didn't ask. Later when it was all over, Enzo could simply say, "But, *cara*, you didn't ask me," as if it was somehow Assunta's fault for not asking as opposed to Enzo's fault for not volunteering the information in the first place. Did he think that Assunta was the kind of woman who would agree to be just one of many? No, he knew she wasn't. Did that make it a challenge—to try to seduce her? Some men, even though they only had one penis, were just like snakes who have two penises—and Enzo was beginning to act exactly like a snake.

"Assunta," said Rosa, using her softest warmest voice, "Did you ask Enzo if he was seeing anyone else?"

"Of course not." Assunta crossed her arms: she said nothing more.

Rosa traced her index finger on the polished desktop. Up and over and down and under and up and...to infinity. "Maybe...it might be a good idea to ask. Just to be sure."

"No," said Assunta. She shook her head. "How would it sound?" she asked, her hands held out, her palms open to Rosa. "It would sound like I don't trust him. I've been out with him four times already, Rosa. The time for asking has long passed."

"Still better to know. To be sure."

"But I *do* know," said Assunta. She dropped her hands to her side. "I know that I trust him. I know that I don't want to create suspicion where there is none."

A soft sound delayed Rosa's response. Assunta was gently kicking the intima bag with the toe of her shoe and the tissue paper was rustling in return.

"Don't say anything," said Assunta.

Rosa held up her hands in mock surrender. "I wasn't going to say a word."

"I mean don't say anything about my seeing Enzo."

"Why not?" The words slipped out before Rosa could stop them.

"Because I'm asking you not to," said Assunta and she pulled out her chair as if she intended to get to work. Rosa said nothing. Not a word. Not another question. But she thought, *Did Enzo ask Assunta to keep the romance a secret?* She wanted to say, "Oh Assunta, don't you see? If a man wants to keep your relationship a secret it doesn't mean it's romantic, it means he's seeing someone else." But she said nothing.

Rosa picked up the note. The pure white paper with the pure black warning. "*He's seeing someone else.*" The note wasn't for Rosa but Rosa's heart was not dancing with joy. She thought about moving it from her desk to Assunta's. But she couldn't do it. She couldn't be the one to break Assunta's heart.

A few days later, Enzo came to the bottling plant as they were closing for lunch. Claudio had already left and Rosa would have been gone too if she hadn't wanted to finish typing the invoices so they could go out in the afternoon mail. Enzo entered so quietly that Rosa didn't know he was there until he cleared his throat. "*Buongiorno, signora.*"

Rosa looked up; she said, "*Buongiorno,*" and she looked at the clock. "Claudio's gone for lunch," said Rosa, returning to her typing.

Enzo looked at Assunta's empty chair. He cleared his throat again. "Are you the only one here then?" he asked. Rosa clicked the keys; she returned the typewriter carriage to the left; she paused. "It looks that way, doesn't it?" she asked and she would have gotten away with her cryptic response if, at that very moment, Assunta hadn't come into the office. Assunta blushed.

"Oh, Enzo," she said.

"At your service, *signora*," he said with a little bow. "What a nice surprise to find not one but two lovely ladies hard at work."

"I'm just going home for lunch," said Assunta, as she lifted her sweater from the back of her chair.

"Allow me to walk you to your car," said Enzo. Rosa said nothing. She was caught in their soap opera but she was an extra, and she had no lines.

"Are you coming soon?" Assunta asked Rosa but Rosa shook her head, waved them off.

In the deserted parking lot, Assunta said, "I don't drive to work anymore. I'm living in the village now so I walk to work."

"Aren't you fortunate?" he said. He leaned against his car but he didn't suggest lunch; he didn't offer to drive her home. "About the trip to Verona," he began. "I have to make a small adjustment. I have some business in Torino for a few days at the end of the week." He waved his hand as if he was dismissing the business as unimportant. He looked around the parking lot but it was deserted. They were the only ones there. "If I take the train from Torino to Verona, and you take the train from the village to Verona, we can meet there," he said. Then he added, as he always did, "If that suits you."

When he had first started to speak, Assunta feared he was going to cancel their weekend together. So when she understood that he was only rearranging the train travel plans, she answered quickly, "Yes, of course. We'll be together on the train coming home."

"I may have to return to Torino," continued Enzo. "I have a customer there and I may have to work on him a little more to get his order. But I'll be back in the village a few days later. While we're in Verona, Assunta, I promise you, we will spend every day together. And every night as well."

She blushed. She was wearing one of her new bras and it made her feel sexy and brave. "I'm looking forward to that."

"Me too, my dear. Very much. You can count on that."

So they finalized their plans and he wished her a good lunch and just before he got into his car, he took another glance at the deserted parking lot and then he traced the scoop of her neckline to the crease of her breasts and hooking his finger there, pulled her to him. The kiss started strong and hard and Assunta thought she might fall backwards, not from passion so much as from Enzo's insistence. She felt his hand at her breast. Assunta stepped back—the parking lot was too public. "Okay, *bella*," he said, lifting her chin, kissing her on her forehead. "I can wait a few more days." And he was gone, leaving nothing but anticipation in the autumn air.

■■■

At *la casa bella*, Fortunato and Bianca lingered over their coffee while the two girls washed the dishes, dried the dishes, and squabbled.

"That was a pretty wreath that you sold Enzo," said Fortunato. "I'm thinking of buying one for my *amore*—the same heart shape but with roses."

"Roses," said Bianca, with a dismissive wave of her hand. "So traditional."

"Some people like traditional," said Fortunato as he stirred the sugar into his coffee. "Some people appreciate it."

"Why was Enzo in the shop mid-week, anyway?" asked Bianca. "Doesn't he usually come in on weekends?"

"*Si*. But he was taking off for a few days. Selling up north somewhere."

"Selling *what*?" asked Bianca and she leaned forward, pushed the espresso cup aside, crossed her arms on the table.

"*Bella*, how would I know? Whatever he sells—bottle caps, tin cans, metal things."

"Maybe his heart is made of metal," said Bianca. "I think he's…"

Giuseppina spoke from the kitchen, "Do you mean like the tin man, Mamma? From *The Wizard of Oz*?"

"*Mamma mia!* Must you eavesdrop on every word I say? Is there no privacy in my own house? I'm speaking to *Papà* not to you."

"*Si*, Mamma, *scusa*," said Giuseppina.

"Enzo always says the lavender is a gift for his mother but I've smelled his mother..."

"What do you mean you've smelled her?" said Fortunato.

"I don't hear any sounds of dishes being washed or dried in there," warned Bianca, calling to her daughters in the kitchen, then she leaned toward Fortunato and sniffed. "Like this." Bianca wrinkled her nose. "When I meet her—usually at the *supermercato* outside of town. Or the Frosinone market. Buying the expensive vegetables for her precious Lorenzo."

"I see," said Fortunato. "And she smells like lavender?"

Now another voice chimed in from the kitchen. "No. She doesn't smell of lavender," replied the older daughter, Antonietta. "That's Mamma's point, isn't it, Mamma?"

"Enough," said Bianca. "This is a madhouse that I live in. Leave the rest of those dishes for later. Go upstairs and do your homework. Don't tell me you don't have any. I don't want to hear that. As for you, Fortunato, and your question about a flower wreath for your *amore*. If it was springtime, I might suggest Voodoo lily—very beautiful but the scent is not good, so I recommend jasmine. Pure white jasmine. An unusual choice but your *amore* is not ordinary, is she?"

Fortunato shook his head. What was there to say? Then, he thought of something.

"Do you think Assunta would go to a restaurant in Ferentino?"

"Why? Did someone see her there? Who was she with?"

"Pietro thought he did. I didn't ask if she was alone."

"Of course. The most important question of all, and you didn't think to ask. Sometimes, Fortunato, I wonder what goes on in that head of yours..."

"Did you deliver Enzo's note to the bottling plant, *bella*?"

"No one was in yet. I left them on the desk."

Bianca gathered the cups and rose to take them into the

kitchen. Fortunato took them from her. "Wait a minute. What do you mean 'them'?"

Bianca took a quick look into the kitchen. The girls were gone but she lowered her voice anyway. "I was going to the plant anyway. That's why I offered to take Enzo's note."

Bianca thought about the arrogance of Enzo. A man so full of himself that he wouldn't stop for a minute to think that perhaps it was dangerous to romance two women at opposite ends of the same village. Of course, men like Enzo were oblivious to women's conversations and intuitions—even Fortunato, loyal and trustworthy Fortunato, thinks he can have his little secrets, thinks that she doesn't notice that he's overly protective and solicitous of Assunta, a woman who has held a torch for Fortunato since they were all at the *liceo* together. Almost twenty years have passed and Assunta is no wiser in her choice of men. Enzo. *Dio mio.* A man who was less than honourable. Bianca remembered her vow to be kinder, less judgmental. After all, the waxing and waning October moon could affect anyone, not just a lonely woman. Perhaps Assunta didn't know it was dangerous to ignore the moon. *Molto pericoloso.* Of course Rosa should have warned Assunta—what kind of a friend was she anyway? Rosa had married under the spell of the full April moon and spent countless moon cycles regretting that decision. Surely, Rosa hadn't forgotten that. And what about Nino? He followed the moon's cycles for planting and harvesting—Nino should have taught Assunta to be aware, to be vigilant. To ignore the phases of the moon is to...well, that would be harsh and judgmental and Bianca was trying not to be.

■■■

Assunta was happy. She hummed a little tune as she walked up the hill. If Simonetta's shop were still open, she'd pop in and make an appointment with the new hairdresser for the day after tomorrow. She already had her new underwear waiting in her train case. She'd also bought an icy blue satin nightgown with a creamy lace insert and spaghetti straps. She might stop at Bianca's herb shop and buy some gardenia petals to sprinkle in her suitcase. The hairdresser's shop was still open but the new hairdresser wasn't at her station. There was no cape folded over the back of the chair; there were no scissors or combs waiting on a spotless white towel; there was only a heart-shaped wreath of lavender tied with a white ribbon hanging on the clips that held the mirror to the wall. The scent of lavender hung heavy in the autumn air. "She'll be back in a few days," said the owner, Simonetta. "This new boyfriend likes to travel."

"Is she seeing someone from the village?" asked Assunta, but she knew.

"Ferentino," said Simonetta. She had her pen in her hand; the appointment book lay open. "Which day, *signora?*"

"Do you know his name?" asked Assunta.

"Lorenzo...I've forgotten his last name. I've never met him but he gives nice gifts." Simonetta pointed to the heart-shaped lavender wreath.

Vendetta

As Assunta reached into her purse for her house keys, she noticed the folded paper slipped halfway under her front door. *Now what?* she thought and, after she opened the door and stepped inside, she kicked the note with the toe of her shoe before she reluctantly picked it up. Assunta imagined the words that the note would contain: *He's seeing someone else.* She leaned one hand against the rough brick of the fireplace to steady herself; she told herself the message wouldn't hurt because she already knew—Enzo was a two-timer and she'd been a fool. A lonely, lovestruck fool. Perhaps she'd crumple the paper in her fist and pitch it onto the grate; maybe she'd tear the note into a million pieces, each one smaller than a teardrop. Instead, unfolding the paper carefully, slowly, Assunta read, "*Cara*, we're home! Come. *Papà* and Elena."

Assunta wiped her eyes. The note fluttered to the floor. She looked around her small kitchen for something to bring to them at the farm. Would they need coffee? Fresh bread? She opened a cupboard, snatched a box of *biscotti*, returned it. She decided she'd grab some supplies on the way. And some flowers. But instead, she ran. Assunta ran out the door, down the steps, up the street, around the bend, down the road, and down the gravel pathway to the farm. She was gulping for air when she reached the gate and saw her father near the pasture fence, patting Zeus. She tried to call out but her mouth was dry and all she could accomplish was a gulp of air. Her father turned. "*Cara, cara,*" he called and then he was beside her and she was safe in his arms and he was holding her tight and both of them were crying. Several minutes passed. Assunta brushed her hand against the rough wool of her father's jacket; she inhaled his smell of soap and hay. She could feel her sweater stuck to her back from the sweat of the run; she could feel the dampness of her armpits; she could feel drops of sweat on her head and neck and forehead and she didn't care. All she cared about was standing safe in her father's arms.

They both looked up at the sound of bicycle wheels sliding across the gravel of the driveway. A crash as the bike hit the ground. The pounding of footsteps as Carlito dove between them, shouting, "*Si ritorna! Si ritorna!*"

Nino managed to untangle himself from the jumble of arms and he looked at Carlito, and he smiled. "How did you know we were back?" he asked.

"I saw Assunta running up the street and I said to Mamma, 'Nino *ritorna*.' And I grabbed my bike." Carlito stopped momentarily to catch his breath and to take Nino's hand, then he continued his story, "Mamma said, 'Wait, we'll go tomorrow. Let them be.' But I took off and Mamma was calling to me that I better be back in half an hour. 'Don't stay,' she said. 'So here I am." Another gulp of air and a small afterthought, "And Mamma said to say *ciao* to Nino and Elena.' So, *ciao*." Carlito rested his head against Nino's side. "I missed you *mille*."

Carlito spied Elena at the doorway and he flew across the yard to her. More hugs. More explanations and after a quick glass of water and a couple *biscotti* shoved into his pocket, Carlito was back on his bike. "Tomorrow, tomorrow," he called as he pedaled down the driveway and out of sight.

Now Assunta came to Elena and kissed her on both cheeks. "How is my new mother?" she asked.

Elena blushed and wiped her hands on her apron and tucked a loose strand of hair behind her ear and hustled Assunta inside. "Come, come," she said. "Nino, the coffee is ready."

Over coffee, Assunta asked all the right questions about their honeymoon trip and listened to their stories of wonderful sights and great meals and everything was going well until Nino said, "So, tell me. What's the matter, daughter?" Assunta tried the usual excuses of being tired and busy at work and Nino put his hand on top of his daughter's and repeated his question. So Assunta tried again but no words came. Just silence, each waiting for the other to speak.

Elena stood and said she'd just go into the other room; said she had a lot of organizing to do with the luggage and as she passed Assunta's chair, she paused to pat her daughter's shoulder and the gesture broke the silence and Assunta began to cry. Elena pulled her chair close and kept her arm around Assunta's shoulder but Nino stood up from the table and went to the sideboard.

By the time he returned, Elena had offered her apron to Assunta and Assunta was drying her tears. Nino poured three shot glasses of whiskey without asking if anyone wanted it. "When you're ready," he said raising his glass to Assunta and downing it in a few quick swallows. He poured another and waited. He moved Assunta's glass closer to her. The tears had slowed and Assunta made a wry smile.

"*Scusa*," she said. "I'm so happy to see you. Both of you. And I wasn't expecting you back until next week. You said a month and it's only been three weeks. I'm just surprised, that's all, and the emotion just caught me. I'm okay now." She reached for her glass and her father said, for the third time, "What's the matter, daughter?"

"It's just a little misunderstanding. Nothing serious." Assunta took a sip of the whiskey and kept her head down so she didn't see the look that Nino and Elena exchanged.

"With who?" asked Nino.

"Do you know Enzo the bottle-cap salesman?"

"Why would I know a bottle-cap salesman?" asked Nino. "Should I?"

"No, no, of course not. He comes to the bottling plant every month to sell, that's all, and I thought you might have met him. He asked me out a few times while you were away and then today, he—we decided not to see each other anymore, and I'm a little sad. That's all."

"Why don't you want to see him anymore?" asked Nino. "I'm sure he still wants to see you."

"Not exactly," stalled Assunta. "We both decided—" Elena lifted her fingers from Assunta's shoulder and shook her head, just slightly, at Nino. "Is he married, *cara*?" asked Elena.

Assunta shook her head.

"Engaged?"

Assunta shook her head.

"A drinker?" asked Elena.

"Gambler?"

Assunta shook her head.

"If my daughter doesn't want to see him anymore," Nino said to Elena, "she doesn't want to see him. *Finito*. His loss." He banged his empty glass on the table, but not too hard.

"Of course, Nino. You're right but why so many tears, Assunta?"

"I'm lonely. And I met him and for a few weeks, I was so happy. Now it's over." She drank the rest of her whiskey, leaned back in the chair and focused on the warmth that was running through her. Warmth from the whiskey but also from her new mother's arm around her shoulder.

"You can always change your mind. It's a woman's right," suggested Elena.

Nino disagreed, "If she doesn't want to see him anymore, there's a good reason. Assunta doesn't change her mind easily." He poured himself another shot, then topped it up a little before he asked his next question, "What's the rest of this story, *cara*?"

"I didn't know...that is, I didn't ask if he was courting anyone else and then today, I found out he is and I feel so foolish. I didn't know."

"Seeing someone else?" echoed Nino and he banged his fist on the table making the glasses shiver. "Who does he think he is? Playing with my daughter's emotions. Staining her reputation. I'm going to have to pay this two-timing snake a visit. What's his name again?"

Now, Elena switched from stroking Assunta's shoulder to patting her husband's hand. "*Calme,*" she advised. "Assunta is a grown woman. She can take care of herself. And she did. She ended it and it's settled."

"It's *not* settled," said Nino. "Not until I pay him a visit. Then it's settled."

"No. There's no need," She shook her head. "People don't do that anymore."

"What people? The *Americani*? With their modern ideas of women's rights and free love. Forget about it. I'll take care of this gigolo."

"Please, I've already ended it," said Assunta, even though she realized as she said it that she hadn't ended it at all. She still had to talk to Enzo and then she never had to speak to him again.

Nino drove his daughter back to her little house in the village but he stopped in front of Rosa's house across the street from Assunta's.

"We'll talk again tomorrow," said Assunta. "*Grazie* for everything. *Grazie mille.*"

Nino brushed his palm over his face, from his tanned forehead over his eyelids and down his ruddy cheeks. He was flush with whiskey and anger. He nodded, touched Assunta's cool cheek, wished her, "*Buonanotte, cara.*"

Rosa's door opened before Nino's car reached the first curve of *via condotto vecchio*. Assunta ran up the stairs and into her friend's warm kitchen. Rosa was alone.

"Carlito?" asked Assunta.

"Gone to bed," she replied but she called out toward the bedrooms, "And you better be asleep if you want to go and see Nino and Elena tomorrow."

Assunta looked past Rosa in the direction of the living room. The room was dark, no warmth or light from the fireplace grate. "Claudio?" she asked. Rosa shook her head. "Not tonight."

They sat at the kitchen table waiting for the other to explain. Finally, Rosa stood and rummaged in the cupboard above the fridge. First she held up the whiskey bottle, golden in the glare of the kitchen light, but Assunta said, "No, *grazie*, I just had." Rosa opened the fridge and closed it again. She reached high and brought out a box of chocolates from behind a copper pot and sat it on the table. When she lifted the lid, the room took on the scent of very dark chocolate, maraschino cherries, and almonds.

"Why isn't Claudio here?" asked Assunta.

"A long story," sighed Rosa. "Tell me your news first. Is something wrong at the farm?"

"No, no. Everything's good," Assunta assured her friend. "They're happy. I'm happy."

"You don't look very happy," said Rosa, observing Assunta's puffy eyes, her pale cheeks. "Have you been crying?"

Assunta wiped her eyes with the back of her hand. She popped a chocolate into her mouth. She chewed. She swallowed. "I had a whiskey with *Papà* so my eyes are a little bloodshot. That's all."

Rosa waited. There were eleven chocolates left in the box. She took one. Let it melt slowly in her mouth. Waited some more.

"You know Enzo came to the plant today," reminded Assunta. "Well, he said he had business up north and was heading there right away. He said he would take a train from there to Verona on the weekend. He asked me to meet him, on Friday night in Verona. At the hotel. He apologized that we couldn't travel there together. I said we'd ride home together but he had to stay on for work. I should have realized something wasn't right. In fact, I think I did realize it but I didn't know what it was. Something seemed suspicious but a man has to work. Work comes first. And he obviously wanted to see me."

"At the hotel," said Rosa. "*Scusa*, I didn't mean to interrupt. I won't say another word. Go ahead. *Per favore.*" She put another chocolate in her mouth.

"I'm not like you, Rosa. I haven't had a lot of experience with men and I trusted him."

Rosa pushed the chocolate box toward Assunta but Assunta shook her head. "I need some water," she said, and she went to the cupboard for a glass while Rosa went to the fridge for the *Santa Serena* bottle. Once they were settled back at the table,

Assunta continued her story. She told Rosa about the lavender wreath, the missing hairdresser, the new boyfriend, Lorenzo/Enzo.

"He's a two-timing gigolo," said Rosa.

"I was longing for romance," said Assunta, reaching for the chocolate box. Assunta chewed slowly but she swallowed hard and said, "I know this sounds a little crazy, Rosa, but I think Enzo really liked me."

"Of course, he liked you. Just not enough to be honest about romancing two women at once. He wanted to have his cake and eat it too—an American expression, but it fits."

"My father threatened to go and have a word with him."

"Your father is sixty-five years old," Rosa laughed. "Plus, this isn't 1940." It was such an old-fashioned idea and yet it was rather sweet that Nino, even at sixty-five, wanted to defend his daughter's honour. "Are you going to talk to him?"

"Who?" asked Assunta.

"Enzo. Or did you break if off already?"

"I didn't put all the pieces together until I was at the hairdresser's, until I smelled the lavender and saw the wreath. You know what? I smelled that lavender in his car the very first time he took me for lunch. So he was seeing her even then."

"So when are you going to talk to him?"

"Now it's all starting to make sense. The way he liked to meet in private places like the picnic lunch by the river. Or dark places like the cinema. That empty little café on the side street. It was all there in front of me. *Mamma mia*, even the note, *he's seeing someone else*; I knew it wasn't about Claudio. I knew the note had to be for me. *Dio mio*—Bianca—Bianca left that note for me. And I never trusted her with her herbs and spells, and now I have to thank her for the warning. Even if I didn't hear it."

"So, you're going to talk to him, right? Do you want me to come too? I have a few words I'd like to throw in his smug little face."

"I'm going to talk to Bianca first," said Assunta and popped another chocolate.

"You're kidding?" asked Rosa.
Assunta shook her head.

Rosa took the last chocolate, tossed it in the air a few times, caught it in the palm of her hand and said, "You're not thinking of having Bianca put some sort of curse on him, are you? Are you?" she asked.

But Assunta was still savouring the sweetness of the chocolate. "*Mmmm*," was all she said.

Later that night, alone in her bed, Rosa replayed the conversation she'd had with Assunta. Mostly the part where Enzo had shown his true colours but Assunta was blind to them until today. How lonely we are. How hungry we are for love. How easy it is to see someone else's blind spots but not our own. Rosa flipped over her pillow, concentrated on breathing deeply to encourage sleep but all she heard was her heartbeat pounding out that message: *he's seeing someone else*. It was easy now for Rosa to say that she knew all along that the note was meant for Assunta but the truth was that she was panicked by the idea that the warning might have been for her.

Rosa thought about the few men in her life she'd loved and the man she'd married, but didn't love. In the end, they'd all disappointed her. She'd blamed her impulsive decision to marry Elgidio on the full moon that had danced on the blue sea of Napoli. But that same moon didn't hypnotize once the honeymoon ended and the reality of married life began.

She thought about those dreary days, almost eight years ago, when she was living in Elgidio's village like a bored and lonely cliché; she remembered how Claudio brought the sunshine back to her life. She'd resisted his declarations of love until one day she didn't. Of course, she'd blamed the beginning of their affair on the purple clouds that streaked the sky that January afternoon but now, in the dark silence of her bedroom, she knew she'd made the decision herself.

Rosa thought about the last three years since Claudio had been back in the village. She thought about both his love for her and for Carlito and her hesitation to marry and she realized she was waiting for the familiar disappointment to strike again. Like lightning in a thunderstorm—you could count on it—it flashed and then, it destroyed. Just last month, Claudio had said, once again, "We can't go on living like this, Rosa. I want to marry you." And Rosa had responded in her predictable manner by fleeing. This time to Venezia.

Rosa flipped over her pillow, felt the cool cotton beneath her cheek, and realized that maybe she'd learned something in Venezia, learned it from the most unusual source: Tony the American who had lost his wife and his two sons in a traffic accident and was wandering around Italy like a man in a trance, waiting to wake up and find out that it was all a bad dream. Then he'd hold his wife and sons so close to him; he'd never let them go. Rosa rolled onto her back, banged her fist against the mattress. What if something happened to Claudio? How many regrets would she have? She thought about the note that had arrived on her desk; the bold black letters still stabbed at her heart. Yes, she might be disappointed once again; yes, she might have her heart broken; yes, marriage was a gamble—in fact, life was a gamble, if you really jumped in, and lived it. It could all go terribly wrong. How long could she continue to blame her decisions on the moonlight, the shimmering stars, the purple clouds?

Rosa tossed and turned until dawn's first light and then, Carlito was at her bedside reminding her that today was the day that they would go to see Nino and Elena, asking if he could ride his bike to school and then ride straight to the farm afterwards, asking what was for breakfast. She performed her morning routine as if she was still dreaming and even the walk down the hill and through the village to the bottling plant did not revive her. Rosa sleepwalked into Claudio's office, ready to recall every detail of her evening with Assunta and her restless night and her...

"Why don't we go away this weekend?" she suggested, her hand on his arm. "Just the three of us."

Claudio had been double-checking an invoice, his mind was full of numbers, but he looked up at Rosa.

"*Scusa,*" he said. "Did you say you're going away again?" His voice was as cool as the early October morning.

"No, *amore,*" said Rosa. "I'm asking you if we might all go away together—for the weekend—the three of us—like a family."

Claudio ran his hand over his freshly shaved chin and then he picked up his pencil and began to tap it on the desktop.

"Napoli?" he asked. He said the word in a way that made Rosa think his next word would be no. And that would be his final word. No.

Rosa put her hand on top of his; interrupted the tapping pattern, repeated her request. "The three of us," she said. "Maybe Sorrento?"

Claudio slid his fingers up the length of the pencil and down again. He rubbed the eraser as if the answer might be found there. Then he asked, "What brought this on?"

"Something Bianca said."

He dropped the pencil. "Bianca? Did you say Bianca?"

"*Il tempo è l'essenziale*—that's an American phrase that Bianca told me," quoted Rosa. "It means, 'Time is of the essence.'"

■■■

Nino was the first customer at Fortunato's barbershop the next morning and after Fortunato tied the barber's cloth around Nino's neck, they got down to business.

"You're growing a few nice curls back here, Nino," said Fortunato as he ran the comb through the silver strands. "Sure you want to cut it short? You look younger with your hair a little longer."

"Cut it the same as usual," instructed Nino. "I feel young enough."

As soon as he saw the scissors moving, Nino addressed Fortunato in the mirror. "What do you know about this bottle-cap salesman who's been romancing my daughter?"

"Bottle caps?" repeated Fortunato. "Salesman?" Fortunato stopped cutting. "Assunta? Do you mean Assunta?"

"Who else?"

"Well, well," sputtered Fortunato. He put down his scissors. "Romancing Assunta? Well, that's good. Sure, that's good news, Nino. Who is he? Have you met him?"

"I'm going to meet him, that's for sure," said Nino. "Are you planning to cut my hair or just look in the mirror?"

"*Scusa, scusa,*" said Fortunato. "I was just so surprised to know that Assunta has an *amore.*"

"*Had* an *amore,*" declared Nino.

"But I was just saying to Bianca last month that I thought Assunta was a little lonely, you know, with you on your honeymoon and Rosa away in Venezia and now boom! Here you are and you tell me she has an *amore*—but it's over already?"

"It will be over when I see him. The two-timing snake."

Fortunato put down the scissors again. "*Scusa,* Nino. Who is this gigolo? We'll go together and pay him a visit. Teach him a lesson he'll never forget. Two-timing a woman like Assunta. I can't believe it."

"I was hoping you'd know his name, Fortunato. He sells bottle caps. I'll ask Pietro down at the bar. I imagine he'll know."

"*Scusa,* Nino," said Fortunato. "Give me a minute. I'll just call upstairs to Bianca and see what she—"

Before he could finish his sentence, Bianca's answer came clearly down the stairs. "Lorenzo Carprara. Also known as Enzo."

She didn't come down to the barbershop to join in the conversation. She had already twisted a piece of muslin around some lavender twigs. Wrapped an elastic tightly around one end to make a ball. Drew a face and several dark curls on the head. Ripped the muslin. Tied two smaller elastics to make legs. Searched through her sewing box for her hatpin—the one with the sharp point—and circled the muslin until she decided the spot that marked a man's kidneys, and stabbed. Bianca opened the drawer where she kept odds and ends: rusty razor blades, tins of burrs, bags of poison berries, and a rooster's skull, and tossed. A few lavender leaves escaped from the wound and scattered in the box. She closed the drawer.

■■■

After school, Carlito pedaled up the driveway to Nino's farm with the same urgency as the evening before, as if he had to affirm that Nino and Elena had really returned even though it was six more days before their planned arrival. Carlito had been marking off the days on the kitchen calendar. He dropped his bike and surveyed the scene; everything was as it should be: Nino was digging in the garden, Zeus was standing close by, Elena was collecting the laundry and dropping the wooden clothes pegs into the wicker basket. Carlito could smell the smoke coming from the kitchen chimney and he hoped Elena had baked her delicious apple cake. Soon there'd be cake and drinks and stories, but not yet. Carlito raced to the shed, waving his hello as he ran, grabbed his special hoe from its hook and almost flew to the garden.

"*Calme, calme*," warned Nino. "You shouldn't run with tools. Who do you think you are? Superman?"

"I wish I *was* Superman," replied Carlito. "Do you think he had to go to school when he was young like me?"

"*Certo*," said Nino. "All children go to school."

"But he was special," said Carlito.

"Only when he was Superman. When he was Clark Kent, he was as ordinary as you, my boy," Nino smiled when he said the word ordinary. "And he helped in the garden and—"

"I don't think he had grandparents," said Carlito. "That's too bad."

"He had good parents," reminded Nino. "That was probably enough for him."

Carlito struck his hoe into the soil a few times before he replied. His voice was as fresh as the newly turned earth. "They weren't *his* parents. Nobody ever says it but he was..." Carlito looked up at Nino for a moment before lowering his head and finishing his sentence, "a *bastardo*."

Nino stopped his work to lean his forearms on his hoe but

Carlito struck the ground with his hoe over and over again. He felt a hand on his sweaty back. "Are you digging to China?" asked Elena. Her voice was light but her face was serious. "You don't have to do the whole garden in one afternoon," she said. "There's always tomorrow."

"We were talking about Superman," said Nino, still leaning on his hoe.

"The comic book boy?" asked Elena.

"He's not just in comic books," assured Carlito. "He's real."

"I see. He lives in America?"

"Kansas," said Carlito. "But he was born on another planet."

"Really?" said Elena, her eyes wide. "How did he arrive on our planet?"

Carlito stared straight into Elena's grandmotherly face. Did she really not know how Superman had come to earth?

"Rocket ship," said Carlito. He gestured to the wide blue sky and then waved his arm across the fields. "Too bad he didn't land right here," he said before he gave Elena the rest of Superman's history, "These people named *signor e signora* Kent—that's an American name—found him and called him Clark. Actually they *adopted* him."

"Sort of like you adopted us as your grandparents?" asked Elena with a glance at Nino and a smile toward Carlito. Carlito couldn't decide if she really knew nothing about comic book heroes and real parents and real adoption, or if she was teasing him. She didn't usually tease him.

"The couple adopted *him*, Elena," explained Nino but he directed his next words to Carlito. "And that made him their real son."

"But he wasn't," said Carlito, with a kick of his shoe at a stubborn clump of dirt. "He wasn't their real son."

Zeus stuck his head over the wire fence and nudged Nino's arm. Overhead, a row of geese veered south, the leader squawking loudly. Nino took his handkerchief from his pocket and blew his nose loudly yet it was Elena who was sniffling a little.

"Listen to me, Carlito," she began. "Assunta is Nino's daughter but now that Nino and I are married, she is my daughter too. Not my *real* daughter but that doesn't matter. What matters is only that I love her and treat her like my daughter, my real daughter. *Capisce?*"

"That American couple—the Kents—they were fine people, Carlito," added Nino, "They gave that orphan a loving home."

"I'm not an orphan."

"Of course not. You're Rosa's son. We all know that." Nino reached over and tousled Carlito's dark curls. "What's really troubling you, my boy?"

Carlito kicked another stray clump of dirt. "What if?" he began. "I'm just saying—like make believe—what if Claudio married Mamma like you married Elena? Would I be Claudio's son like Assunta is Elena's daughter?"

"Claudio would adopt you. You'd be his real son," said Nino. "You'd be like Superman, Carlito."

"Just like Superman," repeated Elena.

Carlito stomped his foot firmly on the clump of dirt. "Well, that settles it," he said.

Elena looked at Nino, raised an eyebrow, but Nino just shook his head and said, "Do I smell apple cake?" And Zeus lifted his head as if to smell the air, as if he knew that apple cake meant apple skins for him.

■■■

Late in the afternoon, Fortunato nipped across the street to the bakery and bought two flaky pastries—the twisted kind that Bianca liked. Then he called up the spiral staircase, "Do you have a minute, *bella?*" As Bianca circled her way down, Fortunato added, "That's a pretty hairband."

She touched the band, an arch of white crocheted daisies, spotted the bakery box, and replied, "What do you want, Fortunato?"

Fortunato busied himself with the bakery box, slipping off the ribbon and unfolding the flaps. A glance in the mirror revealed his flushed face.

"Just a little afternoon sweet for my *amore*," he said.

"I see."

They sat side by side on the bench. Fortunato spread his barber's towel on Bianca's lap, careful not to mention her expanding waist or her spreading abdomen. "Did you know about Assunta's romance?" he asked and then answered his own question. "Of course you did. But what about this two-timer? Do you know the other woman he's involved with? Someone should tip off her father, don't you think?" He offered the box to Bianca. She lifted a treat, held her hand beneath the twisted puff pastry to catch the loose sugar crystals, and bit. Small pastry flakes fluttered into her lap.

"Let Nino take care of it."

"Nino's old. He'll need help to avenge his daughter. It's too much to expect him to take care of advising the other woman's father too."

"Not your business, Fortunato." Bianca licked the sugar crystals that clung to her fingers and folded the corners of the towel to the centre. She lifted the towel, ready to shake the crumbs outside, and return upstairs.

"Wait a minute," said Fortunato. "Just think about it for a minute, *bella*. What if it was one of our daughters? Wouldn't you want to know?"

"Enzo's also seeing the new hairdresser. Her name's Gabriella," said Bianca. "That's all I know."

"Where does Gabriella live?" asked Fortunato. "Nino and I can go and see her father, warn him. Maybe he'll come with us when we talk to this Enzo character."

"Gabriella's father lives in Roma. She's staying here with her aunt and uncle and her cousin. The cousin's name is Angela." Bianca gave an ironic laugh, "A couple of angels: Gabriella e Angela."

"In the village?"

"Outside. Near the bus stop at the edge of town. The aunt knows."

"*Dio mio*, the aunt knows and does nothing. What's this world coming to?"

"The aunt knows Gabriella is away for the weekend. She doesn't know about Enzo, or Lorenzo, or whatever he calls himself when he's romancing her."

"Surely the aunt wouldn't allow her niece to go away on her own," said Fortunato. "Who does she think the hairdresser... Gabriella?..."

"Yes, Gabriella."

"Gabriella couldn't tell her aunt that she's going away with her boyfriend," said Fortunato. "Who does the aunt think Gabriella is with?"

"She thinks Gabriella is with Angela, of course," said Bianca. "The cousins tell the mother that they're going away together. What else? A couple of angels watching out for each other. Perfectly safe."

"But Gabriella is really with Enzo." Fortunato stopped for a moment to shake his head, but his thoughts remained jumbled. "What happens to the other cousin, Angela? Where is that girl?"

"Angela's with *her* boyfriend. Who else? They're spending a weekend in Positano."

"How do you know...?" began Fortunato but instead of waiting for her answer, he put up his hand and shook his head. He didn't want to know. He lowered his sugar twist back into the box. Life was too complicated. Unmarried girls sneaking off for romantic weekends with boyfriends. Cousins lying for each other. The mother knowing nothing; Bianca knowing everything. How to understand women? It was going to be very difficult being the father of two daughters. What if the twins that Bianca carried were also girls? Fortunato wasn't sure he could manage it. Or boys either for that matter. Maybe he should go for a walk and try to clear his head. He suggested to Bianca that he might close a little early today and hike up to Santa Serena but she didn't respond. He looked beside him. She was gone. He looked out the open doorway and saw only a few finches pecking at the sugary remnants of her pastry. He was alone.

An American in Gupino

As soon as Claudio, Rosa, and Carlito were settled in their seats on the train to Sorrento, Carlito opened his new comic book and was instantly immersed in the adventures of Superman. Claudio stretched out his legs and leaned back in his seat, tipped his Borsalino hat over his forehead, and closed his eyes. Only Rosa stayed awake and alert: she watched the Ciociaria countryside flash past, the fields recently planted with durum wheat, the vineyards crowded with dusty vines and heavy fruit, the open pastures interspersed with the undulating hills of Lazio flowing effortlessly into the quarry areas of Campania. Still ahead lay the dark shadows of the Vesuvius. The train rocked; Rosa closed her eyes.

■■■

Tony from America had been to Florence, to Pisa, to some small seaside town whose name he couldn't remember and he was growing restless and thinking it might be time to return to the U.S. He had a sister there, in New York City, who was anxious to take care of him but he was resistant to that idea. He was ready to create his own life—one not built on pity, loss, sorrow. That's what he was thinking about as he sat on the train heading back to Roma. His plan was to stay in Roma for a few days—he still held onto the romantic notion of tossing a coin into the Trevi Fountain to ensure his return and he could do that tomorrow, and climb the Spanish steps once more and people watch at the café—and then book his flight back.

The train was slowing as they approached the next station and Tony stood to stretch his back—these metal seats were anything but comfortable. Some official came walking past, telling the passengers to stay seated until the train had come to a full stop but no one paid him any attention. They were pulling down suitcases from the overhead racks, from under the seats, from the luggage compartment. The blue station sign came into view: Ferentino. Tony recognized the name; it was the station close to the village where Rosa and her son Carlito lived. He had a sudden urge to grab his suitcase, get off the train, and catch a cab to their village and say hello. Stay a night or two at a hotel. Take in the sights. But Tony was not an impulsive man and you'd have to be impulsive to reach under your seat and slide out your suitcase and head for the exit. Without a second thought. Of course, you'd have a moment while you waited for the train to come to a screeching stop when you could change your mind and return immediately to your seat and your sanity. But Tony did not.

And that's how Tony found himself standing on the platform of the Ferentino station looking around at nothing. No cabstand. No bus stop. No telephone booth. In the parking lot, he watched a young woman kiss a man who had tucked her suitcase into his trunk. He watched them get into the car and speed off. He watched another man unlock a battered bicycle from the lamppost and pedal away. He watched a dog stop to piss on the stop sign that marked the entrance to the road. He read the street sign, *via centrale*.

The station man left his booth and locked it behind him. Tony approached, dictionary in hand, although he rarely consulted it anymore. He'd become fairly fluent in the language although once the locals started speaking quickly, Tony was just as quickly lost. "*Tassi?*" he asked the station man. "*Autobus?*" And the man pointed to a building in the distance. The sign on the building said "Bar."

Inside the bar, the mood was hushed. The barman was leaning

on the counter and reading aloud from the newspaper. He announced a letter to someone named Minerva. It seemed to be the Italian version of Ann Landers or Dear Abby and in the same way that Americans were always interested in others' problems, the Italians leaned forward to hear the problem and the response.

The barman held up a finger to signal he'd be with Tony in a moment. Tony had been in Italy long enough to know that an Italian moment could easily stretch to five or ten minutes, so he took a seat at a table and waved his hand to the barman to encourage him to continue.

"*Un momento*," said one of the customers. "I missed that last part. Start again." The customer looked at Tony and Tony nodded: even though he wasn't particularly interested in the letter, he understood it was the polite gesture.

The bartender cleared his throat and started again; his finger tracing the words as he read aloud, "'Dear Minerva: The cherries were in season but my wife was going to be away for the day. I promised that my friends and I would pick the cherries before the birds arrived to do it for us but we got listening to the soccer game on the radio in the kitchen. We had a few beers and ate the pizza that was in the pantry. Somehow the time got away from us—it was a tight game, 1-1 right up to the end. My wife comes home and starts yelling. Seems she was saving the pizza to take to her mother's that night. Seems the cherry tree was bare but the pails were empty. Something about me always promising her the mountain and the sea but never doing anything. Between her and the radio, I couldn't get a word in edgewise. Finally she grabbed the meat pounder from the kitchen drawer and smashed the radio to bits. We didn't even get to hear the final score. What do you think of a woman who smashes a perfectly good radio?'"

Many of the men were shaking their heads in disbelief. What could Minerva possibly say to a woman who deprived her husband from hearing the final score by smashing a perfectly good radio? The room was quiet with expectation. The barman also shook his head before he read aloud Minerva's answer, "'You're lucky she didn't smash you with the meat pounder.'"

The response caused an uproar. Men shared tales of how they would have handled such an outrage. There were a few truths exchanged: women will never understand soccer; only a woman would make a pizza and expect no one to eat it. Women don't realize that you can always buy cherries but you can only listen to the game once. Tony waited until the noise settled a little before he approached the barman. "Can I phone for a taxi from here?"

"*Tassi?*" asked the barman. Then turning to his customers he repeated the request once again, only louder, "*Tassi!*" The customers laughed; they banged the table; they tapped each other's shoulders; they laughed some more.

Someone said, "Ey *signor*, this is Ferentino, not Roma!" Someone else asked, "Ey *signor, Americano?*" Another asked, "Ey *signor Americano*, where you wanna go?"

Tony understood that taxis were not available in this small town but he also understood that they were interested in his destination and hopefully in helping him find alternate transportation to get there. There was obviously no jitney or shuttle bus from the train station to the village but there must be some public transportation. All he needed to know was the bus schedule and where to board it. He spoke first to the barman, "*Caffè, per favore*," then he added, "I'm going to a village near here called Supino."

"Supino?" they asked and looked at each other. Some shrugged; others scratched their heads. Was he at the wrong town? Hadn't Rosa said Supino was near Ferentino? These men didn't seem to be familiar with the village. He poured some sugar into his coffee and stirred and waited. He caught a word here and there. Someone mentioned the *autostrada* and someone else said something about a water fountain but when Tony heard the name of the water-bottling plant, Acqua di Santa Serena, he put up his hand. "*Si, si,*" he said. "That's it." Then he heard more words: bus, too late or perhaps, later, tomorrow, last bus. Customers looked at their watches; the barman consulted a sheet of paper hanging on the side of the cash register and then he glanced at the clock.

He held up ten fingers to Tony—ten minutes to the bus stop? Ten minutes before the bus arrived here?—and then motioned Tony to follow him. Tony downed the last of his espresso, tucked a *lire* note under his saucer, and followed the barman.

They walked quickly across the parking lot, stepping aside to allow a delivery truck entry, and then stopped beside a glossy green laurel hedge. The barman pointed down the road and gave Tony the directions: he said the bus stop, or perhaps the bus itself, was blue. That seemed to be important: to catch the blue bus or to wait at the blue bus stop. "Blue" was the key word. Around the time that the barman asked Tony if he understood, "*Capisce*?" someone called to them from the doorway of the bar. There was a loud, fast conversation, none of which Tony understood, between the customer and the barman, as they called back and forth, and finally the barman took Tony's arm and led him back to the bar.

Inside he introduced Tony to a truck driver who sat at a table with a slice of pizza and a mug of beer. Tony shook the man's extended hand—what was this all about?—and reminded the barman of the time and the bus schedule by pointing to his watch and turning to the door. "No, no," said the barman and the truck driver in unison. They said, "Acqua di Santa Serena," and, "*Finito*," and "Wait," until Tony finally understood that the truck driver was finished his deliveries for the day and offering to take Tony back to Supino with him. "*Poco minuti*," said the driver. Well, Tony already knew that a few minutes could be at least half an hour so he sat down beside the truck driver, ordered pizza and beer and paid both his and the driver's bill, plus an extra *lire* for the barman.

An hour later, they drove out of the parking lot and the driver ground the gears and they were off toward the *autostrada*. The sun was hanging low. They passed over the highway and joined a crush of traffic travelling toward the mountains. At a fork in the road, most of the traffic turned left but they veered right and the driver picked up speed as they drove parallel to the mountain past factories and farms. They slowed once for a stop sign, stopped at the side of the road for a shepherd and some sheep who were crossing from pasture to pasture—the driver had a cigarette; Tony watched and waited. "*Cinque minuti.*" said the driver holding up five fingers.

They started to climb a gentle hill and the farms grew smaller and closer together and eventually gave way to houses. When they stopped at the entrance to the village, Tony saw a blue bus stopped there by a water fountain; the driver turned sharply left and although it seemed that they were heading back in the same direction that they had just come, they soon pulled into the driveway of a stone farm house with lacquered wooden shutters and a large barn out back where the driver stopped. In the parking area, a couple of men were washing delivery trucks. Tony knew better than to offer payment for the drive—that would insult the kindness of the driver—but he offered to help wash the truck. The driver shook his head; pointed to the farmhouse; shook Tony's hand, and walked off to talk to the other drivers. Tony followed the path to the farmhouse and beneath the sign that read, Acqua di Santa Serena, he stopped and knocked and the door swung open so he went inside.

He intended to ask for Rosa, offer to take her and her family out for dinner that night; hopefully get a little tour of the village the next day, and possibly a lift to the train station so he could get to Roma.

His new Italian loafers were silent as he stepped across the cool marble tiles to an open office door. Tony could only see her back—a sweater that might be blue or might be grey and a long neck that was as pale as eggshells. He tapped softly on the door and took a step back so he wouldn't startle her when she turned around. She turned slowly as if reluctant to leave her work or perhaps reluctant to greet a visitor or maybe...her eyes were a startling shade of slate and like the sweater, he couldn't tell if they were grey or blue. She looked a little disappointed when she saw him—Tony wondered if she was expecting someone else. She smiled but Tony noticed that her smile didn't reach her eyes.

"*Buongiorno,*" she said. "*Dimmi,*" using the Italian word that

Tony had come to know as, "May I help you?"

"*Americano*," said Tony, pointing to himself, "I no speak... parlo...Italiano." He reached into his pocket and retrieved a business card. "Tony Baxter," he said, offering the card. He gave a formal little bow. What was the matter with him? First babbling like an idiot about how he didn't *parla* the language, even as he was speaking it, and then pointing to himself as if she couldn't identify him as an American and now bowing like he was some lost Japanese businessman. Her eyes had disarmed him, that's what he told himself, and then it got worse.

She offered her name, Assunta, and her hand and he enveloped her cool small hand in his and couldn't let go. Assunta said, "May I?" referring to her hand held firmly in his.

"You speak English," said Tony. He was delighted.

"Just a little—*poco*," she said. He was still delighted, still holding her hand. She repeated her request, "May I?" and Tony laughed, "*Scusa*," and she pulled her hand from his.

Assunta offered him a seat across from her desk and Tony sat on the edge of the chair and leaned toward her and told her about meeting Rosa and Carlito in Venezia but she seemed to already know. She told him that Rosa and Carlito were away with Claudio in Sorrento.

He said, "That's unfortunate. I was hoping to see them."

"They'll be back in a few days."

"*Bene*," said Tony thinking it would give him a valid reason to hang around the village for those few days. "I've seen a lot of Italian cities, but it'll be nice to see a typical Italian village as well." He asked if Assunta could recommend a hotel and a good restaurant. Then he added, impulsively, "I'm tired of eating alone. Would you like to join me for dinner?" He felt her grey/blue eyes on him while he waited for her answer and when it came, it seemed that he'd made her sad somehow by his impromptu invitation. Had he missed some Italian protocol?

The room grew cooler and so did her voice. She'd shaken her head and said, "No." She'd tightened her sweater around her shoulders; she'd retreated into her chair. Tony wasn't sure what to do next and in trying to do the right thing, he did the wrong. He asked again about the hotel and then, when he saw her eyes brim with tears, he figured she must have thought that he was propositioning her. He'd really stuck his foot in it now. After all he was a complete stranger and Italians were more formal than Americans. He knew that. Tony saw Assunta glance at her watch—it must be closing time—and he got up to leave but instead of saying, "*Arrivederci,*" as he intended, he said, "Listen, before I catch the blue bus back to Ferentino, can I walk you home? See a little of the village along the way?"

"If you walk me home, all my neighbours..." began Assunta but then she stopped. She ran her index finger under her eyelids and said, "Would you like to see my father's farm?"

"Of course," said Tony. "I'd love to." He didn't say I'd love to do anything with you. He didn't say anything to spoil his good luck. "Whenever you're ready to go," he assured her. "I'm ready."

He stood by the back door while Assunta went into the parking lot to speak to the drivers because he didn't want to interfere in her business—plus he was practicing all the Italian phrases he knew so he could talk to her as they walked to the farm. Tony looked up when one of the drivers—his driver actually—called out, "Ey, *signor,*" and waved Tony over to the freshly washed truck, now drying in the pale six o'clock sunlight. The driver looked Tony up and down as if meeting him for the first time and asked, "*Biglietto da visita?*" and as Tony handed the driver his business card wondering why he wanted it, he became aware of the other drivers openly watching. Did they want a card too or were they inspecting him? It felt like an inspection. Assunta raised her hand and called a farewell and the drivers lifted their hats to her, or gave a little salute, and called, "*Buonasera, signorina,*" with such genuine warmth that Tony understood that they were looking out for Assunta like she was their family.

He didn't dare to offer her his arm. He tried to keep an appropriate space between them although he had no idea what an appropriate Italian space might be. He walked on the outside of the sidewalk, closest to the roadway, like an Englishman from the Victorian era protecting the lady from careless carriage wheels and mud splashes. They retraced the route to the spot where he'd seen the blue bus, but there was no bus there now, and Assunta paused for a mere moment to point up the main street, lined with little shops and cafés and spindly trees with only a few brave leaves clinging to their branches. But when Tony took a step in that direction, Assunta tapped his arm and stepped the other way, down the hill, to a narrow side street that curved between beech trees ablaze in autumn-gold. Tony's arm was still warm where she'd touched him. She was talking about something and he was following her, if not her words, and suddenly they were on a paved road with open pastures on both sides. They stepped to the edge of the road to allow a delivery truck to pass, a farmer with a load of straw bales, a donkey cart piled high with bunches of branches, a group of schoolboys kicking a soccer ball back and forth across the street while they called out each other's names.

"The bakery," said Assunta, pointing to a boarded-up building at the end of a driveway strewn with ryegrass. "Angelo—that's the baker—died last December and his son doesn't want to be a baker. He's a lawyer." Somehow Assunta made the profession of lawyer sound much less important or appealing than baker. "So we're left without a baker in the village," she explained.

"Isn't there a bakery on the main street?" asked Tony. "I thought I saw a sign that said, *pasticceria*—that's a bakery isn't it?"

Assunta shook her head. "A *pasticceria* only sells pastries, not bread."

"I see," said Tony although he didn't understand the difference. They were both baked goods. They both required ovens, and bakers.

"All the years I lived on my father's farm," said Assunta, wistfully, "I'd wake up every morning to the smell of loaves baking. Later, we'd hear the truck on the road heading into town to deliver to the stores but I would have already run across the street to collect our loaf. The bread would still be warm and I had to carry it home wrapped in Mamma's tea towel and tucked into the wicker basket. It's funny how much you can miss something as simple as the smell of baking bread."

Assunta seemed so wistful that Tony wanted to give her a little hope so he asked, "Do you think someone will reopen the bakery?" But Assunta looked at him with surprise.

"I already told you," she said. "The son's a lawyer, not a baker."

"But someone else?" asked Tony. "Couldn't someone else learn the business?" Assunta stopped and pointed and they crossed the road to a dusty gravel lane with a few empty milk pod plants still loitering here and there. Tony thought the scene was terribly idyllic: smoke rising from the farmhouse chimney, wood stacked along the side of the house, a small tower of wicker fruit baskets leaning against a shed, a donkey with a straw hat grazing freely, and a man turning the soil in a garden. The man looked up at the sound of footsteps on the gravel pathway and immediately swung the pitchfork he'd been using onto his shoulder and marched toward them.

"*Papà*," said Assunta.

"Enzo?" asked the man, glaring at Tony. He held his pitchfork only inches from Tony's crotch. The man looked like he would definitely stab Tony and do it happily. Tony jumped back. In the distance, the donkey brayed and ambled toward them.

Assunta stepped between Tony and the pitchfork-holding man. "*Papà*," she said. "*Non è Enzo.*" To Tony, she said, "*Scusa...* " and a whole bunch of other words, which he didn't understand. Tony took another step back. Looked toward the roadway. Debated making a run for it. Assunta touched his arm, rooted him to the ground. She turned back to her father, more Italian words spoken quickly and her father stuck the pitchfork into the ground, albeit a little reluctantly as if he'd been looking forward to castrating a foreigner.

He wiped his hand on his pant leg. "*Scusa, signor,*" he said, introducing himself, "Nino, *padre di* Assunta." At that moment, the donkey arrived and butted his head against Tony's shoulder. Like a warning. Tony rubbed his shoulder with one hand, and reached the other to Assunta's father. "Tony Baxter," he said. Assunta's father said something that sounded like a warning, or

137

maybe a threat, but Assunta claimed that her father had said he was pleased to meet Tony. "*Vieni*," said Nino and Tony followed him, while Assunta headed toward the farmhouse and Zeus pulled up the rear.

Some experiences can be understood without the benefit of language and Tony understood that Nino wanted to determine what kind of man Tony was and Tony's actions would tell Nino all he needed to know in the same way that Nino's approach with the pitchfork had told Tony that Nino was a man who was protective of his daughter. This baffled Tony a little because Assunta seemed like a practical and capable woman—except for that caution in her blue-grey eyes and a sense of sorrow that she wore like a sweater.

Nino and Tony walked the farm. Nino showed him the garden where he had been mixing manure into the soil with the pitchfork. The small orchard where Nino patted the trunks of the various fruit trees beginning with springtime apricots and ending with russet apples, now hanging honey-brown and heavy on the boughs. Several rows of grapevines weighted with dusty purple fruit. Nino showed him the shed where the donkey, named Zeus, lived in one half and a dozen chickens were the tenants in the other half. The shed was as tidy as Tony's office back in NYC. Nino named the different logs in his woodpile and Tony nodded even though he hadn't thought until that moment about real logs: cherry, apple, oak. Tony had a fireplace in his home but it was gas, the logs were fake birch. They moved to the back of the house where there was an outdoor sink beneath the kitchen window and it was here that Nino washed his hands carefully with a large bar of yellow soap and the scent of that soap mingled with the aroma escaping from the open kitchen window, of coffee brewing along with something sweet—cinnamon? Brown sugar? Nino left his work boots on a mat inside the back door and Tony slipped off his Italian loafers and followed Nino into the kitchen. Here he met Nino's wife Elena who immediately sat him down at the table and placed a bowl containing a baked apple centred in a syrup of brown sugar and cinnamon in front of him.

She plopped a dollop of cold yoghurt on top and the coolness combined with the warmth woke up all his senses and somehow, he was suddenly able to speak quite perfect Italian to Elena, telling her she was a cook *supremo* and should open a *ristorante* immediately. Elena smiled and when she did, her whole face lit up and her eyes sparkled.

Assunta smiled too as she poured the coffee but she still smiled only with her lips. They were pretty lips, there was no denying that, but the smile was reserved.

It was Assunta who explained that Tony had met Rosa and Carlito in Venezia and Rosa had invited Tony to come to her village if he was ever in the area. No one asked why an *Americano* would ever be in the area of their secluded village. Assunta explained that Tony would stay for a few days until Rosa and Claudio and Carlito returned from Sorrento; she said he'd stay at the *pensione* just outside of town.

"The *pensione*?" asked Elena.

"Where else?" asked Assunta.

"It's too far to walk from the *pensione*," said Elena.

Nino said to Elena, "The blue bus stops outside the *pensione* every half hour, or so, and Tony can take the bus into the village any time he wants." Nino turned toward Tony and asked, "What do you want to see?"

Tony didn't know how to answer. What was there to see? He only wanted to see more of Assunta. Dare he say that?

Elena made a suggestion, "Come for dinner tomorrow night."

Tony said yes immediately. He said he'd take the bus into the village and explore and perhaps he could meet Assunta at the bottling plant at six o'clock and walk to the farm with her, as they had this evening. Everyone agreed; it was settled although Tony felt anything but settled. Plus, how was he to get to this *pensione*? He didn't dare mention the word taxi.

He stood. He thanked Elena for the baked apple and the coffee. He shook Nino's hand. He told Assunta he looked forward to seeing her tomorrow. When Tony picked up his travel bag, Nino said he could harness Zeus to the cart and take Tony to the *pensione*. Tony said not to bother; he thought he knew his way back into the village, where he said he'd take the blue bus right to the door of the *pensione*.

The sun was beginning to dip below the skyline when he got off the bus and crossed the street to the *pensione*. Outside, a few men gathered at tables on the patio drinking and playing a card game. Inside were a bar, more tables, and a telephone with a sign that said "Out of Order." Tony asked the barman about a room and the barman shook his head, "Not here, *signor*. You want the hotel section." He walked Tony through an arched doorway a few feet away where a little table displayed an open book, a pen, and a small inkwell. The barman motioned for Tony to put down his suitcase and he called through the swinging doors that, judging by the scents that wafted out when a young woman exited, led to the kitchen.

"This *signor* wants a room," said the man and he returned to the bar. "How many nights?" asked the young woman.

"Let's say a week," said Tony.

"Let's say?" she repeated, her head tilted sideways, her eyebrows arched.

"A week," clarified Tony.

"Room and meals?" asked the young woman. "Or just room? Meals are ten *lire* more, *signor*." A waiter hurried past them, with plates containing lamb chops, several roasted potato spears and very dark, very shiny, green *rapini*. The scent of garlic and olive oil made his head a little light. "And meals," said Tony. "Starting tonight?"

"Certainly," said the young woman and she reached for Tony's suitcase, tucked it beneath the desk and turned Tony over to the waiter who seated him by the window where the sun was flickering its last shades of red and orange into the room. Tony observed the other tables. A few were couples or families out for a meal but most were workers: blue cotton shirts, work boots, folded caps tucked in back pockets. At the workers' table, the waiter exchanged the lamb plates for empty pasta bowls and put another jug of wine on the table. Then he came to Tony's table.

No menu, no notepad, just a question, "*Signor?*"

Tony decided to make his life simple: he asked the waiter to just bring him what the workers were having.

"*Bene*," said the waiter, lowering his hands as if he'd held a notepad and a pencil and had now finished writing. "Wine?" he asked.

"Yes, red," said Tony.

"Water?" asked the waiter.

"Yes, flat," said Tony.

In a moment, the waiter swung by with a bread basket, a wine jug, and a glass tumbler and Tony was back to watching the workers, the couples, the sunset and, now, the shadows that stretched through the windows copying the inky spires of the cypress trees in the garden.

By the time Tony was served his espresso, most of the other customers had gone on their way. The workers were now out on the patio; Tony could hear their voices, the slap of cards on the metal tabletops, and the occasional clink of beer bottles or coffee cups as the barman served and cleared. Despite the late-night caffeine, Tony felt very tired; he felt that he could pick up his suitcase, climb the stairs to his room, crawl into bed, and sleep for eight hours straight. And that's exactly what he did. Except it was nine hours of dreamless sleep. When he woke, he might have thought he'd dreamt the events of yesterday, starting with the decision to hop off the train and ending with the decision to spend a week in a remote village. But he definitely hadn't dreamed the pitchfork or the angry father and he definitely hadn't imagined Assunta. In fact, since his wife and sons died almost two years ago, he'd never imagined another love in his life but now, he'd met Assunta and she was it; she was the next love of his life, even if she didn't know it yet.

At six o'clock, he walked around to the back of the water-bottling plant and greeted the drivers who were leaning against the wall like weary brooms at the end of a long day. He approached the driver who'd given him a lift yesterday and asked his advice regarding a hostess gift. "Something for Elena who has invited me for dinner," he explained. "I thought I'd stop at the florist shop that I saw on the main street and buy some roses."

"No," said the driver. "Roses are only for romance. Buy Elena a box of chocolate-covered maraschino cherries," he said. "They're her favourite. "

"I didn't see a chocolate shop in town," said Tony.

"Go to the store that sells cigarettes and candies—the *tabacchi* store—they'll have them. Tell them it's a gift and they'll wrap it up for you."

"Okay," said Tony. "Thank you. One more thing. Something for Assunta? A little bouquet of..."

"No," said the driver.

"Inappropriate?" asked Tony.

"Yes," said the driver. "Not right now."

Tony shook his hand and went to knock on Assunta's door. He could hear her voice on the telephone. He remained in the hallway, admiring the curve of her pale neck.

Her voice grew louder, "I already explained," she said. "I don't want to say it all again.... There's no point.... I already said no."

Tony took a step forward but then stopped. It wasn't his business. And what was he going to do anyway? Tell the caller to stop annoying her? Assunta seemed like the kind of woman who could deal with frustrated customers or annoying suppliers. It wasn't his business, not even when her voice grew more ragged. "There's no need to see you... Yes, I do think it's fair... Do not come here...ever." She didn't say goodbye; she just hung up the phone. Tony watched her shoulders slump; he took a silent step back; he watched her shake with little sobs; he took another silent step back. As soon as he was out of sight, he walked back to the entrance, and waited a few minutes. Then he opened and closed the door firmly and began to whistle loudly as he walked slowly toward her office.

■■■

On the way to the farm, they met a girl on a bicycle.
"*Ciao*, Assunta," she called.
"*Ciao*, Giuseppina."
Giuseppina turned her bike and pulled up beside them.
"Where you going?" asked Giuseppina. "The farm?"
"*Si*. We're going to have dinner with *Papà*," said Assunta. Then Assunta added, "Where are you off to?"
"Just riding around," said Giuseppina. "Carlito's coming back the day after tomorrow."
"And nothing to do until then?" asked Assunta.
"Not really," said Giuseppina.
Assunta glanced at Tony: she really couldn't put off the introductions any longer. "This is a friend from America. Actually, he's a friend of Carlito and Rosa's. They met in Venezia. Tony. From America."
"You already said that," reminded Giuseppina and she jumped off her bike to shake his hand, and walk along with them. "Are you waiting for them to come back from their holiday?" she asked, and when Tony said yes, Giuseppina said, "Me too."
"Where do you live?" asked Giuseppina. "In America."
"New York City."
"That's too bad. I thought you might live in Hollywood and know some movie stars."

Tony laughed but when he saw Giuseppina's serious expression, he said, "*Scusa, signorina*, I don't know any movie stars."

They walked along in silence for a while. The sun was weak; the shadows long. Bougainvillea with blooms like blaring trumpets tumbled over a stonewall. Giuseppina tugged at her coat sleeves and said, "Mamma's going to buy me a new coat on Saturday. Navy. I said red but Mamma said I'd soon get tired of looking like a traffic light. Mamma said navy is *classico*."

They reached Nino's driveway. Assunta said, "Say hello to Mamma from me. Antonietta and *Papà* too."

"*Bene*," said Giuseppina. "*Ciao*, Tony from America."

"Nice little girl," said Tony as they walked up the drive.

"Carlito bought her a little glass ladybug in Venezia—sorry, I wasn't supposed to tell. That's Carlito's secret. Please forget I said anything."

Assunta laughed, said, "I can keep a secret," and Tony looked into her grey-blue eyes and wondered how many secrets she was keeping.

He stepped on a loose rock and stumbled. Assunta put her hand on his arm. "Steady there," she said. "The path's a little rough."

■■■

At *la casa bella*, Giuseppina had two pieces of news to tell. She waited until Mamma had served the bowls of penne, waiting until *Papà* had passed the bowl of grated cheese, waited until her sister, Antonietta, had speared her first piece of pasta and then Giuseppina said, "I saw Assunta today. She was walking with a man. *Americano*. They were going to have dinner at the farm with Nino and Elena."

Everyone paused for a moment, forks suspended in the air.

"His name's Tony," said Giuseppina and nonchalantly popped a piece of penne in her mouth, and chewed, and said, "Mmmm."

Antonietta was the first to recover. She said, "Where does he live in America?"

Giuseppina assured her that he lived in New York City, nowhere near Hollywood. "Too bad," said Antonietta, with a teenager's bored sigh, and resumed eating. "Well," said Bianca, choosing her words carefully. "An American in our village. How would Assunta even know an American?"

"Perhaps he's a buyer," suggested Fortunato. "Interested in importing water to America."

"He's a friend," said Giuseppina, and pausing for emphasis, she added, "A friend of Carlito and Rosa's. From Venezia."

"I thought you said he's from America," said Antonietta, pointing her fork at her sister. "You're making up the whole story."

"I'm not," protested Giuseppina. "He's an American from New York City and they met in Venezia."

"So what's he doing here then?" asked Antonietta.

"Waiting for Rosa and Carlito to return."

"And then?" asked Antonietta, "Then what happens in this fairy tale of yours."

"Maybe while he's waiting for them to return," mused Giuseppina, "he falls in love with Assunta."

Antonietta added to the story, "Even though her heart is broken from Enzo, the two-timer…"

"That's enough," said Bianca. "How do you know about Enzo?"

"Oh, Mamma," claimed Antonietta. "Everyone knows."

"I have more news," said Giuseppina.

"Wait a minute," said Fortunato, putting down his fork, "You need to learn there's a difference between gossip and news. And we've heard enough gossip for one day."

Antonietta raised her eyebrows at her younger sister but Giuseppina said, "This is school news. I need you to sign a permission form. For art. And I need a bar of soap and a paring knife."

Antonietta explained how they'd been studying the great sculptors of Italy and now they were going to carve something great too. That's what the knife and the soap were for and the permission form was just in case some eight-year-old was careless with the knife.

"What are you going to carve?" asked Antonietta. "A heart for your boyfriend, Carlito?"

"He's not my boyfriend," said Giuseppina.

"Antonietta, that's enough," warned Bianca.

"Tell us, *cara mia*," said Fortunato. "What will you make with your soap?"

Giuseppina frowned at her sister and then she gave her list of possibilities. "Maybe a turtle shell or maybe a sea shell. I'd like to try a ladybug but I'd need red soap and I'm not sure how to make the spots and a ladybug's no good without the spots, so probably a seashell. Do we have any pink soap, Mamma?"

"I have a brand-new bar—still in the wrapper—you need soft soap. If the soap's too old, it just splinters and you end up with a pile of jagged spears, which can be helpful if you want to mix a... well, never mind, about that. I'll give you a brand-new bar and *Papà* will find the right knife for you."

"I will," said Fortunato. "Now eat your dinner. Mamma has made *panna cotta* for dessert."

Later that night, Giuseppina had her bar of soap, her paring knife, and her permission form all tucked safely in her knapsack ready for school in the morning; Antonietta had her homework done and also tucked safely in her knapsack along with a tube of Perfectly Pink lipstick that Bianca didn't know about, yet; Fortunato was snoring peacefully, and Bianca was still up. From the back of her drawer, she brought an oval bar of olive oil soap that she'd been saving for a special occasion. She spread a tea towel on the kitchen table; she cradled the soap in the palm of her hand while she carved into one side, scraping over and over again. Soap curls cluttered the cloth. When the soap was a perfect kidney shape, Bianca wrapped it in a handkerchief and slipped it in her purse.

The next day Bianca waited until almost closing time before she entered the hairdresser's shop. The owner was mopping the terrazzo floor; Simonetta looked up at Bianca and then at the clock.

"I only need a minute," assured Bianca. "I realized I'm out of your special shampoo and I wanted to pick up a bottle. If you don't mind."

"Not at all," sighed Simonetta as she leaned the mop against the desk and went to the back room where she kept her supplies. She was only gone a minute, or two, just enough time for Bianca to approach the new hairdresser's station and to write a message for Gabriella on her mirror with the bar of soap, and then to stab a hat pin, three times, into the kidney shaped bar and leave it in front of the mirror.

"Here it is," said Simonetta, returning with the shampoo bottle. Bianca handed over the money and was out the door. "I don't want to keep you," she said. Then Simonetta turned, reached for her mop and saw the writing on the mirror. Simonetta only paused for a moment. Gabriella was due in the next morning; let her see the message and wipe it off herself if she wanted to. She'd only learn what everyone in the village already knew, "He's seeing someone else."

When Tony returned to the *pensione* that evening, the bartender immediately put up his hand. "*Momento*," he said and disappeared. He returned with the woman who had booked his room for the week. She spoke some English. She said, "Cold last night?" and Tony said no. She nodded but it seemed that she didn't believe him. "The *copriletto*..." she began, and then she must have realized that Tony didn't understand one word beyond the word "the," and she switched to hand gestures. Apparently, *copriletto* had something to do with a bed cover—a blanket? Bedspread? Specifically the bedspread in Tony's room. And the woman folded one hand over the other like a sandwich. Meanwhile the bartender pulled an imaginary blanket up to his chin. It had been a little chilly last night and Tony had folded the bedspread in two and gone back to sleep. Had he forgotten to unfold it this morning? Did it matter? Apparently it did.

Now the woman was telling him that the cleaning woman had reported the folded bedspread to the owner and as Tony tried to understand why they were having this conversation, the woman continued speaking, entirely in Italian and entirely incomprehensible. "*Scusa*," said the Lavazza delivery man. When did he come in?

"*Signor*," he said to Tony, "if you cold in the night, open the cupboard. There you find a blanket. Wool. Very warm. Okay?"

And Tony nodded and said, "*Grazie*."

And the bartender tapped the espresso into the *portafiltro* and swung it into place. "*Caffè*?" he offered. And Tony and the barman and the Lavazza delivery man all stood at the bar, downed an espresso, and went on their way.

Ask Minerva

DEAR MINERVA: *A BOY CAME to my house to ask permission to take me to the festa. My father took one look at Gianni and kicked him right out of our house. Said Gianni looked like a girl with that long hair. Said he didn't care about the style of The Beatles or The Rolling Stones. "Tutti Americani," my father said even though everyone knows The Beatles are British. And my father also told Gianni to get rid of those balloon pants before knocking on our door again and when my boyfriend said they were bell-bottoms, my father said he'd swing a bell on Gianni's bottom if he didn't get off his property this minute. What can I do? Signed, Unhappy Daughter*

Dear Unhappy Daughter: Say thank you to your Papà *and read the next letter. Minerva.*

Dear Minerva: I just found out that my boyfriend is a two-timing snake who has been romancing another woman. She's not even as pretty as I am. My cousin advises me to break up with him ASAP— that's an American expression that means immediatamente *and I would, except I think I might be pregnant. What can I do? Signed, Unhappy Angel*

Dear Unhappy Angel: First you need to learn the meaning of angel. Then you have two options. Wait for a few weeks to find out if you're really pregnant. Sometimes worry can complicate things. If you are, you'll have to marry the two-timing snake and make the best of a bad situation. If you are not, you can go to confession and say your penance and thank God that you have another chance to learn how to be a true angel. Minerva.

Franco's Story

SINCE FRANCO HAD FIRST SEEN Lucrezia on a Tuesday at one o'clock, he returned the following week on the same day at the same time. She was sitting on the balcony, wearing a wide-brimmed hat, which shaded her face, so when she lifted her head and looked in his direction, where he stood at the gate beside his car, he couldn't see her face. It made no difference. Franco knew it was her by the way she held her head so high, by the way she tucked the book under her right arm and stood, by the way she backed toward the balcony door feeling for the handle with her other hand and by the way Lucrezia slipped inside and closed the door with a soft click of the lock. Franco sighed—he'd have to be patient with her and give her time to get used to his presence in her environment. Lucrezia was like a wild animal; you had to approach her carefully, incrementally—one false move and she'd bolt. He was in her territory now so he'd have to familiarize himself with her habits if he wanted to catch her.

He smiled as he got into his car and rolled down the window. He'd return on the same day at the same time next week. No point in thinking about what he'd do if she wasn't on the balcony. She'd been there today and that was a good sign. She'd retreated when she saw him—this was true—but she hadn't run. She'd locked her door but the soft click of the lock was not definite, it was barely audible; it left room for negotiation. In the meantime, he thought about getting some more information about Bianca—she looked so much like her mother—but he was hesitant. The husband, Fortunato, had been friendly and willingly told the story of Lucrezia and Bianca's arrival in the village, almost twenty years ago, but a second visit with more questions might look suspicious. And he didn't need another haircut. At least, not yet. He drove to the *pensione* on the outskirts of town. Franco had eaten there last week but to be honest, he couldn't quite remember what he'd eaten—he'd been shaken by the sight of Lucrezia after all these years—how many? Thirty since the baby was born; twenty-eight since he'd last seen Lucrezia.

Twenty-eight years ago, Lucrezia had come back to Roma. Just showed up at his classroom door. Franco had walked out of class, books and papers in his arms, and there she was. Leaning against the wall like a weary student burdened down by too many assignments and not enough time. She was dressed in her usual style—*stile classico*—the slim black skirt, the crisp black linen blouse, the leather high heels that accentuated her long legs, the gold watch he'd given her on her twentieth birthday. Her hair was different—pulled back from her face to reveal that widow's peak, those dark arched eyebrows and strong cheekbones. She'd lost weight. Even her lips seemed thinner. Franco stopped outside his classroom door, looked from side to side anxious for a place to drop his books so he could gather her into his arms. He said her name, "Lucrezia?" A question even though he knew it was a fact. Lucrezia.

She put up her hand as if he was taking attendance. "*Presente*," she said. As if two years hadn't passed since she'd left the university, the city, him.

"What are you doing here?" he asked, stepping closer, trying to prepare himself for her answer. Lucrezia was unpredictable—she could be enrolling for classes here at the university; hired as a teaching assistant; suggesting a rekindling of the embers of their romance. Just the smallest puff of air and sparks would fly—he was so hopeful and so foolish. "Just a courtesy visit," she said, her hand up like she was a policeman directing traffic at the Piazza Navona. Franco looked back at his classroom—empty—but he didn't want to take Lucrezia there; they could be interrupted at any minute. The teacher's lounge was always available but it was also always filled with eager ears, pretending nonchalance. Franco nodded toward the exit. "Shall we walk?" he asked and cursed himself when she agreed. How could he properly express himself with his arms full of books and papers?

"I need *un momento*," he said, motioning down the corridor. "To put these things in my office."

"Well, well," she said, with a cryptic smile, "Aren't you important? *Professore importante* with his own office."

"It's a cubby hole, a closet, nothing more than a desk and a chair and a bookcase, or two." Why was he babbling like a lovesick fool? Because he was. Both lovesick and a fool.

On the campus, the pine trees had spread their branches wide. The last of the red roses bloomed bravely in the autumn sunlight. Purple asters were everywhere.

Students crowded onto benches. Some were reading or writing; most were entwined with others. "Nothing's changed," said Lucrezia, pointing to a couple holding hands as they walked along a path layered with brown oak leaves.

"Not for me," said Franco. Must he wear his heart so openly on his sleeve? Must he declare so willingly his constant love for her? Yes. The lyrics of a French song floated through his head, and he spoke the words aloud, "*Je ne regrette rien*."

"So we're speaking *francese* now, are we?" asked Lucrezia.

"At least I'm speaking," said Franco. He pointed to an empty bench beneath a tangerine tree, almost leafless, with its fruit blazing in shades of orange. He surprised himself with his next words. "Tell me about our daughter," he said.

"She's not *ours*. You know that," said Lucrezia. "You know I placed her in the orphanage." She spoke to him like he was a simple-minded student who needed constant repetition in order to comprehend basic facts.

"Listen to me, Lucrezia, this is all wrong. Just the sight of you today and I feel weak. Nothing has changed. I love you. I want to marry you. I want our daughter. I want us to be a family. I..."

"I didn't come here to talk about what you want," said Lucrezia.

Franco knew there was no use asking her why she had come.

Lucrezia would tell in her own time. If he pushed her, she'd clam up. So he waited. A wild canary called and another answered. Franco watched the streak of buttercup yellow as the tiny bird swooped down from his branch and across to a bush where another bird waited. The branch dropped; the birds fluttered their wings; the warbling continued. A pale yellow feather floated to the ground.

A couple of students kicked a soccer ball back and forth en route to the open field behind the philosophy building. They waved at Franco. "*Ciao, professore*," and one of the boys tilted his head toward Lucrezia. "*Che bella*," he said.

"Those were the days, my friend," she said, wistfully, watching the students round the building leaving behind the muffled thumps of soccer shoes kicking the ball, again and again. Then there was silence until Franco spoke.

"Do you have *fotografia*?" he asked.

"Of what?"

"Our daughter. Who else?" Franco leaned forward, gestured with his hands, "What does she look like? Brown hair like you? Strong chin like me?"

"There's no *foto*," Lucrezia lied. "She's not our daughter. How many times must I tell you?"

"Tell me what she looks like." He clasped his hands as if in prayer. "Please."

"I only know her as a newborn," said Lucrezia, lying once again. "Fine blonde hair but that can change. Slate blue eyes—they might have changed too. She was scrawny. Only six pounds. A weak cry like a kitten."

"And now?"

"Gone," Lucrezia said, her third lie of the day. "Just what I wanted for her—a good family. She'll have lots of attention."

"Attention?" repeated Franco, choking on the word. "What about love? Real family? I can't believe you just abandoned her to strangers. I went to the orphanage, you know. Tried to see her."

"Really?" asked Lucrezia, lie number four.

"Those nuns—they're like little Mussolinis. All rules. I said I was the father. I said I want to see my daughter. I said I want to take a *fotografia* for a *momento*. And do you know what they told me?"

Lucrezia shook her head: a silent lie.

"You have no rights. You cannot see her. Against the rules. She will be placed for adoption. I said, 'Let *me* adopt her!'"

Lucrezia leaned back on the bench, moved her legs close together, knees touching, and folded her hands in her lap. Her face was as blank as a black school slate.

"Those black and whites—I don't even want to call them women. They're like cement. Colder than marble. *Immobile*. They told me it's against the rules of the orphanage to allow a father to adopt his child. No rights to his own daughter! *Per l'amor di dio!* Lucrezia, I ask you, what kind of rule is that?"

Silence. Only the sound of Franco's rapid breathing gradually settling down to normal; his heart returning to the regular beats per minute; his face draining slowly from angry red to something more natural, something almost resembling acceptance. Then Lucrezia spoke—the truth or at least her version of it—at last.

"That's what I came to tell you, Franco. She has a family now. The papers are all signed. *Finale*. If you must think of her, Franco, think of her as settled."

"Settled," Franco spat out the word as if it was a piece of rotten pear. He pounded his fist against his heart. "*Amore*. She would have been loved."

There was nothing more to say yet they must have said more because later, Franco would remember that Lucrezia had told him that she had moved north to Genoa, that she had a job in a florist shop there, that she had created a new life and wished him to do the same. Another lie. Lucrezia said she'd come to see him another time. Franco didn't know if her words were all lies although this would become clear in a few years when he travelled by train to Genoa and went from flower shop to flower shop to hear the owners say, "Never heard of her."

The other thing that Franco would remember was the way the autumn sunlight made her brown hair shine and sparkle, the way she crossed one long leg over the other and adjusted her skirt, the way her eyes never revealed the emotion he knew she felt, and the way she touched his cheek with the palm of her hand before she left him with nothing. Nothing but the scent of her Chanel perfume, and a crevice in his heart that refused to heal.

The appealing aroma of tomato sauce flew into his car window and Franco signalled his turn into the *pensione* on the outskirts of the village. Even from the parking lot, he could hear the customers' voices through the open windows. Franco stopped in the doorway and looked for an empty spot. Workers crowded the tables. In the corner, a couple of teenagers held hands across their table. No empty tables. By the window, a solitary stranger sitting at a table for two caught Franco's eye. The stranger lifted his forkful of lasagne and his eyebrows. Franco walked over.

Motioning to the empty chair, Franco asked, "*Permesso?*"

"Be my guest," said the stranger, "I don't suppose you speak English? *Parla l'inglese, signor?*"

"Please," replied Franco, holding up his hand. "I *do* speak English. Unless you want to practice your Italian. *Scusa*, I didn't mean to imply—"

"Believe me, I know my Italian is terrible. I keep putting my New York accent on the words and it creates a completely different language. One that hasn't been invented yet, I'm afraid. My name's Tony, by the way."

"I'm Franco," he said, "How's the lasagne?"

Lucrezia's Tale

THEY'D BEEN YOUNG. WHEN THEY'D met, Lucrezia was one of a few women students at the university and he was one of the many postgraduates. She'd been hurrying back to her dormitory, taking a shortcut across the field, and he'd been lying on his back watching the night sky. "Shooting stars," Franco had said to her even though Lucrezia hadn't asked why he was lying there. In fact, she hadn't even noticed him. Might have tripped over him if he hadn't spoken. Lucrezia slowed to watch a star streak across the sky, dark as indigo, and then she went on her way. Later Franco would tell her, "It was as if the star shot straight into my heart and illuminated it. Wherever I went, after meeting you, I knew my life would never be the same." That's what he told her: she told him, "Franco, you are so *drammatico. Melodrammatico.*" But what could one say? They were young, and soon, they were in love. Him more than her because Franco was more impetuous, unguarded, hopeful, and Lucrezia was not. Lucrezia was cautious but not cautious enough.

As sure as dawn follows night, as certain as an ill wind blows through an open window and bangs the door closed, slam, Lucrezia was pregnant. She definitely didn't want a baby but options in Catholic-soaked Italy were limited in 1940. Lucrezia didn't tell Franco for a few months; fruitlessly hoping that she'd lose the baby somehow but the baby had other ideas; she hung on. Lucrezia certainly didn't tell her parents; her mother would claim she would die of shame and her father, who was permanently disappointed that Lucrezia wasn't a boy, would simply wash his hands of her. They were already on nervous ground because she'd insisted on attending the university and her father had said, "What's the point? You're just going to marry and have children." Her father hated to waste money.

Her mother's opinion was different; she thought Lucrezia's husband choices were better among more educated men. "After all," she told her husband, "Education leads to money and money obviously leads to happiness. Everyone knows that."

Lucrezia finally told Franco the news right after he told her his news. "Wait till you hear this, Lucrezia," Franco began as he reached for her hands and held them tight. "I've been awarded the grant to study Medieval Literature. I can hardly believe it. My heart is dancing with excitement." He put her hand on his heart: *thump, thump.*

Lucrezia said, "I'm pregnant." She held up her hand to halt his words, and continued with her own, "I've made my decision. I have a plan. Don't try to change my mind," she warned. She touched the index finger of one hand to the index finger of the other. "I'll make up some story for my parents," she began, "I'll tell them I have a summer job somewhere up north and I can't come home. Not even for August vacation. I'll tell them I'll come home in the fall for the apple harvest." She moved her finger from her thumb to her index finger. "The baby's due in August." Lucrezia held up her hand in warning. "Let me finish, Franco." Moving to her next finger, she said, "I'll place the baby in the Roma orphanage. I've already been to the orphanage, Franco. I talked to the nuns who live there. They tell me all adoptive parents are well screened and the baby"—Lucrezia was careful never to say "our baby"—"will have a good life. Much better than we can provide."

"But..." said Franco. "I love you, Lucrezia. I'd love our baby too."

"That's what you say now," said Lucrezia, tenting her fingers and tapping. "But when money's tight and the baby's crying all night and you can't do your studying and I can't find work, you'd resent the baby. The baby would be the source of all the problems."

Franco didn't think so; he said he'd like to discuss it some more even though they hadn't really discussed it at all but Lucrezia had her chin set and her shoulders squared. It would be her way in the end. She'd wear him down simply by never changing her mind. "Whatever you want," he said, as if this was the end. And it was. The end of their relationship; the end of honesty between them; the end of unrestricted futures with no secrets; but they wouldn't know that until later.

The baby was born in August and two weeks later, Lucrezia left Roma for a job up north. The official job title had been "caregiver," which Lucrezia didn't like. It wasn't her temperament to be a caregiver; if it were, would she be surrendering her own child to strangers? So she changed the job title to "assistant" and changed her answer to the job offer to *sì*, a reluctant *sì*.

As soon as the baby was born, the baby decreased her own chances of adoption simply by being a female in a world that valued boys. Plus the girl would never win any beauty contests. Her skin was itchy red and blotchy and a few days in the over-heated orphanage nursery didn't improve anything. She cried most of the time and was restless the rest of it. Lucrezia decided not to name her—let her new parents do that—but when Lucrezia stood beside the bassinette and watched the baby wailing, she gave her daughter a little nickname. She called her *poco pomodoro*; she put her cool hand on the baby's chest; she felt the heart beating rapidly and she said aloud, "*Arrivederci.*" She told herself she was doing what was best for the child and if it was also best for herself, *così sia*. So be it.

The first rule Lucrezia broke at her new job was her promise to herself not to write to the nuns at the orphanage to ask about the child's adoption. She wrote every month and the nuns wrote back and every month the story was the same, or a little worse: the child had thrush, had constant diaper rash, had red patches of eczema, wasn't gaining weight, had a growing list of allergies. Couldn't tolerate cow's milk, wheat, tomatoes, strawberries, eggs. Couldn't wear wool. Cried more than she smiled especially with potential parents. Was passed over time and again for the sparkly eyed, curly haired babies who gurgled and cooed in their prospective parents' arms.

Lucrezia's employer was a kind man, a wealthy man. Married for over thirty years to a woman who doted solely on their two grown sons. Giovanni was also a lonely man. He'd broken his leg in a skiing accident and was confined with a burdensome cast and an even more cumbersome wheelchair for six months and for those six months, Lucrezia was his caregiver-assistant. At least she started out that way. Soon she was typing and filing and later she was listening in at business meetings and advising. Eventually she was explaining, when her employer put his hand on her bare leg, that she was not that kind of woman. And then she was. That kind of woman. The kind of woman who Giovanni wanted and, because he was a rich man, found a way to have and to keep. Here's what he offered Lucrezia: a small apartment with a large balcony overlooking the Piazza Duomo in Milano, a permanent job in the office at his textile plant—a real job, not just paid work for the boss's *innamorata*. What cinched the deal for Lucrezia was something that she hadn't admitted that she wanted—a two-bedroom apartment where the second bedroom could be her daughter's. And Giovanni would stay at the apartment occasionally and they could be a family—unrelated and illegitimate—but a family nonetheless. In Milano, Lucrezia became that universal Italian cliché—the other woman, the mistress, *la padrona*.

Here is the list of things Lucrezia doesn't tell Franco that autumn, two years after they'd split up, when they spoke at the university where Franco was working:

- She doesn't mention that her father had died and she was travelling further south to a small village, with a large orchard that her father owned, to arrange with Erminio the *frutticoltore* to continue to prune and spray and harvest and market the apples each year just as before. Only now, instead of sending the proceeds to her father's banker in Roma, he'd send them to Lucrezia's account.

- Lucrezia doesn't say that her mother would sell their Roma apartment, investing Lucrezia's share of the money with the family lawyer, and Mamma will move in to her aunt's apartment—two widows together—to live out the rest of her days.
- She certainly doesn't tell Franco that she was taking the child from the orphanage to raise with her employer, Giovanni, in an apartment that overlooked the Piazza Duomo; didn't say that the child would come to know Giovanni as *Papà* and Lucrezia would never correct her. Nor tell the child they're not married. Nor mention that she hadn't intended any of this—least of all, removing the child from the orphanage—but Lucrezia had seen the girl, alone in the corner of the playroom and the child had walked over to her. She was a skinny-legged two-year old with pale skin and limp hair and cautious, grey eyes. She put her hand in Lucrezia's and simply stood there, and waited. After that, there was no going back.

Courtship: Gupino Style

TONY DIDN'T KNOW HOW TO court Assunta. He'd had dinner at the farmhouse three nights in a row until Rosa returned. Then Tony and Assunta had had dinner with Rosa and Claudio and Carlito. While they'd been on holiday in Sorrento, Rosa had finally accepted Claudio's proposal and all the talk was of their springtime wedding. Something simple but elegant with a role for Carlito. "But no Superman cape," Rosa reminded Carlito. "No flying down the aisle." And they'd all laughed.

Tony had gone with Carlito and Rosa to the weekly market where Rosa had bought russet apples and winter broccoli and shiny chestnuts and Tony had admired the pottery nativity sets while the other villagers looked at Rosa and Carlito, accompanied by Tony, and wondered.

Tony knew that Assunta was not the kind of woman who dated casually. Plus this Enzo character had done something despicable enough that Nino wanted to avenge it with a pitchfork. Tony couldn't afford to make any mistakes in his courtship. He couldn't rush her but he also had to make a move soon; he was only booked for two more nights at the *pensione*. That didn't really matter, he could extend his stay but...he wanted to make his intentions clear.

Tony had taken off his wedding band and his finger seemed strangely bare. There was a faint white line where his ring had been but a few days of Italian sunshine would cover that. He'd expected the ring removal to be a poignant moment but mostly, it just seemed right. The right time; the right place; the right reason. He wanted to begin a future with Assunta and that would require a new life as well as a new ring. He liked the simple gold bands he'd seen on Italian women and some men. If Assunta said yes, he'd happily wear that gold ring. This is what he was thinking about as he sat in his usual spot at the restaurant adjacent to the *pensione*. Slowly swirling the orange slice in his vermouth glass, Tony waited for his *risotto* with *porcini* mushrooms to arrive. Instead Franco arrived.

"How are you, my friend?" Franco asked.

"*Bene*," responded Tony motioning to the empty chair across from his.

"*Bene* is the correct response," said Franco, "but your face tells me differently. Bad news?"

"No news," assured Tony. "I was just thinking about someone."

"Oh, woman problems," sighed Franco as he unfolded the heavy cotton napkin on his lap. "Believe me, we're all in the same boat. Lost at sea."

"I'm going to ask Assunta to marry me," said Tony, surprising them both. Franco straightened his fork infinitesimally.

"Haven't you only known her a week?" Franco said. He aligned his knife with a small tap from his thumb. "That's a little sudden, isn't it? And you don't seem like an impulsive man."

"I *wasn't* an impulsive man," explained Tony, "until last week when I got off the train at the Ferentino station and caught a ride to the water-bottling plant and saw her pale neck and her sad eyes and..."

"When are you planning to speak with Nino?" asked Franco.

"Nino?" repeated Tony as if he'd never heard the name before today.

"*Si*, Assunta's father." Franco motioned to the waiter and then to Tony's vermouth glass. The waiter said, "Momento, *signor*," and Franco turned his attention back to Tony and the ubiquitous topic of *amore*. "We are speaking of Assunta who works at the bottling plant and her father who farms that pretty place at the base of Santa Serena, correct?"

"But Assunta's not a girl. She's a grown woman." Tony drained the last of his vermouth and carefully placed his glass on the tablecloth. "I didn't think I'd have to ask for permission..."

"It's not permission. It's about showing respect for traditions. You want to start off on the right foot, don't you?" asked Franco. To the waiter who'd just approached the table with two glasses, clinking, on a silver tray, he said, "What's good today?" and the waiter recommended the *risotto* with mushrooms. "*Bene*," said Franco.

"I'm meeting Assunta at the bottling plant at six," began Tony. "I'll go to the farm first and talk to Nino. Tell him my intentions. Ask for his blessing."

Franco raised his glass in a toast, "Bravo, Tony. What do you think Assunta will say?"

"Who knows?" said Tony. He put down his glass, ran his finger around the rim. "If she says yes, *bene*, and if she says, no, I'll just have to stay longer and wear her down."

"That's the spirit, my friend. I have had to do that with my *amore* as well. Just keep at it."

"How long did it take you?"

"Thirty years," said Franco. "But believe me, it was worth it."

"I don't know if I have that much time," said Tony. "I'll be an old man by then and...pardon me Franco, I didn't mean to...."

"Listen to me, my friend. *Amore* knows nothing about age. If she's the one for you, you'll put in the time. Perhaps she'll say yes."

"Perhaps," said Tony.

"Of course," added Franco as the waiter placed the plate of *risotto* in front of him. Franco inhaled and smiled before he continued. "There's always the old-fashioned way."

"To ask her father?" said Tony.

"Not quite. In the old days, a suitor and his friends would get together one night and kidnap the girl. The girl would be in on the scheme, of course. She might even be the one who left her father's ladder under her bedroom window but more likely the boys brought their own ladder."

"So they eloped?" asked Tony.

"No, my friend. To elope would be disrespectful to the girl's father. They needed his permission to marry but if the father was slow with his consent and the couple was anxious to...let's say, be together—kidnapping was the answer." Franco took a taste of his *risotto*. "Mmmm," he sighed. "*Divino*."

"Just a minute. I don't quite understand," said Tony, his *risotto* left untouched, his fork waiting in his hand. "The father's certainly not going to give his permission after the boy has kidnapped his daughter."

"That's where you're wrong, my friend. The father *must* give his permission for them to marry, otherwise his daughter is spoiled goods, and obviously no other man would want her," explained Franco. "Really, you must try your *risotto* before it grows cold."

The words swirled around in Tony's head: kidnap, consent, respect, spoiled goods... On the one hand, he'd love to kidnap Assunta; on the other hand, he was pretty sure that she wasn't that kind of woman, who would go away with him willingly and disappoint her father. She was a modern woman in many ways and Tony loved that about her but he also loved her respect for tradition and her love for her little family and her village, lost in a simpler time. He corralled the circle of words to the back of his mind; he'd try the traditional way and simply speak to Assunta's father and ask for his blessing.

"Franco," said Tony. "Would you do me a favour?"

"Name it. I'll try. What did you have in mind?"

"Translating," said Tony and he lifted a forkful of *risotto* and *porcini* mushroom to his mouth, where it spread warmth and pleasure all the way down his throat to his waiting stomach. "You're right. This is delicious. About the translating, I thought you might come with me when I speak to Nino and make sure that I say everything correctly and answer his questions, if he has any, and...well... just be there, I guess."

"It will be my pleasure. Name the time."

"Five o'clock," said Tony.

When Tony and Franco drove up Nino's driveway, Nino was chopping wood at the side of the house. Tony took one long look at Nino wielding his axe and a quick glance at Franco and said, "You better wait here until I explain to Nino who you are. And who you aren't."

"Pardon?" asked Franco but Tony put up his hand and repeated, "Stay here. Maybe lock the door." Tony closed the passenger door as a flushed-faced Nino, with his axe propped on his shoulder, approached the car. Tony motioned to Franco sitting in the car. "It's a friend—*un amico*—of mine," explained Tony and then remembering the phrase Assunta had used, he added, "*Non è Enzo.*" Nino lifted the axe from his shoulder and placed it between his work boots and leaned on it. He looked disappointed. "Do you have a minute, Nino?" asked Tony. "I want to ask you something and *amico mio*—" Tony gestured again to Franco, still waiting patiently in the car "—can translate. His name's Franco. *È un professore.*"

They sat on tree stumps in a circle of pale sunlight. Franco had placed his handkerchief on the stump before he sat, Tony had just adjusted the crease in his pants before sitting, and Nino had simply sat. Nino held his cap between his legs; Franco had rested his fedora on his lap; Tony had no hat. Tony noticed how calloused Nino's hands were compared to Franco's manicured ones: Tony's hands were clenched tightly. He decided to get right to the point.

"Nino," he said, but his voice was high and squeaky like a teenage boy. He started again, "Nino, I want to ask Assunta to marry me and I want to ask for your blessing—*la tua benedizione*—before I do that. *Capisce?*"

"*Si,*" agreed Nino.

Before Tony could absorb the answer and breathe easy, Nino continued. "*Si,* Tony, *capisco,*" he said. "But you have no job. You have no house. You don't even live in Italia."

Now Franco got into the act. "You don't have a job? Or a house?" he asked Tony. "Are you planning to stay?"

"Yes," said Tony and turning to Nino, Tony added what he thought were the most important words of all, the words that any father would want to hear about his daughter, the words that would elicit a smile and a change of heart and a handshake and a blessing. He said, "I love Assunta."

"Of course," said Nino. "But when you go to bed at night, love does not provide a bed or a roof over your head. You need a house. And when you wake up in the morning, love does not provide *caffè e cornetto*. You need money. To get money, you need a job. You're a good man, Tony, but I cannot give my blessing for you to marry my daughter."

Franco interrupted once again. "Tell him your plan, Tony," he began, hoping that Tony actually had a plan, but Nino interrupted him.

"I know your story, Tony," said Nino, "and I'm sorry for your loss but I don't want my daughter to be the cure for your loneliness and sorrow. That's a heavy burden. I know what it's like to lose a wife. It's a sadness that never goes away. Even if you love someone else, marry someone else, like I married dear Elena. You carry that sorrow with you forever like a stone in your heart and you learn to bear the weight. That's all."

Franco tapped Tony's shoulder. "You lost your wife?"

"Yes," said Tony. "And our two sons."

"*Dio mio*. Why didn't you say something?" asked Franco.

"I'm tired of talking about it. Tired of the sympathy. Franco, I want you to translate, word for word." Then, Tony turned to Nino and spoke. "Nino, I know sorrow. I know it well. I'm not looking for someone to make me forget. I'll never forget. For the first time in a long time, I want to take care of someone else. I want to ease her load. I want to make her happy. I love Assunta, Nino, and I want to make her happy."

Nino had nodded his head all through Tony's words and Franco's translations. Now he ploughed his rough hands through his thinning hair as if he might unearth the correct words there before he answered. "You need a house. You need a job. Then we can talk."

"Give me a week," said Tony.

On via del Corso in Rome

ON THE THIRD TUESDAY AFTER Franco had first seen Lucrezia standing on the balcony, he drove again to her house just outside of the village. He was a little early and it was a good job that he was because as he pulled to the side of the road, the front door opened. Lucrezia stepped out wearing a simple dress of green and white swirls that clung to all the right parts of her body. There was a jacket and a hat too but Franco's eyes were stuck on the dress. The gardener came around the side of the house, hat in hand, and opened the passenger door of his truck. She took his hand; she climbed in. What on earth was this all about?

Before Franco had time to think of an explanation for Lucrezia going off with the gardener in a truck that looked to be about two decades old, the driver turned left out of the driveway and Franco lifted his foot from the brake, and followed. Kept his distance. Watched the rakes, shovels, and hoes rattle in the back of the truck every time it hit a bump. After ten minutes or so, Franco began to ask himself what on earth he was doing, following Lucrezia like he was some kind of crazed fool. And what would he do when she got to her destination? Franco had no answer: he'd wait and see what he would do. As if he was a man with a love fever that had lingered for thirty years and might be about to break out of remission once again.

The dilapidated truck pulled onto a side street that led to the train station. Franco slowed; let a few cars pass him; idled beside some cypress trees and watched as the truck shuddered to a stop and Lucrezia stepped out and lined up at the ticket booth.

Someone behind Franco beeped his horn. The driver called out his window, "Ey, *signor*, move or pull over." Franco released the brake, pulled into the parking lot and stopped. Then he walked to the ticket booth.

"*Dove?*" asked the ticket master. A valid question: where was Franco going? Franco motioned to the train that was slowly approaching the station.

"Roma," said the ticket master. "With a dozen stops in between."

Franco exchanged a few *lire* for a one-way ticket. He'd sit in a spot on the train where he could see Lucrezia without her seeing him. He'd get off whenever she did. It was that simple. Franco bought a copy of *Il Corriere della Sera* newspaper—more to hide behind than to read—and as he walked along the platform, he kept his eye out for a green and white dress. There she was. Near the front of the car, on the far side, with a triangle of her dress flowing over the seat into the aisle and the tip of her open-toed shoe swaying back and forth like a pendulum, or perhaps a ticking time bomb.

From eight rows back and from behind his newspaper, Franco sat and watched. Every time the little inner voice told him he was acting crazily, he suppressed it. He ignored every thought that taunted him: *This is real life not some detective novel. If she gets off in Roma, you'll lose her in the crowd for sure. All she has to do is turn around and see you and it's all over.* Franco read the same headline a thousand times and never once absorbed the meaning. He glanced over the newspaper's edge when the train slowed as it approached the stations: *Anagni, Colleferro, Bagni di Tivoli*...but Lucrezia remained on the train, and so did he. Finally, they came to the end of the line, *Termini*.

On the platform a fast-flowing river of bodies moved toward the various Roma exits, which announced, Piazza Cinquecento, Porta Maggiore. Franco kept his eye on the green and white dress, on the sway of her hips. Lucrezia headed straight for the north exit, stopping only once to turn and check the seam of her stocking. This small gesture affected Franco so strongly that he had to stop and lean his fevered forehead against the cool marble column for a moment, before he dared to peek out cautiously. A flash of green and white swirled out the door. On the street, Lucrezia hailed a cab; he hailed the one behind her. Franco said to the driver, "Follow that cab."

The driver turned around and said, "This isn't *il film, signor.*" Gesturing to the Fiats and Vespas that jammed the street, he added, "This is the real traffic hell of Roma."

"Just try," said Franco. He took his linen handkerchief from his pocket and patted his brow, touched the cool linen to his burning neck, let it rest there a moment to absorb the sweat and suspense. It was a film and Franco was simply watching to see what would happen next.

Lucrezia's cab stopped on *via del Corso* in front of the bank; Franco's cab stopped a discreet distance behind. "Let me know where she goes," said Franco hiding once more behind his newspaper.

"Into the bank, *signor*. Where else?" replied the driver. "Thirty lire, *per favore*." Franco gave him forty, bolted for the bank's revolving door. He caught a glimpse of her shaking hands with some bald-headed banker wearing the obligatory grey pinstriped suit. The banker motioned to the offices. Lucrezia disappeared into one with him. Franco sat in one of the leather chairs. Behind his newspaper he pretended to read while he inhaled other people's cigarette smoke and waited. Twenty minutes later, the scene was repeated in reverse. Lucrezia and the banker came out of the office, shook hands, and Lucrezia went directly outside with her arm already raised to hail a cab. Only she didn't.

As Franco continued to circle in the bank's revolving door—outside, inside, outside again—he saw Lucrezia lower her arm and walk slowly down the street. The revolving door spun him onto the sidewalk, where Franco caught his breath, tried to balance his dizzy head. His heart was beating fast; he could hear his blood pounding in his ears and perhaps that's why he didn't hear Lucrezia's words when she turned and spoke. She repeated, "This has to stop." So Franco stopped.

They stood opposite a café, the sidewalk littered with tiny intimate tables and chairs with their legs touching each other. Franco thought, *The taxi driver's wrong. This is definitely* il film. *The only question is whether it's to be a tragic Roman melodrama or a Hollywood fairy tale.*

Then Lucrezia spoke again, "What do you want now?" as if Franco had been following her for years, constantly haunting her days and nights, bombarding her with requests.

He pulled out a chair, offered it to Lucrezia, watched the familiar way she smoothed her skirt, crossed her long legs, folded her hands in her lap. Franco covered his heart with the palm of his hand—a fruitless movement to try to hide its frantic pumping. His chest moving in and out, in and out. The waiter arrived, pen poised over his notepad.

"*Caffè?*" asked Lucrezia but Franco shook his head. "This calls for a drink. Prosecco. Two glasses. An antipasto board. Two plates." The waiter looked at Franco; he looked at Lucrezia; he nodded. From that moment on, the waiter would serve as silently as a movie extra without lines. Love was blooming in the cool autumn air but not a November sort of love. The woman was as fiery as the orange leaves that lined the sidewalk and the man— oh my! *Tutto amore.*

"What are you doing here?" Lucrezia asked. "Other than following me."

Franco had so many words to say that they crowded into his throat, causing a traffic jam. Letters hooked onto question marks. Short words got caught between longer ones. Entire sentences curled tight and rolled into ridiculously romantic expressions of love. She took off her hat; set it on the table; smoothed her hair over her widow's peak.

"Are you married?" he asked.

"Are you?"

"No."

"Then, I'm not either," said Lucrezia, as if she wasn't married if he wasn't but could be if he was.

Franco wasn't sure where to begin. He knew that it wasn't a

good idea to simply blurt out the question that had troubled his days and disturbed his nights since he'd met Bianca, the herb woman, who looked so much like Lucrezia. Who was her father? No, that wasn't the question. The real question: was he, Franco, Bianca's father? Then there were a thousand questions that would follow. But not yet. He couldn't begin with that specific question so he tried a more general one.

"What have you been doing all these years?"

"Nothing remarkable," said Lucrezia, as she pulled off her white gloves and laid them on the table. Her nails were as red as a ripe tomato; a dull gold ring circled the finger on her left hand. "I'm a farmer. I farm my father's apple orchard."

"Yes," said Franco, without thinking, always without thinking, "I saw the trees."

"There are laws against spying you know."

"Let's not begin this way, *cara*. With harsh words." Franco laid his hand, palm up on the table between them. Lucrezia poked her finger into his palm, but not sharply—almost playfully—but removed her finger just as quickly.

"What have you been doing, Franco? Still teaching?"

"That's how I met Bianca, the herb-store woman—you know her, right?" He hadn't meant to introduce Bianca into the conversation just yet but here she was, a name hanging in the air between them. The silent waiter stretched a hand and placed the plates, the antipasto board, poured the wine, and disappeared. Cold bubbles from the prosecco dissipated in the October air; the name, *Bianca*, hung over the table like a third guest.

"Of course, I know her," said Lucrezia, twirling the gold band on her finger. "She's my daughter."

"You said you never married," reminded Franco.

"Well, no," began Lucrezia. "Not exactly..." But she never finished her sentence. Instead she reached for an olive and slipped it between her lips. She lifted her glass, tilted it toward Franco. "To old friends," she said.

"I was more than your friend," replied Franco but he drank nevertheless.

They ate; they drank; some birds chattered in the distance; a street sweeper brushed down the roadway and scattered discarded leaves. In the distance, through the crack of an open window, a radio sputtered some unrecognizable melody until someone tuned it in. One of the sad songs of Naples drifted lazily through the air. Melancholy notes lingered here and there. The waiter refilled the glasses. He twirled the bottle when he finished pouring as if he could turn off the sadness that had begun to settle.

"Tell me about her," said Franco.

Lucrezia let the bubbles of prosecco dance in her mouth before she began. Once she started, she couldn't stop and Franco sat forward in his chair catching and swallowing every sentence.

"I left her at the orphanage as we agreed. I went up north to work and forget. But I couldn't. I thought some childless couple would adopt her quickly but nobody seemed to want her. She wasn't a pretty baby. Lots of allergies and skin rashes. The nuns wrote on her chart that she was always sick, seldom smiled, rarely laughed. After a while she got too old to appeal to the childless couples who wanted a baby. And who could blame them? I didn't intend to take her. Two years after I left her, I went to see her. She was in the playroom with the other children but standing off by herself. I don't know what happened, Franco. She saw me and walked over and took hold of my hand—and she didn't let go—and I was hers."

So many questions tumbled through Franco's mind. They somersaulted so quickly he couldn't catch hold of any of them. Nor did he want to. He reached for Lucrezia's hand and held it, and didn't let go. He said, "I'm yours."

A December Romance

WHEN BIANCA ARRIVED AT HER mother's house, Lucrezia greeted her cautiously. "This isn't your usual day, *cara*," Lucrezia said, glancing at the mantel where a large bouquet of maroon roses was displayed in her best cut-crystal vase.

"No," said Bianca. "Where did you get the flowers?"

"Is everything okay?" asked Lucrezia.

"*Si*," said Bianca. "The flow...?"

"Fortunato? The girls?" asked Lucrezia, with another quick look at the fireplace.

"*Si*," said Bianca. "Why do you keep looking at the mantel? Are those roses from—?"

"I don't think Teresa is cleaning the mantel clock properly," responded Lucrezia. "Those angels around the clock face—you have to dust between their wings and the folds of their robes otherwise the dust collects in there and they look grey and grimy when they should be pure white. To tell you the truth, I've been thinking of getting rid of Teresa. She cleans too little and she talks too much. Gossip, gossip, all the time."

"Really?" said Bianca, pulling a letter from her purse. "Do you think she might have written this?"

Lucrezia sat down on the armchair. She smoothed her skirt and reached out her hand for the letter. "Sit, *cara*," she said to Bianca but Bianca said she preferred to stand.

Bianca said, "Go ahead, Mamma. Open it."

Lucrezia slid out the letter, read it quickly, and returned it just as quickly to its envelope. "So?" she said to Bianca.

"Anything you want to tell me?" asked Bianca.

"I've already told you. Teresa gossips too much and doesn't dust enough. That's all I have to say."

Lucrezia flicked her fingers beneath her chin in that familiar gesture, which meant the conversation was finished.

Bianca stood near the fireplace; she observed the dust-free mantel, inhaled the intoxicating scent of the unusual Tuscany roses. "Mamma, I don't think that's all. I think this letter—whether it's from Teresa or not—is about you."

"About me?" repeated her mother. "That's *ridicolo*." She stood up and moved toward the kitchen. "Do you want a drink, *cara*? *Limonata* perhaps? Good for the digestion."

"I want an answer to this letter," said Bianca.

"Very simple," said Lucrezia. "Tell the writer to mind her own business."

"That's what I intend to say to the writer but I'm asking you if the information in this letter—" and Bianca put out her hand, inviting her mother to return the letter "—is my business."

"Because she writes about a widow?" asked Lucrezia, raising both her voice and her eyebrows. "Am I suddenly the only widow in the area?"

"A well-to-do widow," reminded Bianca. "A widow who lives in a house with a circular driveway even though she doesn't own a car."

Lucrezia returned the letter to Bianca, who slipped it into her purse. After a few seconds of silence, Lucrezia brushed an imaginary crumb from her dress and said, "Erminio has a truck. A gardener has to get into the property to do his work, doesn't he?"

"The letter writer doesn't say anything about a man driving a truck," said Bianca. "She says the man who visits the widow drives an expensive car."

"Truck, car, expensive car. What difference does it make? The writer's still a gossip. Tell her to mind her own business."

"Let's just imagine, for a moment, Mamma, that you *are* the wealthy widow who lives in the house with the circular driveway." The scent from the flowers distracted Bianca momentarily. Stunning antique Tuscany roses—maroon rather than the more common red—the sender knew her mother well. "Who could this man who drives an expensive car and comes to visit *very frequently* possibly be?"

"How should I know?" asked Lucrezia. "Really, Bianca, I'm tired of this conversation. It's giving me a headache. I'm going to have to go and lie down for a while. We'll visit another day, *cara*. I'm just going to go up..."

The rest of Lucrezia's words were lost beneath the sound of the door chimes.

Bianca looked at her mother but Lucrezia made no sign of moving to the door. Instead, she rubbed her fingers in small circles on her forehead.

The bell rang again. "Aren't you going to answer that?" asked Bianca.

"I don't think I will," Lucrezia replied. "It's probably the peddler and I'm tired of telling him to go away." She called out to Teresa "Can you come down and..." but it was too late. Bianca had entered the front hall and opened the door.

It's hard to say who was more surprised. Bianca or Franco. He stared at her so intently that she stood rooted to the floor and it was only when Franco glimpsed the swirl of Lucrezia's burnt orange dress behind Bianca's caramel-coloured one that he lowered his gaze and began to twirl his fedora. "Well, you might as well come in," said Lucrezia. She led them into the living room where they sat and looked at each other and waited for someone to speak.

"What are you doing here, *professore*?" asked Bianca. "How do you know my mother?"

Franco looked at Lucrezia. "You look a great deal like your mother," he began. "When your mother was younger, of course. I knew her..."

Lucrezia interrupted, "We met at university in Roma a long time ago. And we just bumped into each other at the bank the other day." Lucrezia waved her hand to indicate that the other day might have been last week or last month or yesterday. "Franco is interested in apple trees so he came to see. Right Franco? You came to see the trees?"

A pause hung in the air while they waited for Franco's response. Bianca noticed her mother had sat forward in her chair, was twisting her wedding band round her finger. "No," said Franco. "I came to see you." Addressing Bianca, he continued, "I am courting your mother. She didn't want to tell you just yet but I think the time is right now, don't you, Lucrezia?"

"Oh Mamma," said Bianca, her eyes wide with surprise and then delight. "I'm happy for you. It's been twenty years since *Papà* died—too long to be always on your own."

"I'm not on my own," said Lucrezia. "I have you." .

"Died," repeated Franco, and then a little louder, "Died?" He looked at Lucrezia.

"It's very warm in here," said Lucrezia. "Shall we have something cool to drink?"

"Shall we have the truth, Lucrezia?" asked Franco.

Bianca looked from one to the other. She touched her handbag, which contained the anonymous letter about the widow who was seeing someone. This man was more than a casual old friend; there was a history here, a history that Bianca knew nothing about, yet.

"So, you met at university and didn't see each other for thirty years, is that right?" asked Bianca. "And you just bumped into each other by accident in Roma? I know you're a *professore* at the university there, but tell me a little about yourself. Are you a widower, do you have children?"

"I never married," said Franco. "I have a daughter."

"Franco," cautioned Lucrezia.

"Is it a story you'd rather tell, Lucrezia?" asked Franco, as if Bianca's mother already knew the professor's story.

"Mamma?" said Bianca. "What is this all about?"

Lucrezia said, "It's just an old story—not even worth telling, Franco—but I'll tell you all about it later, Bianca. Why don't we talk about something more interesting now?" She glanced at her fingernails, painted with deep burgundy polish, as if for inspiration and asked, "Has Fortunato painted the babies' room yet?" To Franco, she said, "My daughter's expecting twins in the springtime."

"And you already have two girls," added Franco.

"And you, *professore*, have a daughter," said Bianca, and they were right back where they started.

So Franco began the story. "Your mother and I were very young, very much in love but not in a position to begin a family when your mother told me..." Here he adjusted the decision to place their baby in the Roma orphanage to sound more like a mutual decision than a unilateral Lucrezia decision.

That's where Bianca interrupted, the first time. "Orphanage," she repeated, looking at her mother. "You left me in an orphanage?" Before Lucrezia could form a response, Bianca spoke again. "Wait a minute. You're saying that you, *professore*, fathered me? Is that true, Mamma? What about *Papà* Giovanni da Milano? Did he adopt me when you married? Is that what this is all about? You neglected to tell me that I'm adopted?"

"I think we better have some tea," said Lucrezia. "Peppermint. To calm everyone down."

"I don't need any tea. I *am* calm," said Bianca but her mother had already gone into the kitchen, leaving Franco and Bianca to stare at each other. Franco sat with his hands planted on his knees. His fingers were long and lean like her own. Bianca touched her hand to her ear; Franco's ear mirrored her own—a little spot at the top of the left ear where the skin had never folded over. Fine hair like hers. Mamma's hair was thick. But none of these physical similarities mattered. No one would claim to be a father unless he actually was. And if Franco was her father, who was Giovanni and why hadn't Lucrezia ever told her? Instead of letting her live a life of lies. Bianca noticed that while she asked herself these questions, Franco sat patiently and waited.

The teacups rattled relentlessly as Lucrezia returned with a tray containing tea that no one wanted and biscuits that no one would eat. They all did the polite thing, accepting the cups of tea, refusing or consenting to sugar, stirring. Franco was the first to speak and he directed his words at Bianca, "I know this must be difficult for you. May I continue with the story or would you prefer your mother to tell you?"

"My mother's had thirty-two years to tell me," said Bianca. She stared at her mother: Lucrezia sipped her tea. "You may as well go on."

"I want to assure you that you were wanted and you were loved. It was just a matter of economics and...of timing. I had just accepted a study position and your mother wanted to finish her degree, of course. It seemed the best solution..."

"For who?" asked Bianca and her eyes were only on her mother.

Lucrezia tapped her fingers together impatiently but her voice was calm enough, "For you, *cara*. We wanted you to have a loving stable family and we just weren't in a position to provide it."

"But you did provide," said Bianca. "Only you switched out my real father for Giovanni and never mentioned it to me. All these years, you've let me think that *Papà* Giovanni was my father when this other man was," she pointed to Franco, "Where were *you* all this time? Why are you just showing up now?"

"I didn't know where *you* were," said Franco, looking at Lucrezia and then Bianca and then Lucrezia again.

"We lost touch with each other," explained Lucrezia. Here she paused once more to twist her wedding band. "Then I met Giovanni and we...well, we decided to create a family..."

"*Momento*," said Franco and Bianca in unison.

"You *married*, didn't you?" asked Bianca.

"You *didn't* marry him, did you?" asked Franco.

"Marriage," repeated Lucrezia. "So much fuss just to have a man dressed in robes swing incense around and declare you married."

"I can't believe this," said Bianca. She rose from her chair to stand right in front of her mother's. "All these years. Not one word to say I had a real—a birth—another father. Alive. I could have had a father walk me down the aisle. My girls could have had a grandfather. How dare you, Mamma. To keep such a secret. It's *incredibile. Incredibile*," she repeated. She shook her head. Her eyes were wet. "I'm leaving, Mamma. I need some time to be by myself—to be away from you."

"I know, *cara*," said Lucrezia. "When you're ready, I'm here."

Bianca turned to Franco. "*Grazie, professore*," she said as she shook his hand, the hand with slender fingers like her own.

"I hope we will meet again, Bianca," said Franco. His voice was steady and calm even if his eyes revealed a lifetime of longing.

"We will," said Bianca. "I appreciate your honesty. It's just... right now... I can't...." And she was gone.

The mantel clock ticked its steady heartbeats; the roses emitted their soothing perfume; Lucrezia and Franco sat in silence. Lucrezia moved first, gathering the teacups onto the tray. "Don't worry about her," she said. "Bianca needs time to think things over. Then she'll come back. We'll just give her time."

"So," said Franco, "In this way, she is exactly like her mother." His voice held more resignation than happiness until he added, "I've waited a long time to meet her, to see you again, Lucrezia. I can wait a little longer." And this time, there was a hint of happiness combined with hope.

A week passed before Bianca knocked again on her mother's door. They kept their distance, each gauging the other's mood. "More flowers I see," said Bianca, gesturing to the mantel where the Tuscany roses had been replaced with a small bouquet of pink miniature roses, the kind you'd send to celebrate a baby's birth. "Interesting choice," Bianca said. "*Il professore?*"

"*Si*," said Lucrezia, touching the tiny petals with her fingertip. "From Franco. From your father, Bianca. I'm sorry I didn't tell you, *cara*. I always meant to. When you were a little older. After *Papà* Giovanni died. When we moved here but it never seemed the right time. It seemed unnecessary to upset our home and our little family and I thought, *How could it help for her to know about Franco? It was all a lifetime ago.* So I said nothing and saying nothing came to be the truth."

"Truth?" repeated Bianca. "I don't think you know the meaning of the word truth, Mamma."

"Perhaps not, *cara*, but I know I'm your mother. There's no other. That's the truth."

"Yes, Mamma, you're right. There's no one quite like you."

"*Grazie, cara.* Are you here to work on your column? I put all the letters on *Papà* Giovanni's—on the desk upstairs. Everything's waiting for you."

Along with the letters on the desk, there was a duplicate bouquet of miniature pink roses with her name on the envelope that was pinned to the pink bow. The envelope was sealed but that didn't mean that Mamma hadn't steamed it open, read the card, and resealed it. Mamma...well, you could never predict. The message written on the card was simple: "Bianca, it was so wonderful to finally meet you after all these years. I hope we can meet again soon—whenever you say. Many good wishes, Franco."

Franco had included his business card and Bianca noticed he had put a line through his Roma address and telephone number and printed in, very neatly, the name and number of the *pensione* at the edge of the village. So he was staying nearby. Was he on holiday? It seemed early for the Christmas vacation—barely the first week of December—but perhaps the university...she had to get to work.

Bianca put the note in her purse and reached for the first Minerva letter. The envelope was printed with large letters. The note was brief.

Minerva—Papà *is dead. Mamma is going to marry a new man. Who's my REAL father? S.M.*

For a crazy minute, Bianca thought she had written the letter to herself and she only relaxed when she reread the signature, S.M. Who did she know who was engaged to be married? Rosa had returned from her trip to Sorrento wearing a diamond ring that was not only larger than Bianca's but was the same pear-shaped style as the one Richard Burton had given to Elizabeth Taylor. As if Rosa was some kind of movie star.

The printing was the printing of a schoolboy. But the initials were not C.C. for Carlito Corsi, but rather, S.M. There was something oddly familiar about the letter, S. The top half of the letter S was drawn larger and thicker than the bottom. Then, she got it and she knew for certain that Carlito had sent the letter because the initials S.M. stood for Super Man. It could only be Carlito. Rosa was marrying Claudio—and about time too—and Carlito was asking the question, "Who's my real father?"

She wasn't sure how to answer. If it was an adult, who had written, Bianca might use words like "birth father" or "natural father" but a seven-year old wouldn't understand. Bianca wasn't sure she understood. She thought about using the age-old expression about how we are all God's children but that wouldn't help Carlito. In fact, it didn't even help her. It was just avoiding the question. Perhaps she could say that if the man marries his mother, he becomes the boy's father—*automatico*—would that reassure him? Maybe she could suggest that the man wanted to marry the boy's mother just so he could become the boy's father. Would he believe that? Did she? Perhaps she could write that if that man's *willing* to marry your mother...but that was petty. And Bianca was trying to be kinder. Carlito needed to know that Claudio would become his real father when he married Rosa: Carlito also needed to know that Claudio, not Elgidio, had fathered Carlito so he was already Carlito's real father but it wasn't Bianca's job to tell the boy what everyone else already suspected. Before he found out for himself. That was Rosa's job and so far, she hadn't been doing a very good job of telling the truth but...

Dear SM: Your REAL father is the one who loves you and cares for you every day. It's his love that makes him real and real love is as powerful as the yellow sun. Minerva.

P.S. *If others tease you about your new father, they're just jealous because your father is young and handsome and theirs are old and fat.*

Ask Bianca

BIANCA, WEARING HER NEW BROWN swing coat and a dark chocolate scarf, walked past the barbershop on her way home from the hairdresser's. The barbershop door was still open. Bianca checked her watch; Fortunato must have a late customer. Bianca quickly decided she needed a drink of water before climbing the hill to *la casa bella*. Maybe she and Fortunato could walk home together and she could educate him about revenge. Subtle methods like curses, spells, and kidney problems were more effective on two-timers than a black eye here and a broken leg there. Vague aches and pains would lead to stress, stress leads to impotency, and impotency was just what Enzo needed. Along with less arrogance. She'd thought about filling Enzo's pocket with caraway seeds to stop infidelity but how could she fill his pockets every day? Unless, of course, she told him the caraway seeds increased potency. It was a lie—undeniably—but it obviously didn't really count if you were advising a gigolo. Bianca parted the beaded curtain of the barbershop and then, she stopped for a moment.

A stranger was in Fortunato's chair. The man had his chin lowered so Fortunato could trim the hair at the back of his neck. Even without seeing his face, Bianca knew he was an American. His suit was definitely Brooks Brothers even if his soft leather loafers were Armani.

"*Scusa, signor*," Fortunato said to his customer. "Bianca, I thought you'd gone for the day. Sit, *cara*, I'll be finished in fifteen minutes. Do you want some water? You look a little flushed."

Bianca unwrapped her scarf, unbuttoned her coat and as she folded them over the back of the chair, she motioned with her chin toward the stranger but the stranger responded before Fortunato did.

"*Buonasera, signora,*" he said. "You must be Fortunato's wife. He's been telling me all about you. I'm Tony Baxter."

"From America?" asked Bianca even though she already knew the answer.

"*Si.*"

"What brings you to our little village?" Bianca asked. To Fortunato, she said, "*Si*, I'll have some water."

"Well, I've met a few people here and I've been looking around a little," began Tony. "Sightseeing, you know."

Bianca laughed, "Sightseeing in this village would take you less than a day." She accepted the glass of water from Fortunato and continued her conversation with Tony, "Tell me, who have you met?"

"Bianca," interrupted Fortunato as he picked up his scissors. "Let me finish *signor* Tony's haircut."

"A person can still talk while the barber's cutting," reminded Bianca. "As you well know." She took a sip of her water, and waited.

"I don't mind," said Tony. "Let me tell you in the order that I met them. First, I met Rosa and Carlito in Venezia, then, Assunta at the bottling plant, her parents Nino and Elena at the farm, Claudio who is Rosa's *amore*, and then a man at the *pensione*—from Roma—*professor* Franco Portobello—"

"Portobello?" echoed Bianca. "I met him too—just a few days... weeks ago. Do you remember, Fortunato?"

"*Si*, the man with the Lancia Flaminia," said Fortunato.

"Yes, that's him," confirmed Tony. "And then the last person I met was a little girl named Giuseppina. She was riding a bicycle. And now I've met you, Fortunato, and Bianca. Everyone's made me feel very welcome."

"How long are you staying?" asked Bianca. She wanted to ask why he was staying but that was too forward and Bianca prided herself on being subtle, and polite. "If you don't mind my asking."

"I don't mind at all but I can't really say," said Tony. "It depends. Fortunato was telling me about your herb store upstairs, Bianca. When I'm finished here, perhaps I could take a look. I'm having dinner at Nino's farm tonight and I thought I might take a little gift."

"Nino grows his own herbs," said Bianca.

"Not herbs for cooking. Fortunato tells me you make very pretty herb wreaths," explained Tony. "I was thinking more of Assunta. A little gift..." Bianca could see his flushed face reflected in the mirror.

Fortunato reached for his brush, swept the soft bristles across the palm of his hand a few times and then swept the stray hair clippings clinging to Tony's neck. His neck was red too.

"Let's walk upstairs and see," suggested Bianca. "While Fortunato sweeps up."

Upstairs, the first thing Bianca said to Tony was, "You don't need a gift for Assunta. First of all, she's not the kind of woman who can be romanced with gifts and second of all, she's not in the mood for romance right now."

"But," began Tony but then he stopped as if he wasn't sure what his objection was. "Is there something else you could suggest?" he asked.

Bianca looked him over from his obviously new loafers to his gold Cartier watch to his silk necktie. Healthy skin, eyes as shiny as chestnuts, good white teeth. She said, "You seem like a good man. Why don't you come back next year and try then?"

"Next year?"

"*Si*. If you and Assunta are *simpatico*, you'll still be *simpatico* next year," said Bianca as she stepped toward the stairs.

"Wait a minute." Tony put his hand on Bianca's arm, which was reaching for the railing. "I can't wait until next year," he said. "I realize I've just met her and I certainly don't want to rush her. I'm happy to court her for a year but I'm not going to go away for a year and then come back and start from page one. I don't have that kind of time."

"What's your hurry?" asked Bianca, turning to stare at his face once more. "You look healthy enough. Do you have some disease? Some condition?"

Tony sighed. "Worse than any disease. I've fallen completely in love with her. Just like that," and Tony snapped his fingers.

"Do you often fall in love—just like that?" repeated Bianca, mimicking his finger snap.

"Never."

Bianca moved away from the spiral staircase and stepped instead to a tall cupboard and ran her finger along the labels on a row of assorted bottles and jars. "What you need," she said, "is a love potion. Something fast-acting."

"I'm already in love," said Tony.

"Not for you," said Bianca, with her finger resting on a bottle of red hibiscus flower petals. "For Assunta."

Tony shook his head. "She's not the kind of woman who'd drink a love potion. I'd have to trick her into drinking it. Slip it into her tea or something like that, and I'm not that kind of man."

"Are you sure?" asked Bianca, her hand now on a narrow jar labelled, Black Snakeroot.

"It's dishonest," said Tony and he shook his head once more. "But thanks for the offer. I appreciate it."

"My pleasure," said Bianca. "But one more suggestion. Crush the petals of a flower in one pocket. Sprinkle an envelope with your aftershave and put it in the same pocket. Inside the envelope, put the love letter. Carry it with you for three days. Then kiss the seal and slide it into her mailbox. *Capisce*?"

"Love letter?" asked Tony. "Anything specific?"

"I'll tell you what not to say," said Bianca. "No *bella, bella bella*. No talk of moonlight and starlight. Write the first thing you noticed when you met her—write only that."

"But, but," said Tony. "I noticed her neck—long and pale."

"Don't waste your words on me, my friend," said Bianca. "Write it for her. Dip the pen in your heart and write."

How to Buy a Bakery

THE FOLLOWING WEEK, TONY CAME to the barbershop again. Fortunato was already sweeping up and Bianca was upstairs unpacking and jarring some spices she had bought at the Frosinone market that morning. After the *good evenings* and the talk of possible rain, Fortunato tilted his head toward Tony's and said, "Not time yet for a trim, *signor*."

"No, I thought you might give me some advice," said Tony. "Do you have time? Are you pretty well done for the day?"

"All the time in the world," declared Fortunato as he swept a towel over the leather seat of the barber chair. "Have a seat or..." Fortunato glanced at the circular staircase that led up to Bianca's herb store. "Would you rather walk down to the bar and have a coffee?"

"No, I'd like the privacy, if you don't mind."

A half smile crossed Fortunato's face. Privacy? Such a foreign word. A faint scent of cinnamon floated down the stairs. With a small shrug of his shoulders, Fortunato motioned Tony to sit in one barber chair and Fortunato swivelled the other to face him and then he sat too. Between them lingered the aroma of cinnamon and the spicy scent of shaving cream, shampoo, and English Leather aftershave.

"Do you know the man who had a bakery across from Nino's farm?" Tony began.

"Such a fine baker. God bless his soul." Here Fortunato stopped to cross himself quickly and the motion was reflected in the mirror, a double blessing. Then Fortunato shook his head sadly, "Too bad his son didn't carry on the family business."

"I understand the son's a lawyer," said Tony.

"*Si*," sighed Fortunato. "Such a shame but what can you do? Young people these days!"

"A lawyer is a good profession," said Tony.

"When your father is a fine baker and you grow up surrounded by flour, salt, yeast, your future is clear. You have an opportunity to carry on the legacy of bread baking. Anyone can be a lawyer but to be a baker—that's an art—you can't learn that in textbooks."

"I see," said Tony even though he didn't. "I want to contact the son. Do you know where he works in Roma?"

"Why do you want to contact him?" asked Fortunato.

"I need a job."

"*Mamma mia*," said Fortunato. His brow wrinkled; he leaned forward in his chair, his voice was whisper soft, "Are you a lawyer too?"

"No," Tony assured Fortunato. Then Tony bent forward in his chair to confide, in the same *sotto voce*, "I'm going to buy the bakery."

"Congratulations, my friend," said Fortunato as he jumped from his chair and came to Tony's where he shook his hand vigorously and patted his back at the same time. "Congratulations. So, *you* are a baker."

"No. I'm not a baker. I'm going to hire a baker. Do you know anyone?"

Fortunato returned slowly to his seat. He swung the chair to face the spiral staircase and called up, "*Cara*, do you have a minute? Can you...?" Before he had finished his sentence, Fortunato saw Bianca's foot on the top step, the next one, and then she was in the room in a swirl of cinnamon and cardamom and advice.

"Do not hire anyone who uses commercial yeast," began Bianca. "Do you understand, *signor*? This is essential. They must produce their own yeast from the air." Here, Bianca waved her hand as if wild yeast was everywhere, which as it turns out it is, but Tony would find that out later. "Do you know about flour?" asked Bianca and before Tony could shake his head, she continued, "Don't use bleached flour to make white bread like the *Americani*. *Mangiacakes*. No wonder they're so pasty-faced. Only use the best flour, which is double zero—*doppio zero*—you know that, right?"

Tony shook his head. He explained, "That's why I'm hiring a baker. He'll know."

"Where are you going to find this baker?" asked Fortunato.

"Why do you say he?" asked Bianca. "What's wrong with a woman baker? As long as she has strong arms."

To both questions, Tony answered, "I don't know, yet."

■■■

Tony met up with Franco at the *pensione*. The waiter had just placed Tony's chicken dinner, with a side of roasted potatoes and carrots, on the table. It smelled delicious. Franco asked the waiter to bring him the same.

"Bring a bottle of red too," said Franco. To Tony he said, "Don't wait for me. Eat before it gets cold."

Tony passed the bread basket: the waiter brought the red wine and a couple of stubby glasses and poured; Tony proposed a toast, "To the future," he said, touching his glass to Franco's, "And to whatever it may bring. *Buona fortuna*. New adventures. And, of course, *amore*. How are you doing with your thirty-year quest to marry your *amore*?"

Franco drank before he responded. "*Bene*," he said. "I'm just waiting a little longer. There's a daughter and I want to be sure I have her permission before I ask for her mother's hand."

"I have the opposite situation," said Tony as he sliced into his roast chicken, allowing the heat and the aroma to escape. "I have a grown woman that I want to marry and, as you know, I have to ask her father for his blessing. So many traditions."

"Traditions keep us civilized, my friend. Otherwise the world would be in chaos," said Franco and he moved his glass aside to make way for his dinner plate. The waiter arrived to put Franco's plate in front of him. The scent of roasted potatoes and rosemary rose to mingle with the soft scent of garlic already floating in the air.

"I need a translator," began Tony. "And I was hoping you'd be willing to do that for me. Wait, wait," he said, holding up his hand. "Let me finish. I need to meet with a lawyer in Roma and I want to be sure that everything is clear. Here's my plan," but before Tony elaborated, he ate a few more forkfuls of the chicken, interspersed with the roasted potatoes—what *did* they do to get them so crunchy on the outside yet soft on the inside? The chicken was exceptionally flavourful as if he'd been eating pale, mock chicken all his life and only now was he discovering the real thing.

Franco poured more wine; he said, "I'm glad to see you're enjoying your meal."

"It's delicious. Everything I've eaten here has been delicious. Who does the cooking here anyway?"

"The owner's mother. The aunt makes the pasta. They buy the desserts, and the bread, from Frosinone."

"So here's my plan, Franco. There's a deserted bakery across the street from Nino's farm and I'm going to Roma to talk to the lawyer, who is now the owner of the bakery since his father died—"

Franco paused with his fork full of potato half way to his mouth and said, "God rest his soul."

"Yes, of course," said Tony. "I'm hoping to buy the bakery and get it up and running again. Hire a baker and a deliveryman and...well, whatever else I have to do. I'll have to learn as I go—that will be my job. Nino says I can't ask for his daughter's hand when I don't have a job. So, that's step one, to have a job."

"I see. Do you know anything at all about bread?"

"I know I like to eat good bread," said Tony as he ripped a piece of bread in two, the crust showering the tablecloth with crisp, golden flakes.

"Well, that's a start. When do you want to go to Roma to meet with the lawyer who owns the place?"

"As soon as possible," said Tony, scraping the last of the chicken from the bone. "I asked Nino to give me a week so hopefully the lawyer can arrange the sale quickly and I'll be able to—"

"Tony, listen to me. This is Italy. Nothing gets done in a week. It might take you a week to even get an appointment. The lawyer will want a week to decide if he wants to sell and if he does, to set a price. The price will be too high. You'll need to negotiate. There's another week. Then there's the banker. Do you know the bank's hours of operation? Of course not. No one does."

"It doesn't matter," said Tony, placing his knife and fork on his plate. "If the lawyer agrees to sell, that will be a start—I can tell Nino that much so he knows I'm serious. Then I'll work on finding a house and making official arrangements to live in Italy."

"All of this takes time, Tony. More time than you can imagine. In Italy, nothing is simple. Nothing is as it seems. Take that chicken that you enjoyed so much. It's not chicken, of course, it's rabbit."

"Rabbit! They eat rabbit?"

"You, Tony. You eat rabbit. And you think because it looks like chicken and is roasted like chicken, that it is chicken but—"

"It doesn't matter. I enjoyed it. I can adapt. The thing is, will you come to Roma with me and translate?"

"Yes, as long as you understand that it won't be fast. It won't be easy. It won't—"

"Thank you," said Tony. "Are you in the mood for dessert? I saw something that *looked* like pudding."

Friday Full Moon Dinner

THE NIGHT THAT ROSA INVITED Tony and Assunta to come for dinner was the first night that Tony went to Assunta's house rather than the farmhouse. Assunta had warned him that her neighbours would probably all be watching out their opened windows. Tony had said, "Won't they be preparing their own dinners?" "Isn't it too cold for open windows?" "Won't it be dark by seven-thirty?" but Assunta had just shaken her head and said, "You'll see."

His soft leather loafers were almost silent on the cobblestones; it was so quiet on the street he could hear the soft sounds of classical music on a radio, the clink of a metal spoon tapped against the edge of a pot, the sound of water spraying from a shower head, and yet the neighbours still heard his approach. Shutters creaked open, silhouettes appeared in windows. From a silent, darkened window, a spiral of cigarette smoke escaped. Tony didn't mind; he thought it rather charming that they were so interested in his affairs; of course, he'd come to change his mind.

He tapped on Assunta's door and began to whistle while he waited. He whistled, "I'm in the mood for love..." He did it purposely but the first thing Assunta did after she opened the door was to put her finger to her lips. She motioned with her chin; he stepped inside and followed her into the kitchen. "This is a nice little place," said Tony, looking around the small space. "The kitchen looks brand-new."

"*Si*," said Assunta. "I had it remodelled before I moved in last month. I don't feel at home, yet, or maybe I never will. Who knows? It's dreary," she said, pointing vaguely to the beige walls, the pale pine kitchen cabinets, the neutral terrazzo floor. But Tony wondered if she was really referring to the dreariness of living alone. He knew that feeling.

She motioned to a kitchen chair, with a laddered back and woven wicker seat, and invited him to sit. "What can I get you?" she asked. Tony didn't see any glasses or espresso cups set out ready on the counter. In fact there was nothing on the counter except a glass of strange-looking flowers, or maybe weeds, with their blooms closed tight. "Carlito picked them for me," explained Assunta. "They're chicory blossoms but they close up once they've been cut."

Tony checked his watch: he was nervous and he didn't know why. Other than the fact that he wanted to make a good impression on Assunta, wanted her friends Rosa and Claudio to like him and think them a good match, needed to find a way to show how much he was attracted to Assunta without overwhelming her, intended to overwhelm her. Not with a love potion. But how?

"What time are they expecting us?" asked Tony even though he knew she'd said eight o'clock and it was barely seven-thirty.

"We can go now if you want," said Assunta and she paused as if she was waiting for Tony to respond but when he didn't, she reached up to the cupboard and pulled out a bottle of vermouth. "Or we can have a drink here first. Whatever you like."

Tony couldn't gauge her intentions. Did she want to spend some time alone with him? Is that why she was suggesting the drink? Or was she just being polite? He couldn't tell; he couldn't tell and if he couldn't decipher her actions, or inactions, how would he know what to do?

"In America, we have that same brand of vermouth," began Tony—why was he talking about brands? What was the matter with him? When Assunta stopped with her arm halfway between the cupboard and the countertop, he added, "But I like it."

Assunta put the bottle on the counter, reached again for a

couple of stubby glasses.

"I see those glasses everywhere," said Tony. "It's like they're the national Italian drinking glass."

"I know in America they have a different glass for every drink," explained Assunta, turning the glass over in her hand and then turning it upright again. "We have that too in the bars but in the home, with family and friends, we—"

"They're fine. I was just making a comment," assured Tony wishing he could kick himself under the table. Stop saying the wrong thing. Maybe stop talking altogether.

"Lemon?" asked Assunta. "Or perhaps you prefer orange?"

He looked nervously from one end of the bare counter to the other but saw no fruit bowl to tell him what was available. Then he reasoned that she wouldn't offer both unless she had both. Next he noticed that the clock was ticking almost as loudly as his heart. Finally he recognized a drop of sweat had met up with another and was sliding down his back in a slow, steady trickle. In the meantime, Assunta had opened a drawer and pulled out a small cutting board. Now she held a knife in her hand. Waiting. Tony wished she would stab him and end his misery.

"You're the reason I'm still hanging around the village," he said. "And..." What else was there to say? Let her say something, anything.

"My father and I have this drink at Christmastime with a slice of orange and a maraschino cherry," said Assunta. "To make it more festive."

Had he missed something? Were they now talking about the holiday season? Wait a minute. Had he spoken those words about hanging around the village out loud? Or just thought them?

She sliced and slipped the circle of orange into the glass, topped it with vermouth. She pulled a jar from the refrigerator and unscrewed the cap. She captured a maraschino cherry, dropped it into one glass, reached for another. Then she licked her fingertip and Tony slid back his chair and went to her. With his thumb he wiped a tiny drop of sticky juice from the corner of her lip and she leaned in and kissed him. A wonderfully sticky-sweet, cherry-scented kiss. Tony heard bells ringing and it took a few seconds before he realized it was her doorbell; someone was pushing it *ring, ring, ring. Ring, ring, ring.* Carlito came bounding into the room like a boy on a mission.

"Mamma says, do you have an extra—hey, what happened to the flowers?" asked Carlito. "Are they dead?"

"No," said Assunta. "They'll open up again soon—probably in the morning, in the sunlight."

"Mamma says it's going to rain tomorrow. She read it in the clouds."

"Then the next day," assured Assunta. "Be patient."

"Why are you looking at Tony like that?" asked Carlito. He directed the next question to Tony, "Are you *impaziente*?"

"What did Mamma want?" reminded Assunta and Carlito remembered. "A lemon," he said. "If you have."

They walked across the street, hand in hand in hand. Carlito was in the middle, Assunta carried the bag that held the lemon and Tony carried the black box strewn with silver stars that contained a bottle of *limoncello* he had bought as a hostess gift. After they'd handed over their respective parcels, the women retreated to the kitchen and the men to the dining room.

"Those are nice," said Tony pointing to a vase of pretty pink carnations spicing up the evening air.

"*Papà* bought them," explained Carlito, emphasizing the word, "for Mamma."

"Let me give you one," said Rosa as she carried an antipasto platter to the table. She broke off a bloom with one quick snap and pushed it through the slit of Tony's lapel.

Tony would smell the spiciness all through the meal, and later into the evening. He'd save the flower in his jacket pocket as a memento. He'd crush the petals of the flower in his pocket.

As they gathered around the table, the talk was mostly about Rosa and Claudio's upcoming spring wedding. Claudio had given Rosa a ring that was quite spectacular and Rosa wore it with confidence. Tony thought Assunta would not want that kind of ring. She'd want something very traditional, something classic. He was thinking about a ruby set in the Venetian style but obviously he was getting ahead of himself. One spontaneous kiss didn't necessarily lead to an engagement.

"Did you see the full moon?" asked Rosa.

"The sky's a little cloudy," said Assunta. "Not like the summertime when the sky's so clear that the moon's a—"

"Giuseppina says that if you gaze into the light of a full moon, you can gain superhero qualities," said Carlito.

"And if you start howling at the moon?" teased Claudio. "Then what?"

"You turn into a werewolf, of course," said Carlito. He wrapped a thin slice of prosciutto around a breadstick and waved it as if it was a magic wand. "Everyone knows that."

Claudio wrapped his own slice and pointed the breadstick wand toward Tony. "Beware, my friend, a full moon can dazzle you. Make you fall madly in love. And tonight is Friday. Friday night plus a full moon. *Mamma mia!*" Claudio winked at Tony and said, "*Fare attenzione*, my friend."

"We're making a moon at school," said Carlito. "Out of cardboard. And a star too. For the nativity play. And I need a towel, Mamma. Maybe a brown one to look like a shepherd's robe. Or stripes. I'm a shepherd."

"Do you need a shepherd's hook too?" asked Assunta.

"Too dangerous," said Rosa and Claudio in unison. "Seven-year-old boys and sticks—"

"I'll be eight next week," reminded Carlito. "Want to come to my party?" he asked Tony.

Tony looked at Rosa who insisted that he was most welcome. Nino and Elena were coming; Assunta was coming. Maybe they could come together? So, it was agreed. First, the birthday party next week and then next month, the nativity play and so Tony's social calendar began to fill.

After the guests had left, Claudio collected the espresso cups onto the tray, stacked the dessert dishes, gathered the silverware, and made a suggestion, "Why don't we leave these until the morning?"

"*Impossibile*," assured Rosa. "*Sfortuna*. Even if it isn't bad luck, do you want to wake up to the sight of dirty dishes?"

"I don't mind," piped up Carlito.

"No one's speaking to you. Aren't you supposed to be in bed?"

"Well," stalled Carlito. "I could help to dry the dishes..." He paused, overtaken by a gigantic yawn.

"Bed," said Rosa. "If you want Claudio to take you to the market in the morning and look for—"

"*Papà*," corrected Carlito. "He's *Papà*."

"*Si*," said Claudio. "I'm *Papà* and you're as tired-looking as a bag of last fall's potatoes. Lucky for you that your *Papà* is young and strong." Claudio bent down and tucked his shoulder into Carlito's abdomen. He rose slowly, with Carlito slumped over his shoulder, and headed to the bedroom. Rosa heard the bed squeak, heard the opening and closing of the dresser drawer, heard the fluff of Carlito's pillow and the rustle of crisp sheets, and she smiled. How lovely it was going to be to have a husband like Claudio, a father who willingly tucked his son into bed as if it was a pleasure rather than a chore. Before Claudio closed the bedroom door, she heard him promise, "*Si*, Carlito, tomorrow we go to the market and see if the travelling comic-book man has his pushcart there."

Rosa stood with her hands submerged in lemon-scented dishwater, wiping the insides of the glasses and cups with her dishcloth. Claudio stood behind her with his arms around her waist. She said, "That boy! Always comics and superheroes!"

"He's growing so fast—eight next week." Claudio nuzzled his lips beneath her ear, down her neck. "Tell me, *cara*, do you ever think you might like another child?"

Rosa's hands stilled. Her face was flushed from the humidity of the dishwater. She pursed her lips and tried to blow a stray hair from her forehead. Tilted her head slightly as if listening for the sounds of Carlito's breathing.

"Did you hear me, *cara*?"

"*Si*."

"*E così*?"

"Did you mean right now? Because I really want to do these dishes first," said Rosa.

"*Cara*, why do you joke? Say yes. Say no. Don't make a joke. I'm *serio*."

"If I say yes, you will say no—don't shake your head at me, Claudio—you know you will. You'll say not another baby until I have explained to Carlito that you are his real father even though I was married to Elgidio when he was born."

"And you think this is unreasonable? I *am* his father. He has the right to know the truth and I have the right to be called '*Papà*.'" Claudio let go of Rosa's waist, reached for the linen tea towel waiting on the counter.

"It was just a slip of the tongue when I called you Claudio. It didn't mean anything." Rosa swirled her hands through the water: it was getting chilly. "I've been referring to you as Claudio for almost eight years. That's all."

"It's long enough, Rosa. You must tell him. It's as simple as that."

"Simple for you," said Rosa, her fingers swirling the suds in a circle. "You become his real father and I become an unfaithful wife."

Claudio wiped the inside of the cup, the outside, the inside once again. "I can tell him. He's old enough to understand. He already told me all about cupid's arrow and love and chemistry." He hooked the cup handle over his forefinger and set it on the kitchen table. "It's never good to keep secrets, *cara*, everyone always finds out in the end."

Rosa rested the final cup on the dish drainer: her finger touched a tiny chip on the rim, which could easily turn into a thin crack. She had a cup like that, now pushed to the back of the top cupboard shelf, that had chipped, then cracked, then one day just separated into two pieces in her hand. She'd glued it back together. Glued it very carefully, yet every time she reached for that cup, she was aware of the repair—a break so fine she could barely feel the invisible glue with her fingertips, and yet, she knew the crack was there. Rosa turned on the hot water tap and her words were muted by the sound.

"Did you say yes?" asked Claudio.

"Sì."

"To tell Carlito or to another child or to both?" His words came in a rush followed by a pause as he stood beside her, holding his breath, waiting for her answer.

"Sì," she said. "Both. *Tutti e due.*" She bumped her hip into his. "But not tonight."

By the time she'd switched from washing cups and glasses to dinner plates, the conversation had also changed.

"I'm glad Carlito invited Tony to come to his birthday party along with Assunta. Don't you think?" asked Rosa.

"*Certo.* He likes Tony and of course, Tony likes him."

"I wonder sometimes," said Rosa, wiping her dishcloth once more over an already spotless plate. "Do you think it's uncomfortable for Tony? To be with our son when his own sons are dead. You know, happy to be here but also the reminder of his own family. Their birthdays."

"*Dio mio!* I forgot his story. You know, I don't think he sees it that way. Look at him. All he sees is Assunta. Here's what's going to happen—Tony will sweep Assunta off her feet. They'll fall madly in love, get married, and live happily ever after here in the village," said Claudio.

"That's our story—"

"I know."

"*Pazzo romantico!*"

"Who are you calling a romantic fool?" asked Claudio, flicking his tea towel lightly at Rosa's backside. She scooped a handful of suds and tossed. The suds landed on the stone floor and Claudio stepped forward, pretending to fall, clutching onto her apron so that she came down too. Two lovers on a soapy floor with the dishes still undone.

■■■

It was the night of Carlito's eighth birthday party and Tony was walking Assunta home. Since she lived across the street from Rosa, Tony had suggested that they take the long way home: up the curving street, past *la casa bella*, where Fortunato's family lived, beyond the water fountain and around the bend toward Nino's farm. From there they could cut through the laneway lined with beech trees and be at the bottom of the hill near the blue bus stop. They could walk past shuttered stores spaced between squares of lamplight from the three bars on the main street, and eventually be back in front of Assunta's house. They walked in companionable silence under a night sky sprinkled with stars and a sliver of moon. A tinge of frost was in the night air. Assunta watched Tony turn up the collar of his coat and burrow in. "Warm enough?" he asked, digging in his pockets for his leather gloves.

She adjusted her scarf and made a suggestion. "If you don't mind a different short cut, we can cut across the bakery property and come out on the street behind my house."

"Of course," said Tony. "Lead the way"

He put his hand on her back. Just for a moment. To guide her onto the path. Dead grass crunchy with winter's first frost. She stopped. A jolt sizzled up her spine. For a crazy moment she thought he'd touched her with one of those vibrating joy buzzers that feels like an electric shock but isn't. Right through her woolen winter coat. Now the vibrations tingled beyond her spine to circle her rib cage. She put her hand on her heart as if to keep it in place. Assunta turned to look directly into Tony's eyes.

"I..." she said.

"Me too," he said before he kissed her so slowly and deeply, kissed her so slowly and deeply that she felt she would dissolve onto the ground were it not for Tony's arms around her holding her so firmly and his body pressed so strongly against hers. All her uncertainties disappeared and she could only think of this moment, this sensation of trust and decency and passion.

Tony loosened his hold on her and Assunta saw him fall to the ground.

"Tony, are you all right? Did you hurt...?"
Then she realized that Tony had not fallen; he was kneeling. Kneeling on one knee. He had one hand in his pocket and the other hand outstretched to her. So she took a chance and grasped his hand. She could steady him as he rose again or she could listen to what he had to say to her. It couldn't be a proposal because where was the ring? Everyone knew you couldn't get engaged without a ring—surely an American knew this too. He had one hand in his coat pocket. Did he also have a ring box? Was she being a little ridiculous? Expecting a ring from a man she'd known for only a few weeks and...

"Assunta," Tony said as if wasn't the first time he'd repeated her name. "Are you listening to me?"

Sensible, responsible Assunta reappeared. She straightened her shoulders, calmed her aching heart, and tilted her head toward Tony. "I'm all ears," she said even as her breath was ragged and her heart was banging against her ribs, and her lungs were threatening to run out of air. She bit her bottom lip so she wouldn't blurt out something stupid, like "I love you too."

Tony did not talk about romance or love. She gave her head a shake: he seemed to be talking about bread and flour and catching yeast from thin air. Then she heard her father's name, and Tony's list of her father's expectations of any man who wanted to marry his daughter: a job, a house, a forever love. Each of these words was teamed with a shake of Tony's head. Then a smile, a smile as wide as the sliver of moonlight in the night sky.

"Excuse me," she said. "Did you say you are going to buy the bakery across from *Papà's* farmhouse? Do you know anything about running a bakery? Do you know, for example, that there is one bakery for pastries and a different one for bread and focaccia?"

Tony answered her but his response had nothing to do with bread.

He said, "*Ti amo*, Assunta. No. *Io sono inamorato da te*. I am in love with you, Assunta."

Assunta shook her head. Had she drunk too much wine? What

did love have to do with a bakery? And why was he buying a bakery?

Tony was still talking; phrases lined up like a math problem searching for the total from all the sums listed:

- buy the bakery
- Rome lawyer
- paperwork and money
- hire a baker
- right flour.
- bakery delivery trucks
- drivers
- customers
- bakery name

Then the list changed to include a house near the bakery, near her father's house, still in Supino. A house with three bedrooms. "I could build a house for you Assunta. We'll talk about that later," said Tony. "But first ..."

Now Assunta realized she was not drunk; she was just frozen, frozen in place in the middle of a farmer's field in the middle of the night. But her hand was warm in Tony's hand. His words although jumbled were somehow very clear. He'd stopped talking. Was it her turn?

"Tony," she began. "I'm impressed that you have spoken with my father—that was so respectful of you—and I'm a little stunned that you have put all the requirements into action. But..."

"Do not say but," said Tony.

"We have only known each other for..."

"You know that doesn't matter, Assunta. You know."

"I know that love needs time to reveal itself and not to be..."

"I'm revealing my love for you, Assunta. It's not an impulsive love. I'm being completely honest and open with you. It's not infatuation, or loneliness or the influence of the night sky and the slim moon and the sprinkle of stars above us."

"We have time to…"

"We don't need time, Assunta. I love you. I will have you, or no one. I will own a bakery and buy you a house. Your father will give his blessing. We will be married—somewhere—wherever you want. And we'll be happy. We'll leave sorrow behind and embrace happiness. We'll do it together. All you have to do, Assunta, is say yes. Say yes to me. To love. To forever."

"Yes."

"Yes?" Tony said. "Did you say yes?"

"Wasn't that what you wanted to hear?" asked Assunta and her laughter floated like the sound of tiny bells during Sunday mass.

Tony finally removed his hand from his pocket to offer a few dried carnation petals, a rubber band, and a couple of coins. They both looked at the collection but neither spoke. A wind blew a few petals into the field and Tony closed his hand.

"I was thinking," he began. "You might like a ruby stone set in antique Venetian gold. Something traditional and unique, Assunta, just like you."

And so their fate was decided. In the almost frozen field of the deserted bakery that lay between Nino's farm and Assunta's house.

Tutto Bene

FORTUNATO SAT AT THE KITCHEN table, reading the Ask Minerva column in the newspaper to Bianca.

Dear Minerva: Some little flirt has got herself pregnant and is spreading rumours my son is the father. She's planning a shotgun wedding. How can I stop her? Reluctant Future Mother-in-Law

Dear Reluctant Future Mother-in-Law: First of all, what makes you think she got herself pregnant? Surely your son, the Saint, had something to do with it? Second of all, why would any woman resort to trickery just for the pleasure of marrying your son? What makes him so speciale? And third of all, any woman who's desperate to marry your son also gets you as a mother-in-law. I hope this foolish girl has considered that. Minerva

"These letters worry me a little," Fortunato said. "It's a crazy world, Bianca. All these new ideas about free love, girls tricking men into marriage—what if he marries her and she isn't pregnant? Then what happens?"

"How should I know?" asked Bianca. "I have enough to do with raising our own girls. I can't be advising this stranger as well. I can't feel sorry for her if she wants to marry a two-timer. Leopards never change their spots—Minerva should have told her that."

"It doesn't say he's a two-timer," said Fortunato, running his finger along the words in the newspaper. "How do you know...?"

Their conversation was interrupted by the mailman's knock on their kitchen door. Fortunato returned with a small pile of the usual bills and a large white envelope, addressed in ink the colour of pomegranates. He handed it to Bianca and said, "You might like to open this one, *cara*," and Bianca reached for her paring knife.

"I don't even want to go to this wedding," said Bianca, dropping the invitation on the kitchen table.

Fortunato was slowly unfolding the hydro bill as if he wanted to put off the shock of the total as long as he could. "What now?" he asked.

"I don't like the date—two weeks before Mamma's wedding. So typical of Rosa to try to upstage—"

"I'm sure she didn't know," said Fortunato. "*Coincidenza.*"

"*Coincidenza?*" repeated Bianca. "*Improbabile.* In this village, where everyone knows everyone else's business, you think she doesn't know? Fortunato?"

"Bianca, look at this hydro bill," said Fortunato, his finger firmly on the word, *totale*. "Sky-high! Can't we use less *elettricità?*"

"*Certo,*" said Bianca, turning the wedding invitation over and back and over again. "We can eat in the dark. Instead of using the washing machine, I can boil water on the stove—no wait, on the fire and scrub the clothes by hand and then you, Fortunato," Bianca tapped the invitation like a gavel on the wooden tabletop, "can shave with cold water and—"

"Okay, okay, it was just a suggestion." He slipped the bill back in its envelope and pushed his worries to the back of his mind.

The girls arrived home from school chattering and calling out, "What's for lunch? Do I smell meatballs, Mamma?" and Bianca replied, with a glance at Fortunato, "Close the door. *Papà's* not paying to heat the outside."

"It's nice out today," said Antonietta. As a teenager, she felt it was essential to contradict everything her mother said. "Spring is definitely in the air."

"You can't trust March," declared Bianca. "Warm spring breezes one day and cold North wind the next. Make sure you keep your coat done up properly. You don't want to catch a spring cold and—"

"Oh, Mamma," said both the girls in unison. Then Antonietta spied the mail. "Is it Nonna's wedding invitation? It looks awfully plain."

"See the rose in the corner?" replied Bianca. "It should be two gold wedding bands or a gold cross or even some white lilies but no, Rosa has to always—"

"Bianca," warned Fortunato.

Sometimes Bianca was sorry that she had ever told Fortunato about her resolution to be less critical. To be kinder. It seemed that she was constantly tightening her lips to keep back her words and she wasn't at all sure that it was worth it. Kindness might be an over-rated virtue.

"Will we have new dresses for the wedding?" asked Antonietta hopefully.

"*Certo.* Matching dresses."

"But Mamma, I'm thirteen years old—almost fourteen. Why do I have to wear the same baby style as Giuseppina?" asked Antonietta, who was really much closer to thirteen than fourteen.

"I'm not a baby. I'm eight and a half," declared Giuseppina.

Fortunato reached for his copy of *La Repubblica* newspaper. As sure as thunder follows lightning an argument was coming. Fortunato gave the paper a solid shake and began to read about the Lazio soccer team practices scheduled for this week.

"Mamma, there's a pretty dress in my magazine," suggested Antonietta, pulling out her latest copy of *Teen Magazine*. "Maybe the dressmaker could copy it? Annette Funicello wore it in her latest—"

"That girl's always dressed in a bathing suit," replied Bianca, ignoring the magazine that her daughter held out. "And not one that you're ever going to be allowed to wear."

"But Mamma, Annette's a Mousekeeter. Walt Disney said she's—"

"What do I care about *signor* Disney and his mouse girls?" asked Bianca, lifting her eyebrows and turning up her palms.

"You want to copy someone's style, copy Bernadette. She may be a French girl but she's *modesto*."

"Mamma, she's a nun. I can't dress like a nun!" Antonietta hugged her magazine to her chest like a shield from her Mamma's words.

"It's not that I want you to dress exactly like Saint Bernadette. I just want you to copy her style. Be *elegante, modesto*."

"Maybe I should just wear a flour sack," responded Antonietta. "Then you can be sure none of the boys would ever look my way."

"You want to dress like these go-go girls *Americane*?" asked Bianca. "They look like they're wearing flour sacks. Just two rectangles of cloth, and not very much cloth either. No, no flour sack for you. A nice Peter Pan collar and a skirt with box pleats—that's for you. Maybe, if you can stop pouting for two minutes, a pair of new shoes with those little heels—kitten heels. How's that?"

Antonietta thought it over. She could roll up the skirt once she left the house. She could unbutton the top two, or maybe three buttons. Kitten heels—that was something.

"Red kitten heels?" Antonietta asked eagerly.

"Red is not a colour that virtuous women wear."

"Rosa wears red heels," added Giuseppina, wanting to get into the conversation even though she wasn't sure what kitten heels were.

"*Essato*," said Bianca.

Antonietta stuck her magazine under her arm and took her almost fourteen-year-old self upstairs to her room where she could flop on her bed and contemplate the unfairness of being born in a small village to an even smaller-minded Mamma. But Giuseppina stayed in the kitchen: she had more news to give.

"Carlito is getting a new suit for the wedding," said Giuseppina. "Claudio, his *Papà* is buying it for him."

"Is that what Carlito calls Claudio now?" asked Bianca. "*Papà*?"

"*Sì*. Why not?" Giuseppina put her hands on her hips as if she might be anticipating an argument. "Claudio is his father as soon as he marries his mother."

As always with Bianca, you never knew what she might say and today was no exception.

"*Si*," said Bianca. "His real father." And she smiled her real smile, not the one she used to be polite but the one she used when she was truly pleased about something.

The smile encouraged Giuseppina to share her other bit of news, which was kind of a secret, but not really.

"Rosa said that Carlito isn't allowed to wear his Superman cape for the wedding, even though Carlito really wants to," began Giuseppina, and then she lowered her voice for the full effect of her next words, "So Carlito will wear his Superman T-shirt underneath his white shirt, and no one will know."

"Like Clark Kent," said Bianca with another real smile.

"Mamma," exclaimed Giuseppina. "You know about Clark Kent and Superman."

"Of course," said Bianca—a third smile. "Now, that's enough for today. Go and get your sister so you can set the table. Fortunato, get that mail off the table. How are we going to eat with your papers all over the place?"

■■■

At her mother's house, Bianca had settled down with Lucrezia into a routine of finishing their respective activities: Bianca writing her Ask Minerva column in the extra room upstairs and Lucrezia studying the Diane von Furstenberg dresses in the latest Vogue magazine, before enjoying a cup of tea together on the balcony, if the weather was still warm enough. Today, an unpredictable April wind was blowing from the North and so they sat in the living room by the fireplace. The logs crackled. The aroma of apple wood slowly filled the room.

"Erminio says," began Lucrezia, "that some of the original apple trees are too old to bear fruit and he's had to cut some and replant. These logs are probably from trees that my father planted."

"Nonno planted the trees?" asked Bianca. "I didn't know that."

"Well, he didn't actually *plant* them," said Lucrezia with a wave of her hand to indicate how she'd slipped off the truth and into the imaginary. "He had Erminio plant them. But *Papà* gave the instructions to plant. What's the point of having a *frutticoltore* if you don't let him do his job?"

Bianca watched the tea leaves settle in her cup. Her mother's stories of the past often changed slightly with each telling.

"How old is Erminio anyway?" asked Bianca. "I think he may be younger than I am. Wouldn't he have been only a boy when Nonno was alive?"

"*Certo*," said Lucrezia. "I'm not talking about this Erminio. The one that you know. I'm talking about his father. The first one, Erminio Primo. He taught his son all about caring for an orchard. More tea?"

Bianca gestured toward her cup, which was still full.

"What's the matter?" asked Lucrezia. "Trouble with the Minerva column?"

"It's a letter that Minerva can't answer—" began Bianca.

"Give it to me. I'll answer it."

Bianca put her hand in her mother's outstretched one and gave it a squeeze. "It's not that I *can't* answer," said Bianca. "I just can't answer in the newspaper."

"I see. What is it, Bianca? Birth control? *La bambola voodoo*? Recipe for deadly..." said Lucrezia.

"Money."

"Tell her to ask her banker. That's what they're there for. When they're actually in the bank and not fooling around with their—"

"It's not advice a banker could give," assured Bianca. "It's... well, here, listen."

Bianca took the letter from her pocket. The lined paper was ragged as if someone had ripped it from the pages of a school notebook. The query was brief: *My husband is cheap. I need money for the children's clothes but he won't give. He counts every penny in his pocket, so I can't—what can I do?*

"What's the problem?" began Lucrezia and then she stopped.

"Oh, I see. You can't print the answer in the newspaper that men read. Didn't I warn you that this would happen? This is *molto serio*, Bianca. What are you going to do?"

"What can I do? You said yourself that it's not advice that can be published. I can't answer her letter, that's all."

"If you could," said Lucrezia, leaning forward at the table, looking straight into Bianca's eyes, watching for the correct response. "What would you say?"

"I would say talk to the butcher's wife," began Bianca. "Get her to charge an extra chicken leg or string of sausages to the monthly bill. If the woman has chickens, tell her to sell a few eggs every week to the butcher's wife and tell the husband that the chickens aren't laying well. At the end of the month, the husband will pay the butcher's bill, the butcher's wife will give the woman the extra money and the children will get some new clothes. Of course, the woman will have to make up some story about the new clothes—if the husband even notices. Of course this advice cannot be published for husbands to read."

"Very good, Bianca," said Lucrezia as if Lucrezia was the *professore* and Bianca was her *studente*, which in a way, she was. "It's important to always have a story ready—for the clothes or for anything really—but you forgot the hairdresser."

"Mamma, I hardly think this woman has money to go to the hairdresser."

"It doesn't cost to go and sit and listen. Where else will she get this kind of advice about cheap husbands or cheating husbands? Bedroom problems? Effective herbs for ailments? How to cause ailments and—" Lucrezia stopped momentarily to pick up her teacup and drink. "Tell her to go to the hairdresser's. Maybe she'll want to leave *il bastardo economico* one day and the women at the hairdresser's can give advice on that too."

Bianca lifted her cup too, and drank. "Thank you, Mamma. You're always a great help to me."

Lucrezia said, "I hear that young Gabriella, the hairdresser, is to marry that two-timing bottle-cap salesman next month. Soon she'll be writing to you for advice about a cheating husband—

like it's a surprise. Once a cheater always a cheater. Too bad she has to learn the hard way. Now, Bianca, let me read your tea leaves."

Bianca didn't have a lot of faith in teacup reading, even though she knew that Mamma had followed the steps perfectly in order to get an accurate reading. Maybe it was just the prediction that Bianca didn't want to believe. Mamma had swirled three times; she'd taken three breaths before turning the cup to position the handle. She read the first symbol aloud.

"Letter M," said Lucrezia. "For Minerva."

"Not necessarily," said Bianca. "It could be for you, Mamma."

"*Essato*," said Lucrezia. "Mamma will be Minerva."

"But *I'm* Minerva," protested Bianca and Mamma had said, "Who will write the Minerva columns when you're busy with the babies? Wait, I see a basket. No, two baskets. Those are the twins."

"We know they're twins," sighed Bianca.

"Here in the middle section," said Lucrezia, "which represents the near future..."

"I know what it represents," said Bianca with another sigh.

"*Madonna mia*," said Lucrezia. "Two lions. Plain as day. Both exactly the same."

"Females?" asked Bianca.

"Worse. Manes. Two males as clear as the nose on your face."

Bianca put her index finger to her nose and tapped a few times. Almost as if she was about to tell a lie, and wanted to prevent her nose from growing long. It was a gesture left over from her childhood.

"You could be wrong."

"I'm never wrong."

"*Va bene*. I can handle boys," said Bianca.

"*Va bene*," said Lucrezia. "And I can handle your columns while you're taking care of the boys."

"We'll see," said Bianca but they both knew it was decided. Their future was crystal clear: Bianca would reluctantly give up writing her column to mother two baby boys and Lucrezia would write Bianca's Minerva columns and that was that.

A few weeks later, they were back in the same chairs having a different conversation. "I want to speak to you about Rosa's wedding," said Lucrezia to Bianca.

They'd already discussed Rosa's wedding dress—a silver and white sequined affair that made her look more like a mermaid than a bride—very low cut in the front. Bianca had said, "Rosa may be *Napolitana* but she's no Sophia Loren."

Lucrezia had added, "And that white feather boa Rosa wore to cover her bare shoulders. *Non appropriato.* Completely Hollywood."

Bianca said, "I'm still shocked that the priest didn't tell her to cover herself with a shawl."

"You forget, *cara*," said Lucrezia. "A priest is still a man. Now tell me, how are you feeling? Any more false labour pains?"

"Is that what you want to talk about?" asked Bianca. "I know it was early for labour but I really thought—"

"Did you, *cara*?" asked Lucrezia.

The week before, Bianca had sat in the cool church with her hands folded innocently over her swelling belly. The twins were due in six more weeks but when the priest reached the part of the marriage ceremony where he raised his eyes from Rosa's cleavage and looked out at the guests and asked the age-old question, "If any...has any just cause why these two should not be lawfully wed...speak now or forever..." Bianca leaned forward to grab the wooden pew. "*Scusa,*" she called out, panting a little. "Is *Dottor* Volpone here?" Then she lowered her head onto her outstretched arms and moaned.

"*Madone,*" said Fortunato. "*Dottore? Dottore? I bambini stanno arrivando.*"

The wedding guests gathered around; some offering advice, others just watching. Holding his black bag above his head, the doctor made his way slowly through the crowd, repeating, "*Scusa. Per favore. Scusa.*"

Giuseppina waved to Carlito who was still standing beside Rosa at the altar; Carlito responded with a Superman gesture: pointed elbows, hands planted firmly on his waist, a puffed-out chest, which might reveal the S of his Superman T-shirt, but only if you had X-ray vision. With their fingers entwined, Rosa and Claudio waited by the altar but the priest had deserted the bride and groom to administer to Bianca.

"*Ambulanza?*" asked Fortunato when the doctor finally arrived to pull out his stopwatch, to lay his hand on Bianca's belly, and assess.

"Give us a minute," said the doctor. To the priest, the doctor suggested, "Have the organist play something." The priest gestured to the organist who began to play Mimi's death scene from La Bohème. "Handkerchief," the doctor said to Fortunato and when Fortunato produced a spotless square, the doctor instructed, "Fan her neck. Stay calm, Bianca. Breathe easy. In and out. In and out. *Mantenere la calma.*"

"*You* stay calm," replied Bianca. "I don't want to have these babies in the church, *per l'amor di dio.*"

Thirty minutes passed before Bianca, her face flushed but calm, sat back in the pew and the doctor made his announcement, "False labour." To the priest, he gestured and said, "Continue."

Everyone returned to their seats. Claudio straightened his silver tie. Rosa adjusted her headdress of yellow and white daisies *alla* Elizabeth Taylor and Carlito checked the button on his white dress shirt, patted the Superman T-shirt beneath. The priest looked at his watch. He had another wedding in half an hour— the young hairdresser, dressed in virginal white and hiding her belly behind a bouquet of baby rosebuds and lavender would be arriving soon. In less than six short months, the hairdresser and her husband would be back in church for the baptism of their son, Renzo. An affectionate derivative of the name, Lorenzo.

The priest couldn't have the next expectant bride waiting in the vestibule before the recessional hymn had even begun for this one, plus there was some bad blood between the next groom and some of the current guests. Nino, in particular, but also

Fortunato, Pietro. The priest sped through the First reading and skipped the Second as well as the Profession of Faith. He kept the Sign of Peace. After a hurried communion distribution, he skipped straight to the Blessing and Dismissal. At the first strains of the Recessional hymn, the priest touched his hand to Carlito's shoulder and said, "Go," and Carlito fairly flew down the aisle.

"I don't want any false labour pains at my wedding on Saturday," warned Lucrezia. "The babies aren't due for another month and if they want to arrive early, it will have to be after the ceremony."

"Yes, of course, Mamma," began Bianca. "I'm sure—"

But Bianca's words were cut off by the sound of the door chimes. "Let me get that," offered Bianca, to be kind but also to escape her mother's unkind suggestion that she might try to redirect the spotlight from her mother on her wedding day. That would definitely be mean-spirited when Bianca was trying so hard to be kind, even though practising generosity was incredibly difficult.

As soon as Franco saw Bianca open the door, his face lit up. "Just the person I was hoping to see," he began and then with a quick look at Lucrezia, he amended, "My two favourite women."

"Teresa," called Lucrezia. "*Caffè. Biscotti. Presto.*"

"*Si, si, signora,*" said Teresa as she passed through the hallway and into the kitchen, moving at her usual snail's pace.

"I wanted to talk to you about something," Franco said to Bianca and he directed her to the armchair in the living room. "And I have a little gift for you." Franco reached into the breast pocket of his tweed sports jacket and pulled out a long, narrow box. It looked like a jewellery box, the kind that held a necklace, a bracelet, a strand of pearls.

Lucrezia frowned. "What's this?" she said.

"Just a little gift for our Bianca, my dear. But first I want to explain something." Then he added, "To both of you."

"So explain," said Lucrezia with a glance at the kitchen doorway. "Where is the coffee, Teresa? I could have travelled to Colombia and..."

After Teresa had served the coffee and passed the biscuit plate, and after Lucrezia had shooed her back upstairs, and after she heard the roar of the vacuum cleaner, Lucrezia turned back to Franco. "So explain."

Franco took Bianca's hand. "Don't be upset with Mamma, Bianca, but she told me that you have *il segreto*..." Bianca pulled her hand from Franco's but Franco quickly reassured her, "Mamma didn't tell me the secret itself. Only that you have one. *Va bene*?" When Bianca nodded, Franco continued, "I know you come to Mamma's house once a week and do your secret work in the office upstairs. I know Mamma has been worried about how you will be able to do that work once these babies arrive."

"But Mamma already decided," began Bianca.

Lucrezia interrupted, "Franco, Bianca and I have already sorted this out. Don't interfere."

Franco put down his cup, "When a man has a concern about his own family, Lucrezia, it is not *interferenza*. Let me finish what I have to say and then you, of course, can say what you wish. *Va bene*?"

"*Si*," said Lucrezia. She crossed her legs and her arms but she held her tongue.

"Continue."

"Mamma thought it would be impossible for you to do your work in the office with two babies but I have come up with a simple plan," said Franco. A smile spread across his face. "Would you allow your Mamma and I to care for the babies one day a week? Perhaps even two? Then you could do your work and we could have the pleasure of caring for the babies."

"I don't—" began Lucrezia.

"Mamma doesn't babysit," said Bianca.

"Babysit is a word *Americana*," said Franco. "We don't even have that word in the Italian language and I'll tell you why. Because it is not babysitting when you care for your own grandchildren." He directed his next words to Lucrezia. "I wasn't here to be part of Antonietta and Giuseppina's childhood but I want to be involved with these next two. If you will permit us,

Bianca. Believe me, it would be our pleasure."

The only sound in the room was the hum from the vacuum cleaner upstairs and the tick of the mantel clock. Finally Bianca broke the near silence, "What do you think, Mamma?"

Lucrezia directed her words to Franco, "Are you going to give her the gift?"

Franco laughed. "I almost forgot." He lifted the narrow box from the table and put it in Bianca's hands. She untied the indigo ribbon and unwrapped the gold foil paper and lifted the lid of the box to reveal pencils. A dozen wooden graphite pencils, all sharpened and ready to use. "I know you type on your father's typewriter," said Franco. "But I thought you might like to write by hand sometimes too."

Bianca stood up, and hugged him. It was the first time she'd touched him in such an affectionate way. Franco had to wipe away a few tears. "What do you think, Mamma?" repeated Bianca. "About babysit—about taking care of the babies?"

"Why not" said Lucrezia, throwing her hands in the air. "It will be an adventure. Your father can push one stroller and I can push the other—or wait, maybe we can go to Roma, Franco, and buy a twin stroller at Baby Mondo. I saw one there last month—navy blue with an awning with a fringe—just like that song from the American movie—what was the name?"

"Oklahoma," said Bianca.

"Okay," said Franco and it was all settled.

■■■

Everything was set for a perfect wedding for Lucrezia and Franco. Potted pink azaleas decorated the altar steps. The granddaughters in their matching white organza dresses with pale pink sashes and bows at the back would sprinkle azalea blossoms on a pure white cotton runner as they preceded Lucrezia down the aisle. Fortunato would accompany Lucrezia, who would be dressed in a soft, warm-grey Chanel-style suit. Franco would be waiting at the altar with Tony the American as his best man and

Bianca would be sitting in the front row. The boutonnieres and corsages were all baby's breath and hot pink azaleas. Later the guests would come to the apple orchard, with the trees abloom in apple blossom white, for a catered buffet and endless Italian champagne served by waiters in white jackets and black ties. The wedding cake was five layers high. Lucrezia and Franco's wedding would be a day to remember but not for the clothes, the food, or the flowers.

"Are you feeling well, *cara*?" asked Fortunato when Bianca came down the stairs, dressed for the wedding.

"*Si*," said Bianca. "Girls, hurry up. Nonna will be waiting for you."

Giuseppina pounded down the stairs in her white Mary Jane shoes and Antonietta followed, happily tapping her kitten heels on every single step. "We're ready, we're ready," they called as they ran out the door to jump into Franco's car.

"*Va bene*?" asked Fortunato as he helped Bianca into the front seat.

"*Si*," said Bianca. "Stop worrying."

Fortunato took a moment to wipe his forehead—the day had turned warm—before climbing into the back seat with the girls. "*Andiamo*," they called to Franco. "Let's go."

Franco drove to the church. "*Va bene*?" asked Franco as he helped Bianca from the car.

"*Si*," said Bianca. Franco and Bianca went into the church, Franco to stand and wait at the side of the main altar and Bianca to sit and wait in the front row. Fortunato took the wheel and drove to the edge of town to pick up Lucrezia. The bells were chiming eleven when Fortunato returned to the church with the bride and the flower girls.

It was stuffy in the vestibule; Fortunato asked one of the altar boys to hold the door open for a few minutes so they could catch some breeze. "I'm not hot," said Giuseppina hopping from one foot to the other.

"You're spilling your flower petals," said Antonietta. "Give me your basket." The girls collected the spilled petals and lined up in order, waiting for the first organ notes to signal that it was time to begin. Bianca sat peacefully in the front row. Giuseppina almost skipped down the aisle but Antonietta stepped carefully, keeping pace with the organ music and allowing the petals to sift through her fingers and flutter leisurely to the floor. Fortunato wiped his forehead once more and offered his arm to Lucrezia. He was shaky; she was calm as they headed slowly to the altar where Franco stood waiting.

Fortunato clutched the end of the pew as he took his seat beside Bianca. Then he took her cool hand in his to ask once more, "*Va bene?*" She smiled and the ceremony began. When the priest arrived at the fateful lines, "...why these two should not be lawfully..." a moan travelled from the front row, past the Stations of the Cross, beyond the curtained confessionals, to the holy water fonts at the back of the church.

Lucrezia, her face flushed red with anger, turned quickly to Bianca. This time the priest remained rooted to his spot as Bianca called out, "*Scusa*. Is *Dottor* Volpone here?" This time, the villagers, glancing from one to another with raised eyebrows, leaned back in their seats as *Dottor* Volpone lifted his black bag and walked up the main aisle. Another moan filled the church. "Hurry," called Bianca.

Fortunato's forehead was damp with sweat; his face was ashen. He clutched his stomach, bent over in pain, and moaned once more. *Dottor* Volpone spoke into Fortunato's ear and Fortunato nodded before the next moan. By now Franco, Lucrezia, and the girls had deserted the altar and crowded around the pew. The priest was fanning Fortunato's face with his golden stole. "Pain every few minutes," *il dottore* said to no one in particular. He tried to lay Fortunato down on the pew but Fortunato only curled up into a ball. His moans were escalating toward screams. "Stop that fanning," said the doctor to the priest. "Call for *ambulanza*."

Franco came to Bianca and put his hand on her shoulder. "*Va bene?*" he asked and she nodded but her eyes were full of tears. "What are we going to do?" she asked. "What are we going to do?"

"The ambulance will come," said Franco. "You and the girls and Lucrezia will come in my car to the hospital. It's all going to be fine. Everything's going to be *tutto bene*."

"Oh," Bianca said.

"Here's Mamma," said Franco, putting out his arm for Lucrezia. "See, it's like I told you. *Tutto bene*."

Franco was right, in a way. Before they left for the hospital, Franco had a quick word with his best man, Tony, who then invited all the guests to come to the apple orchard for the wedding dinner even though the bride and groom were neither married nor available to celebrate. "The food's already prepared and paid for," he said in his casual American style. "So we might as well enjoy." The ambulance arrived with sirens shrieking and took Fortunato to the hospital in Ferentino where they rushed him into surgery and operated before his appendix burst. Bianca and her family crowded the hospital waiting room.

One week later, Fortunato was released from hospital and two weeks after that, when Bianca did go into labour, he was back at the hospital with her. When the doctor came into the waiting room to announce two boys, Bianca and babies all well, Fortunato cried. He shook hands with the other fathers-to-be, who were waiting for their own news, and then he rushed to the phone booth to announce the news.

In a few weeks, two small but healthy boys, Onesto and Valerio, would be baptized at the village church, right after their grandparents Franco and Lucrezia were finally married.

■■■

In May, Bianca received a letter but not in any of the usual ways. It wasn't included with the other Ask Minerva letters delivered to Mamma's house. Nor had the mailman delivered it to her herb store, since there was no stamp. Yet the letter was propped on the wooden counter in Bianca's herb store. A sprig of rosemary, the herb of remembrance but also the herb of love, was lying casually in front of the envelope. It was addressed, most familiarly, in

Fortunato's handwriting—Fortunato's handwriting—to *Cara Minerva*.

Cara Minerva:
Tony and Assunta plan to be wed next spring, as you know. But perhaps you don't know yet that Tony's sister will travel from America to meet his fiancée. The sister is not happy about his plans and he fears that she may try to interfere. Of course an Americana *knows nothing of voodoo dolls, curses, or spells but she can use her American ingenuity to disrupt the wedding plans, if she wishes. Certainly, a New Yorker is no match for you,* mia cara Minerva. *I'm sure you will instruct her about how we do things here in Supino.* Buon fortuna, *from your devoted fan.*

And now Bianca would await Tony's sister who thought she might *interferire* in the wedding. Obviously this—what was the word *Americana*? Oh yes, busybody—didn't know the ways of the village, or of Bianca. Bianca would make a small cotton doll and dye it red, white, and blue. Fill it with fresh angelica, and a few pins. Best to be well-prepared for the *Americana's* arrival in Supino.

Acknowledgements

My first thanks must always go the villagers of Supino and those whose ancestors came from Supino, for their love and support. Although this is a work of fiction and the characters are imaginary, the village itself remains the main character. *Grazie, Supino, grazie mille.*

I'm grateful to the team at Inanna Press led by Rebecca Rosenblum who have welcomed me into the world of publishing. Luciana Ricciutelli, who has since passed away, accepted my book originally and I know she'd be so proud to see this book in print. Thank you Courtney Hellam, who designed the fabulous cover. *Che bella!*

Members of my writing group (Maria Cioni, Debi Goodwin, Janet Looker, Shelley Saywell, Barbara Tran, Jamie Zeppa) have read and commented and reread various drafts of this book and they have been encouraging all through the process. Thank you also to the people who wrote blurbs for this book, especially Barbara Kyle who gave me excellent editing advice when the characters were a little lost in Supino.

Thank you to everyone who read *My Father Came From Italy* and *Summers in Supino* and sent emails and notes and recommended the books to others. I consider these readers as my friends.

Thank you to my family here in Canada, in the U.S.A., in Italy, and in Australia for your support. Thank you to members of the Supino Social Clubs—everywhere.

Special thanks to my youngest daughter, Kathryn, and her

family, who housed me during Covid, and gave me time and space (and great meals) to write.

Thank you to my cousins, Assunta and Johnny Paglia, for their unlimited support and their excellent translations of English words into Italian.

And thank you, dear readers, for your ongoing interest.

Credit: Debi Goodwin

Maria Coletta McLean is the author of the best selling memoir, *My Father Came From Italy* and the sequel *Summers in Supino: Becoming Italian*. She's been featured in the National Post, the Toronto Star, the Globe and Mail and USA Today. In 2002, she was awarded the Queen's Golden Jubilee Medal for her contribution to the Canadian literary landscape.

Maria is a graduate of York University and the University of Toronto; she lives in Toronto where she teaches English as a Second Language and Creative Writing at Seneca College. She maintains a home in the village of Supino, where the patio is still under construction. www.mariacoletta.com